The Trail

of the

Wild Rose

ALSO BY ANTHONY EGLIN

The Blue Rose
The Lost Gardens
The Water Lily Cross

The Trail
of the
Wild Rose

Anthony Eglin

M

MINOTAUR BOOKS
New York

A THOMAS DUNNE BOOK FOR MINOTAUR BOOKS.
An imprint of St. Martin's Publishing Group.

THE TRAIL OF THE WILD ROSE. Copyright © 2009 by Anthony Eglin. All rights reserved. Printed in the United States of America. For information, address St. Martin's Press, 175 Fifth Avenue, New York, N.Y. 10010.

www.thomasdunnebooks.com
www.minotaurbooks.com

Design by Kathryn Parise

LIBRARY OF CONGRESS CATALOGING-IN-PUBLICATION DATA

Elgin, Anthony.
    The trail of the wild rose : an English garden mystery / by Anthony Eglin.—1st ed.
        p. cm.
    ISBN-13: 978-0-312-36547-9
    ISBN-10: 0-312-36547-0
    1. Botanists—Crimes against—Fiction. 2. Accidents—Fiction. 3. Gardeners—Fiction. 4. Gardening—Fiction. 5. England—Fiction. I. Title.
    PS3605.G53T73 2009
    813'.6—dc22

                                                    2008036023

First Edition: April 2009

10 9 8 7 6 5 4 3 2 1

For Russ & Sherry

ACKNOWLEDGMENTS

I consider myself fortunate indeed to have had the extensive resources of Quarryhill Botanical Gardens at my disposal to research the plant-hunting aspects of my story. As a result, the description of the fictional Ravenscliff is based in large part on Quarryhill.

In particular, I am deeply grateful to William McNamara, Quarryhill's executive director, who gave so generously of his time, helping me craft parts of my story to reflect true-to-life conditions in the field and providing accurate botanical data and facts. Over the last twenty years, Bill has led or participated in twenty-five plant-hunting expeditions to China, Japan, India, Nepal, Taiwan, and North America. The results of these remarkable, often hazardous, journeys can now be seen at Quarryhill's extraordinary twenty-acre garden, sculpted from a mountain slope, overlooking the vineyards of Sonoma County. Today, Quarryhill is home to one of the largest collections of scientifically documented wild-source

Asian plants in North America. Almost every plant, shrub, and tree flourishing in this botanical wonderland has been grown from seeds brought back from expeditions by this "Indiana Jones" of the plant world.

A special thanks to Charles Erskine, former Curator of the Arboretum Royal Botanic Gardens, Kew, for help with staffing information about Kew.

My thanks to DC Claire Chandler, Hampshire Constabulary, and Andrew Heath, Thames Valley Police, for keeping me straight with UK police procedures.

At St. Martin's Press: A heartfelt thanks to my editor, Pete Wolverton, for his steadfast support and guidance from the beginning. And lucky me to have the keen eyes of copy editor Cynthia Merman to add the finishing touches.

By no means last, my gratitude for the invaluable contributions of my wife, Suzie, and friends Roger Dubin, John Joss, and Dave Stern.

AUTHOR'S NOTE ON
SOURCES

My thanks to Howick Hall Gardens and Arboretum for horticultural detail extracted in part from their excellent brochure.

For information on ancient Chinese ceramics, I am indebted to the Percival David Foundation in London. The foundation, now part of the University of London, is home to one of the finest collections of Chinese ceramics outside China, comprising nearly two thousand objects dating back to the tenth century A.D. Starting in 2009, the collection will be on display permanently at the British Museum.

Additional botanical and horticultural details concerning roses are excerpted from *The Quest for the Rose* by Roger Phillips and Martyn Rix (Random House, 1993).

Historical plant-hunting references are excerpted in part from *The Plant Hunters* by Toby Musgrave, Chris Gardner, and Will Musgrave (Sterling Publishing Co., 1998).

Partial descriptions of Jade Dragon Snow Mountain are derived from Travel Yunnan China's Web site: www.travelchinayunnan .com/city/Lijiang/attraction/yulong.htm.

Linda Stratmann and her excellent book *Chloroform: The Quest for Oblivion* (Sutton Publishing, 2005) proved me woefully misinformed on chloroform and its use in the commission of a crime. Thanks, Linda, for setting me straight.

Thanks also to biologist, photographer, and writer Beatriz Moisset for the excerpt from *The Midge and the Chocolate.*

The section on the Museum of Garden History is excerpted from the museum's Web site and from the author's experience.

The quotation on page 242 is by Ben Macintyre, the *Times,* London.

The crossword puzzle clues are from the *Times,* London.

Good God. When I consider the melancholy fate of so many of botany's votaries, I am tempted to ask whether men are in their right mind who so desperately risk life and everything else through the love of collecting plants.

—CARL LINNAEUS, *Glory of the Scientist* (1737)

The Trail
of the
Wild Rose

PROLOGUE

October 2006, Yunnan Province, China

They walked more slowly now. Signs of fatigue from the steep climb and the thinning air were starting to show on their faces. In the last hour the sky had blackened, and the once distant rumble of thunder was now loud. Now and then cannonlike fusillades echoed between the jagged peaks around them. An ice-cold rain that had arrived with the thunderstorm had made the rough going even more arduous, the footing more treacherous. They would have turned back long ago had not the Chinese botanist in the lead assured them that the ancient roses and the seeds they sought were not far ahead.

Two hours earlier, they'd left their vehicles in care of one of their guides, at the seven-thousand-foot elevation. This was the ninth day of a two-week plant-hunting expedition that had started in the ancient city of Lijiang, in a far-flung corner of China, under the shadow of Jade Dragon Snow Mountain. Its unconquered peaks are sanctuary to animals that have never known the scent of man and a superabundant flower kingdom that was old when the Gardens of Babylon were new. For centuries the region has been a botanist's paradise.

Anyone observing the single file of nine men—not that there would be, in this remote area and at this altitude—might have questioned their sanity. Less because of the weather than the hazardous route. Barely six feet wide, the trail was flinty and slippery in places where the rain had turned to ice. Like a thin strand of ribbon, it wound its way in a shallow spiral up the face of the mountain: on one side, a wall of gray granite; on the other, a dizzying drop of more than three thousand feet.

No words were spoken. They would only be lost in the fury of the wind. It was just as well because they had to concentrate, to tread carefully.

Only the last two men in line witnessed the man in front of them stumble and fall. They shouted to the others, who by this time had forged ahead by several paces. Now the leaders stopped and returned to see what had happened. One of them knelt and spoke briefly to the man on the ground, then helped him to his feet. A discussion followed among the men; some were in favor of abandoning what had clearly become a foolhardy mission, others were intent on continuing. In the end, it was the man who'd stumbled who convinced them that he was fit enough to go on and that they shouldn't give up, especially now, when they were so close. In a minute, they were all on their way once more, pressing into the storm.

Not many paces farther on, the man stumbled again. But this time, he managed to stay on his feet, swaying drunkenly for a few seconds. Then he stiffened, and before anyone could reach him, he toppled sideways—disappearing without a sound into the yawning abyss.

ONE

June 2007, England

The road south out of Little Stanhope village could have been any one of hundreds that spider the picturesque Thames valley, south of the city of Oxford: narrow, with dense hedgerows—often blocking the view on both sides—and fraught with un-remitting curves.

To anyone following the Vincent Black Lightning motorcycle, it would be apparent that the leather-jacketed rider was familiar with the quirky road, its capricious twists and turns. Allowing for the light drizzle, he maintained a steady but not excessive speed, barely slowing for some of the shallow bends, and swaying fluidly from one side to the other, like a boxer dodging blows, as he coaxed the sleek machine through the blind hairpins.

He was headed for the market town of Wallingford, one of many picture-postcard towns and villages that straddle the Thames on its slow-flowing journey southeast to Windsor, thence to London, and to the sea.

Despite his familiarity with the road, he knew that concentration was critical: The margin for error, for both him and the driver of an oncoming vehicle, would be slender. Physically and mentally committed, setting up his line through a particularly long curve, he was at first unaware of the car that had appeared suddenly from behind. Only when he emerged from the curve, accelerating for the straight stretch of road ahead, did he spot the fast-approaching car in his side mirror.

He heard a swish of tires on the wet road and glanced over his shoulder to see that the dark-colored car had closed the gap and was now on his tail. He sensed a road rage situation in the making but was in no mood for a confrontation—or the inclination to outrun the car, which would have been easy. He slowed and pulled over to the left as far as the narrow road would permit. The hedgerow leaves whipped the sleeve of his jacket as he beckoned for the car to pass. He glanced in his mirror again to see why the driver, a man wearing a cap and wraparound sunglasses, wasn't taking what was a clear opportunity to pass.

Suddenly the hedgerow stopped; in its place was a raised grass verge with a post-and-barbed-wire fence farther back. The road widened, too, and there was no oncoming traffic. Now the drizzle had turned to rain. Wiping his face shield with his glove, the bike rider waved again for the car to pass. At last it accelerated and pulled alongside.

The rider glanced to his right, curious to get a closer look at the hot-footed driver, careful to make it quick. He wasn't about to give the man the slightest reason to think that he was being challenged.

The instant their eyes met, the car swerved hard to its left, slamming the rear wheel of the bike, spinning the 450-pound machine into the verge. Sliding on the slick road, it careered off the grassy mound in a twisting somersault, hurling the rider several feet into the air. The bike landed first, fragments of metal, chrome, and glass showering the road. Two seconds later, beyond the mangled machine, the rider plummeted headfirst to the ground. He crossed his arms in front of his face, but it did little good. His helmet hit the tarmac with a sickening crack, and his body rolled several feet before coming to rest facedown, unmoving.

An eerie silence fell on the scene. The white sound of gentle rain was foreboding.

Then flames started to lick around the ruptured tank.

Suddenly, a roaring explosion, as the motorcycle's twisted remains erupted into a searing ball of flame and smoke.

With a screech of tires and the smell of burning rubber, the car sped off.

Approximately forty-five minutes later, an NHS Oxfordshire ambulance arrived at the Accident and Emergency unit of St. George's Hospital on the outskirts of Oxford, where the unidentified rider, on life support, was rushed to the trauma center.

TWO

Two days later, London

The knees of Kingston's old corduroy trousers were damp muddy blotches, his Wellingtons still wet from the hosing off he'd given them before leaving Andrew's garden. He was tired, his back ached, and he had never been happier to see the shiny black front door of his flat on Cadogan Square in Chelsea. For the best part of the day he had been helping his bachelor friend Andrew double-dig a long border, transplant a camellia, and install an old moss-covered stone trough—a recent auction purchase—in the garden of Andrew's small brick Georgian house on the banks of the Thames in Bourne End.

Andrew—despite countless "auditions" over the years—had never found the woman who measured up to his idea of the perfect wife, never minding that he would make an impossible husband. He had made a small fortune with a dot-com business, bailing out and retiring at the hoary age of fifty-five, just before the bubble burst. Soon thereafter he'd bought the house for cash and proceeded to line the pockets of a reputable garden designer to refurbish the original garden that was first laid out by a former set designer in the early twenties. He jokingly called it his country estate, spending only a few weeks and weekends there, mostly during the summer. He also let his older sister use it, occasionally. The rest of the time he lived in his flat, three doors from Kingston.

When Andrew had said that he could do with a little help, Kingston was only too ready to oblige. No longer having a garden of his own, he seized every opportunity that arose to visit other people's gardens or, as in this case, to help out in whatever way he could. Being a former professor of botany, the demands on his time were all too frequent. These days, though, he pitched in physically only for friends, and never for money.

What Andrew hadn't told him was that the trough weighed four hundred pounds minimum, the border was ten feet deep and thirty feet long, and the camellia was an eight-foot-tall senior citizen with roots that had antipodean ambitions.

Kingston turned on the shower and went into the bedroom to shed his dirty clothes. It was a little after five, plenty of time before the weekly rerun of *As Time Goes By*—his all-time favorite television sitcom—that started at six. Pullover halfway off, he was surprised to hear the phone ring. Not so much because it was unexpected, but more because the call invariably came ten seconds *after* he had just stepped into the shower or bath. Half dressed, he walked barefoot to the living room and picked up the phone.

"Lawrence Kingston," he said, more abruptly than intended.

"Hello, Lawrence, it's Clifford. Hope I'm not calling at a bad time."

"No, not at all," he lied.

Clifford Attenborough was Curator of Horticulture at the

Royal Botanic Gardens, Kew. He was also a former colleague of Kingston's at the University of Edinburgh, and a friend of long standing.

"Good," said Attenborough. "It's about a phone call I received this morning. A Dr. Banks from St. George's Hospital in Oxford contacted our office, asking to speak to someone about recent plant-hunting expeditions initiated by Kew, perhaps. Since I'm also a member of the Field Work Committee, which has an overview of all the expedition work that our staff is engaged in, the call was passed on to me."

"An unusual request, coming from a doctor."

"That's what I thought, until Banks told me why. He said that the night before last, they'd admitted a young man who had suffered serious head and other injuries in a motorcycle accident. He's in a coma and bad shape from all accounts. Here's the curious part, Lawrence. In the small hours of this morning, the man emerged from the coma for a brief period and broke into what one of the nurses described as incoherent mumblings. According to the nurse on duty at the time, the patient's fragmented comments, mostly unintelligible, were about a plant-hunting expedition."

"Did he mention Kew?"

"Not that I'm aware of. One of the doctors up there is an avid gardener apparently, and the minute plant hunting was mentioned, Kew automatically came to mind, hence the call to us." Clifford paused, as if waiting for some kind of response from Kingston. None came.

"Come on, Lawrence. Even you must admit that it's damned intriguing. The office is checking, as we speak, to see what expeditions have taken place in the last—"

"Damn!" Kingston interrupted. He had forgotten all about the shower running. "Hold on a tick, Clifford."

In half a minute he was back.

"Sorry about that," he said, knowing now that the conversation was going to drag on longer than he'd at first hoped. "Sounds intriguing, Clifford. But why call me?"

"In addition to our trying to identify the man, Banks suggested that one of our staff go up to Oxford to meet with him and to observe the patient. With luck, to be present during one of the man's talking spells. He said the man's heavily bandaged, but they'll e-mail me some photos of him anyway."

"Wait a minute, Clifford. You're not suggesting—?"

"Here's the rub, Lawrence. I can't get away right now. Even if I could, I'm not the person to be involved in this. Not only that, I simply don't have anyone to spare right now who's qualified to deal with such a situation. It struck me that—"

"Slow down, Clifford. What on earth do you think I could accomplish that one of your people couldn't?"

While Clifford had been pleading his case, Kingston was starting to have second thoughts. He was doing sod-all right now. A trip up to Oxford in the TR4 might be a nice break for a couple of days. He hadn't visited Oxford Botanic Garden for some time, likewise Blenheim Palace and the gardens and park there. The more he thought about it, the more he realized that he could also make a detour on the way back and stop off to see his old school friend Bertie Conquest, a retired army colonel who lived with his wife on a respectable spread called Pigeon Farm, near Princes Risborough, where they raised miniature horses. By the time Clifford replied, Kingston had talked himself into what was shaping up to be a week's break. Why not?

"Come on, Lawrence, this is right up your alley. You've been on plant-hunting expeditions. You know as much as or more than any of our people about botany and horticulture. Plus, I happen to know you well enough to appreciate your sense of ... well, curiosity, shall we say. You must admit it's a rum set of circumstances."

"Hmm." Kingston had been half listening to what Clifford was

saying. "I suppose they want someone to go up there immediately?"

"They do, yes. Banks said the next forty-eight hours are critical, whether the fellow's going to survive or not. Mind you, for all
we know, the poor chap may have said all he's going to say."

While listening, Kingston had been racking his brain to think
of any good reasons why he should turn Clifford down. He drew
a blank.

"All right, Clifford. I'll run up to Oxford first thing tomorrow.
Dr. Banks, you said, right?" He jotted the name on the pad by the
phone.

"Yes. I'll call him back and tell him to expect you. What time
shall I say?"

"Let's say ten thirty to eleven. You might want to suggest that
they also set up a voice-activated tape recorder in the room."

"Good idea. If Banks has any further questions, or the situation has changed, I'll let you know. Give me your mobile number."

Kingston provided it, saying that he would report back after
his meeting with Dr. Banks and having visited the "mystery" patient.

Clifford thanked him, and the call ended.

THREE

Kingston's decision to take a few days off immediately after his visit to St. George's was looking better by the hour. The weather forecast for the rest of the week was fair and sunny, with little or no chance of rain—which, translated, meant pack an umbrella anyway. With the TR4's top down, under white puffs of cumulus clouds bright against the blue sky, he drove out of London on the A40. Instead of merging onto the Motorway at Uxbridge, by far the fastest route to Oxford, he would stay on the A40. It was too nice a day to be in an open sports car inhaling diesel fumes, and dodging BMWs and Mercedes overtaking at 100 miles an hour.

At ten thirty, Kingston was ushered into Dr. Banks's office. The conversation was brief. Banks reiterated what Clifford had told him, adding that the man had a name, at least for now. He said that the police had informed him that since the man had no wallet, driver's license, credit cards, et cetera, on his person, it was assumed that these had been carried in a tank-top bag, a practice common with bike riders. The only things in the bag that had survived the combustion were two sets of keys and scraps of metal believed to be parts of a mobile phone. The motorcycle license plates identified the owner as a Peter Mayhew, age twenty-seven, of Arundel, West Sussex. So providing somebody else wasn't riding his bike, the police were going on the assumption, for the time being, that the patient was Mayhew.

In answer to Kingston's first question, the doctor said that he'd talked with one of the nurses only twenty minutes earlier, who said the patient hadn't spoken again since his earlier ramblings. The voice-activated tape recorder was on all the time and checked every hour or so. Nothing had been recorded thus far.

Banks suggested that first they visit the patient, and afterward Kingston could speak with Jane Churchill, the nurse who had been present when Mayhew had talked about the expedition. After declining the offer of a cup of tea or coffee, Kingston accompanied Banks through a maze of glassy-floored corridors to a lift that took them to level one, where they were buzzed into the neurological critical care unit. After checking the patient's chart, Banks stood on one side of the bed, Kingston on the other. For a few moments, words seemed gratuitous.

The only part of Mayhew's body not covered by sheets, blankets, and bandages was the area of his face from his brow to just below his lower lip. His eyes were closed and he appeared, to Kingston, to be breathing normally, aided no doubt by the oxygen line to his lungs through a nasal feed. Tubes and cables of varying size, some carrying liquids, were attached to sundry parts of his anatomy. Like thick strands of spaghetti, they looped and coiled their way across and up the bed, each ending at one of the dozen instruments, monitors, and contraptions in the battery on the wall above the headboard, or at the portable stand of medical apparatus on Banks's side of the bed. The only sound was a steady hum, accompanied by the intermittent blips of the monitors as the LCD lights blinked and flickered. In the midst of it all, Kingston spied the portable Sony tape deck, its recording light on.

"The chap's lucky to be alive," said Banks, turning his gaze to Kingston.

Rarely at a loss for words, Kingston was having difficulty framing a response that didn't sound like a platitude. "What are the chances of his making it?" he asked after a while, looking at Banks.

"Still too early to tell. With cases like this, it's impossible to predict the outcome. It could go either way. On the plus side, he's young and before the accident was no doubt in good physical condition."

As Banks was speaking, Kingston was wondering how long he should plan on staying in Oxford. He was booked into the Randolph Hotel for two nights, and the hospital staff were alerted to call him on his mobile the minute Mayhew spoke or regained consciousness. Even without Banks's prognosis, just by looking at the comatose man, Kingston could tell that there was no saying when and if he might talk again. And even if he did, there was no guarantee that he would continue where he'd left off, talking about a plant-hunting expedition. In an altered state of consciousness there was no telling what he might dredge up—his childhood, his school days, almost anything. That prompted another thought, which Kingston was surprised hadn't occurred to him before. Was it concluded that Mayhew had actually been on an expedition? Or had he been harking back on one that he'd read or heard about? Neither Clifford nor Banks had made that clear. He took one last sorry look at Mayhew. Next, he needed to talk with Nurse Jane Churchill. She was the only person who might be able to resolve that question.

The meeting, with Banks present, took place in his office. Jane Churchill had just finished her eight-hour shift and had swapped her uniform for a fleece jacket over a turtleneck sweater, and tan slacks. After a minute or so, describing Kingston's academic background in botany and plant sciences, and explaining to the nurse Kingston's temporary role as a Kew designee, Banks excused himself, leaving them alone in the office. Kingston sat in Banks's chair with a notepad in front of him, Nurse Churchill, hands clasped in her lap, facing him on the other side of the desk.

Kingston ran a hand through his unruly mop of white hair, leaned back, and crossed his legs. "Is it all right if I call you Jane?"

"Of course," she replied.

"As Dr. Banks explained, this is not my usual line of work. I'm here merely as an observer in an attempt to gain further knowledge about your mystery patient, Peter Mayhew."

"I understand. The doctor clued me in earlier."

"Good." Kingston put on his best smile. "So if I come off sounding like a policeman, just let me know."

"Don't worry, I will," she replied, smiling back.

"All right, Jane. Perhaps it'll make it easier if I ask a few questions."

"That's fine."

"Was anybody else with you when the patient started to speak?"

"No, I was alone."

"How long did the episode—for want of a clinical word—last?"

She smiled. "Episode is fine. About a minute—two, at the most."

"Tell me as best as you can recall, Jane, what did the man say?"

"First, I should make it clear that he wasn't speaking normally. His voice was quiet, almost inaudible at times, and there were long pauses between some of the words. He never uttered a complete sentence."

Kingston nodded and jotted something on the notepad.

She looked into middle space for a few seconds. "I believe his first word was 'mountain,' or 'high mountains,' perhaps. Then he mumbled something about a narrow path or trail." She thought for a moment. " 'Vertigo,' I remember that. It's difficult for me to remember the exact sequence."

Kingston scribbled some more notes, then looked back at her. "What words or phrases did he use that led you to believe that he was talking about plant hunting?"

"He mentioned 'plants' and 'seeds' and the word 'expedition' twice, I believe. Also the phrase 'herb specimens.' At least, that's what I thought it was at the time. One of the doctors who's into gardening told me later that it was more likely herbarium specimens."

"He's right. Any others?"

She rubbed her chin, thinking. "He referred to 'field notes' and to 'bloody awful weather.' "

"Anything to suggest where the expedition might have taken place? The country?"

She shook her head. "No, there wasn't."

Kingston uncrossed his legs and leaned forward. "One last question, Jane, if I may. And I realize that it may be unanswerable. Thinking back on it, was there anything the man said that might have led you to believe that he'd been on an expedition? Or did you come away with the impression that he was recalling something that he'd either been told or had read about?"

Jane looked away, mulling over the question. "Of the two," she said, turning back to meet Kingston's blue eyes, "I would say that he *had* been on an expedition. I got the distinct feeling that he was reliving it. As if it were painful to him."

"Good. That's significant." Kingston was silent for a moment, then said, "I'm sure Dr. Banks would have mentioned it, but I'll ask anyway. Has Mayhew had any visitors?"

"No. I would know if he had."

Kingston got to his feet, extending a hand. "Thank you very much, Jane. You've been most helpful."

They were at the office door when she stopped and turned to Kingston. "There was one other thing. I forgot," she said.

"What was that?"

"He mentioned a man's name, Peter. He said it twice as I recall. Soft and drawn out."

"Odd that that's his name, too. Could be more than one Peter, I guess."

"I suppose so. I wondered about that, too."

"Did he say anything about this Peter? I mean, was his name part of a sentence, connected to anything?"

"No, just the name. It was as if Mayhew were calling out to him, perhaps."

"To himself, maybe? But that doesn't make sense."

In the corridor they said goodbye, afterward heading in opposite directions: Jane Churchill to the car park exit, and Kingston to the main entrance, where he would have Dr. Banks paged.

Kingston checked into the Randolph Hotel at 12:30. Over the years, it had served admirably as his pied-à-terre whenever he was in Oxford. He had been told when he'd phoned in the booking that the venerable hotel had recently undergone a face-lift. Now, looking around the ornately appointed lobby and reception area, he was reassured to see that it had lost none of its former warmth and elegance.

The Randolph was located conveniently in the heart of the city, directly opposite the famous Ashmolean Museum. Kingston knew the museum well, also. It was established originally to house curiosities collected by John Tradescant the elder, the seventeenth-century botanist and gardener to royalty. Ironically, Tradescant happened to be one of Britain's first plant hunters.

FOUR

After an undisturbed night's sleep, Kingston phoned the hospital from his room at seven thirty. Put straight through to the critical care ward, he was told that there had been no change in Mayhew's condition and no further outpourings. The news was not surprising and suited Kingston's immediate plan—to repair to the hotel's dining room for a full English breakfast, the works. He picked up the *Times* that the hotel had provided, checked his appearance in the mirror, and left the room. Making his way down the elegant staircase, rather than taking the lift, he remembered to turn off his mobile. He doubted that the hospital would call in the next hour.

Ten minutes later, Kingston was engaged in his daily joust with the *Times* crossword puzzle while tucking into his bacon and eggs, sausage, grilled tomatoes, and toast and marmalade—Cooper's Oxford fine cut, his favorite. At the same time, three miles away on the other side of the city, Peter Mayhew had started to talk again.

Kingston had finished his breakfast and was on his third cup of tea when he looked up from the newspaper to see one of the hotel staff approaching. He recognized the young woman as one of the receptionists.

"Dr. Kingston?"

He nodded.

"Excuse the interruption, sir. St. George's just phoned, asking for you—the hospital. They would like you to call back right away. Here's the number." She handed him a slip of paper.

He thanked her and took the message.

"I do hope everything's all right," she said as she turned and left.

Kingston signed the check, left the restaurant, and headed for the lobby. He found a chair away from the reception area and phoned the number he'd been given.

It was as he expected. The nurse, who had clearly been waiting for his call, said that approximately one hour earlier, Peter Mayhew had broken into another "talking spell." In answer to Kingston's questions, she said that the episode had lasted approximately one minute and was much like the first one, which she and the other nurses in the ward had been briefed about. Nurse Churchill, she added, wouldn't be coming on duty until later that morning. To Kingston's relief, she said that the tape recorder had been checked, and that the episode had been recorded. "His voice is really clear, and they've made a copy for you," she added.

Kingston thanked her, saying that he would be at the hospital within the half hour to listen to the tape.

On arrival at the hospital, Kingston was directed to Dr. Banks's office. Kingston took a seat as Banks pressed the Play button on the portable tape recorder on the desk between them, and the tape started to run.

After a few seconds of ambient sound—the now familiar muted hum and pinging of the electronic instruments—Mayhew's voice cut in. As the nurse had said, his voice, albeit in a low monotone, was surprisingly clear. His first two words were "too dangerous." He repeated them a few seconds later. After a short pause, he mumbled "Peter," the name that Nurse Churchill had mentioned. A longer pause followed, then came a jumble of words strung together: "*Rosa chin* [unintelligible word] . . . important . . . no, no . . . we can't."

Kingston, who had been listening intently while staring at the desktop, glanced at Banks. But before he could make a comment, Mayhew spoke again. His voice had changed. Now it had an edge of urgency, agitation. "Turn back . . . too late now . . . David tried . . . ask Guan Yong."

"There's one more bit," Banks said during the next, longer break.

"Call Lijiang . . . my God . . . accident . . . he's gone."

"That's it," said Banks, stopping the tape. "What do you think?"

"China. That's where he was."

"That would be my guess, too."

"There's no doubt about it. Lijiang is a town in Yunnan Province. It's close to the northwest corner. Several years ago I was on a field trip in that region. The mountain scenery is breathtaking, and the diversity of plant species is amazing. China has more abundant plant life than any country in the world. Last time I checked, there were over thirty-two thousand plant species and nearly three thousand species of trees in China alone. To give you an idea of comparison, there are approximately eight hundred and fifty natural species of rhododendron in the world. Of those, China has six hundred–plus. As a matter of fact, Royal Botanic Garden, Edinburgh, has seen fit to establish a permanent field station in Yunnan."

"I'd like to hear about it one day," said Banks. "You're sure I can't get you coffee or tea?"

"No thanks. I've already had my morning's quota."

Banks was frowning. " 'Guan Yong'? Do you think that he or she was one of their group?"

"Most likely one of the guides, yes. Mayhew's Chinese pronunciation is surprisingly good."

"I wouldn't know," Banks muttered. "The accident? I wonder what that was about."

Kingston shrugged. "It's a dicey business, Doctor. Traipsing through remote parts of that region can be dangerous—certainly not for the faint of heart. It's hardly like a weekend stroll through the Dales. They were probably in an area called Jade Dragon Snow Mountain. Eighteen-thousand-foot elevations are common."

"Sounds like a barrel of fun," Banks said, grimacing.

"I remember one mountain road we encountered was literally cut out of the side of a vertical slope. If you have vertigo or acrophobia, forget it."

"Jesus. If you're trying to impress me, Lawrence, you've succeeded."

Kingston smiled. He couldn't resist one last "Indiana Jones" shot. "The weather can be a bugger, too. You see, nearly all seed-collecting expeditions take place in the autumn. And in that part of the world you never know what to expect: torrential rains, the constant threat of typhoons, the occasional earthquake, just for starters."

"Good God. All this, to collect a few seeds and plants?"

"It sounds irrational, I know, but men have been risking their lives doing it for three hundred years."

Banks was shaking his head. "Not a lot to go on."

"Right. But at least we know the locale and we have a name. That might be sufficient for Clifford and his people to determine who organized the expedition, who was on it, and what Peter Mayhew's role was." Kingston stood, ready to leave.

"Here's a copy." Banks got up from his chair and handed Kingston an audiocassette.

"Thanks." Kingston took a small address book from his inside jacket pocket. "I don't think there's much to be gained from my staying on in Oxford. If Mayhew talks again in the next couple of days, perhaps you could call me at my friend Bertie Conquest's. I'll be staying there tomorrow night through Friday." Kingston tore a perforated page from the back of the address book and wrote down his mobile number, Pigeon Farm's address and phone number, as well as his own in Chelsea. "Also, it might be a good idea if you could have any future taping sessions copied and the cassettes or transcripts sent to both Clifford and me," he said, handing Banks the addresses. "As a matter of fact, I understand there are ways now to e-mail audio messages." He broke into a smile. "Still having one foot in the mid-twentieth century, I haven't the foggiest idea how it's done, but I'm sure someone on your hospital staff will know all about that kind of stuff."

Banks smiled back. "They will, I'm sure. It was a pleasure meeting you, Doctor," he said as they shook hands.

"Likewise," said Kingston.

"Next time you're in Oxford, stop by and say hello." He winked. "I'll show you a few of Morse and Sergeant Lewis's hangouts."

"I certainly will, and I'll let you know how this all works out," Kingston replied, motioning with the cassette before putting it in his pocket. "Most important, I hope your patient makes a full recovery. One day, God willing, he can give us the full story."

Kingston crossed the hospital parking lot, got into the TR4, and checked his watch. It was not yet eleven. He would return to Oxford, park the car in the Randolph's nearby lot, and drop off the tape at his room. After calling Clifford Attenborough and reporting on the day's events, he would spend a leisurely couple of hours strolling around the city, followed by a late pub lunch. The remainder of the cloudless but breezy day would be spent revisiting Britain's oldest botanic garden, the University of Oxford Botanic Garden.

· · ·

The next day, Kingston was settled in the guest cottage at Pigeon Farm, the charming Edwardian country house, home to his friends retired Colonel Bertrand Conquest and his pert wife, Penelope. After the episode at the hospital, he planned to enjoy every minute of his three-day stay. He was looking forward particularly to reacquainting himself with their quintessentially English garden that had been listed in the National Garden Scheme's *Yellow Book* for the last half dozen years and was open to the public on most summer weekends.

As on his previous visits, he knew that Penny would never let him leave without their making the rounds of the stables and paddocks. Like it or not, he was duty bound to spend what customarily amounted to an hour or two fraternizing with the current crop of miniature horses. The concept perplexed him. He couldn't imagine why anyone, other than children, would want to own a miniature horse. Hers were not only miniature but also Falabellas, a relatively rare breed of Argentinean origin that must conform to a strict height requirement at the withers—the ridge between the shoulder bones—of no more than thirty-four inches by the time they reach four years old. Or, as Kingston exclaimed, roughly six inches below his belly button.

Naturally, the number one topic over the roast Aylesbury duckling dinner on the first night was St. George's mystery patient. With a setup that already had the makings of a BBC whodunit, there was no reason for Kingston to add any embellishments. He did anyway, and by the time coffee was served there was much speculating on what might have transpired on what he had volubly portrayed as a plant-hunting expedition gone awfully wrong.

A couple of preprandial scotch whiskies and several glasses of wine had lulled the colonel into a mild state of anesthesia, his responses limited mostly to nods and the occasional grunt. For reasons unknown, the wine had the opposite effect on Penny, not that she'd consumed anywhere near her husband's intake. Before long she had commandeered the conversation with a blitz of questions that would have made a trial lawyer appear tongue-tied.

Kingston soon found that steering the conversation away from the plight of the unfortunate Peter Mayhew and the dangers of plant hunting in faraway parts of the globe was no easy matter. After two hours and far more wine than he was accustomed to drinking at one sitting, it was clear that Penny still didn't fully grasp the concept of plant hunting. Though he was drowsy and ready for bed, he decided that a story might serve to convince her and to close out the night.

"Let me tell you about George Forrest," he said.

"Please do," she replied, wide-eyed.

"Sadly, few people know about him, even dyed-in-the-wool gardeners. Forrest was one of many British plant hunters who changed the face of horticulture in this country. He went on his first serious plant-hunting expedition to China, in 1905, to the northwest corner of Yunnan."

"Same place as the Mayhew expedition?"

"The same region. Yes. Whether he was aware or not at the time, it was a particularly dangerous assignment because the entire area was in a state of political turmoil and civil unrest." Kingston paused to take a sip of water; no more wine for him. "Forrest was a guest of a small French mission, and while he was quietly hunting in the area, lamas—Tibetan priests, that is—were on a rampage in the immediate countryside, committing atrocities and murder."

"Good heavens," Penny muttered.

"Forced to leave the mission, he and his assistants and about sixty men, women, and children set off for the next village several miles away. At midday, on a patch of high ground, they watched as their mission was burned to the ground. Forrest left the group to reconnoiter, looking for a way of escape, but it was too late. From his position on a ridge he watched with horror as the Tibetans rushed forward with their swords and bows with poisoned arrows. The entire group, numbering about eighty, was picked off one by one or captured. Some of the women committed suicide by throwing themselves into a nearby stream to escape slavery."

Kingston now had Penny's rapt attention. "What a horrifying thing to have witnessed," she said.

"Of Forrest's seventeen collectors and servants, only one escaped. The lamas hunted Forrest for eight days and nights. Traveling by night and hiding in the daytime, he managed to subsist on a handful of wheat and dried peas, which he'd found earlier and had the presence of mind to save. Starting to hallucinate, suffering cuts and bruises and limping on swollen feet, he had a number of close calls, including one in which two poisoned arrows passed through his hat. He finally shook off his pursuers and eventually stumbled across a small tribal village."

Bertie interrupted, announcing gruffly that he was "going up the wooden hill" for the night. After he'd left the room, Kingston continued.

"Where were we?" He was having trouble remembering now.

"He'd arrived at the village."

"Right. So, with the aid of friendly villagers, who fed and took care of him for several days, at great risk to themselves, he was able to continue. He was not out of the woods yet, though. With the villagers now helping and hiding him, he discovered that to escape the region required climbing a mountain range with a snow line of eighteen thousand feet. Reaching the summit, Forrest and his party then traveled for six days over glaciers, snow, ice, and jagged limestone until his feet were 'torn to ribbons.' This was not the end to his misery, though. Descending the mountain he stepped on a fire-hardened bamboo spike set by villagers to protect their crops. The one-inch-diameter spike passed straight through his foot, sticking out two inches on the topside."

"Good grief," said Penny.

"Hobbling for several more days, he and the party reached a friendly town where his wound was attended to, and he was fed and rested. When recuperated, he disguised himself as a Tibetan and managed to escape by accompanying a troop of soldiers to the safety of a larger town. There, he learned that, during his nightmarish period of escape, the Foreign Office had declared him as missing, presumed dead."

Kingston folded his arms and leaned back. "So you see, Penny, plant hunting's not exactly for the weekend gardener."

Penny was shaking her head. "I should say not. All to collect seed and find new plants. It's hard to believe."

"Forrest was one of the best. Over the next twenty-seven years, he went on eight more excursions to Yunnan. On his final trip— 1932, I believe it was—he died of a heart attack and was laid to rest in a little churchyard there. In his nearly thirty years of plant hunting, George Forrest collected thirty thousand herbarium specimens and three hundred new introductions of rhododendron."

Kingston had no difficulty nodding off that night.

The next day passed seamlessly. The morning was devoted to a leisurely stroll through the garden with the colonel as guide. Kingston knew of few private gardens with a better collection and display of old roses. Mixed in with perennials and shrubs, they hugged the ground and clambered up old apple trees in the orchard. The walk through the garden was followed by lunch at a local gastro pub: another concept that Kingston found meretricious at best. He found the phrase itself not only oxymoronic but also begging for the insertion of the word "intestinal." By and large, British pubs, along with their excellent beers and ales, were the last bastion of honest-to-goodness, decently cooked, predictable food in the country. Kingston had no problem with landlords stepping up the quality and widening the selection of their menus, but—much as he appreciated fine food—in no way did truffles, duck confit, and foie gras belong in the local pub.

What remained of the afternoon was dedicated to miniature horses.

The following morning, Kingston was sitting in the conservatory with a cup of tea, reading the local newspaper, when he heard the phone ringing in another part of the house. "Phone for you, Lawrence," Penny called out a few seconds later.

He went into the living room, where he found Penny pointing in the direction of the hall. As far as he could recall he'd given the Conquests' number only to his friend Andrew and Dr. Banks. On the hall table he saw the phone, off the cradle, and picked it up.

"Lawrence Kingston," he said.

"Hello, Lawrence. It's Donald Banks. Sorry to call so early, but I've got some rather bad news."

It must be about Mayhew, thought Kingston. Why else would Banks be calling?

"Peter Mayhew died last night."

"That *is* bad news. I'm sorry it had to go that way."

"Yes. It was quite a shock. I was convinced he would pull through. We all were. So much so that we'd moved him out of ICU. That's why we decided to establish the cause of death."

In the pause that followed, Kingston was wondering if that was standard procedure in such cases. Before he could ask, Banks spoke again.

"It's a police matter now, I'm afraid."

"A police matter?"

"Yes. Peter Mayhew didn't die as a result of his injuries. It was an overdose of lidocaine. It's widely used as a local anesthetic, but excessive doses lead to cardiac arrest and death." Banks paused. "It was never administered to Mayhew by anyone on the hospital staff. Someone wanted to stop him from talking, by the looks of it."

"Good Lord!"

"Quite a turn up for the books, eh? By the way, I told the police of your involvement and they'll probably want to talk with you. I gave them your address and phone numbers. I hope that was all right."

"That's fine."

"There was something else. The inspector I talked with—Sheffield—said that another vehicle was involved in Mayhew's accident. They found fragments of glass from a vehicle other than the bike. Skid marks, too."

"A hit-and-run, by the sound of it."

"Inspector Sheffield didn't speculate, but now, with Mayhew most likely having been murdered, it would seem a possibility, one would think?"

Banks's question went unanswered for a moment while Kingston contemplated the inescapable: Someone had managed to slip into Mayhew's room, unnoticed, and given him a lethal injection. "Yes, it would," he replied.

"Well, I'm sorry to have spoiled your day, Lawrence. When are you returning to London?"

"In all probability, tomorrow."

"You'll inform Clifford Attenborough, of course."

"I will, yes."

"Goodbye, then. Don't forget to call me next time you're in Oxford."

"That's a promise."

Kingston put the phone down and stood for a moment, shaking his head, mulling over the grim news and its implications. After several moments, he turned and went through the French doors into the garden to tell Penny and Bertie.

FIVE

Kingston left Pigeon Farm that afternoon after lunch, cutting short his stay by one day. On the drive back to London, with the radio off, he had plenty of quiet time to mull over the troubling events of the last few days, trying to fathom why someone wanted Peter Mayhew silenced and how the assailant managed to do it. In the end, he could think of nothing further that might change his original line of reasoning and first-blush conclusion: Mayhew's murder was linked somehow to the expedition. If so, he could only suppose that something had happened on the expedition that one or more of the other members didn't want revealed. Whatever that "something" was had to be serious enough, so incriminating, to warrant taking a man's life. The police would have heard the tape by now. He wondered if they'd come up with anything. Five minutes later, passing through Beaconsfield, he gave up thinking about it and turned on the radio.

Kingston arrived at his Chelsea flat just after four. Before calling

Kew again, he decided that a cup of tea was in order. He'd called twice from Pigeon Farm, but on each occasion Clifford was away from the office.

He put the kettle on and opened the biscuit tin, to find that he was out of digestives. "Damn," he muttered. In the living room he checked the answerphone. The LCD display showed three messages. Kingston couldn't help but smile. A metaphor for his social life: gone for four days and only three messages. The first was from his friend Andrew, inviting Kingston to lunch. The next, from his garage, was a reminder that the TR4 was due for a minor service the coming Wednesday. The last was a message from Detective Inspector Sheffield, Thames Valley Police, asking Kingston to return his call.

Kingston sat on the sofa and dialed the Oxford number. In no time at all, the inspector was on the line.

"Ah, Dr. Kingston. Thanks for getting back to me so quickly. The people at St. George's said you were taking a few days off. Decided my questions could wait 'til you returned."

"Yes. I just got back from visiting friends in Princes Risborough."

"Dr. Banks told me about your subbing for the people at Kew and what happened when you were at the hospital."

Kingston detected the hint of a North Country accent. Unusual for an Oxford cop, he thought. "Yes. Frankly, I didn't realize what I was letting myself in for."

"You're aware that we have Peter Mayhew's death listed as a homicide?"

"Yes, Dr. Banks told me."

"He informed me that you're a retired professor of botany."

"That's right."

"He said that you'd also been on a plant-hunting expedition in China. That was one of the reasons for Kew Gardens having asked you to provide assistance, if I'm correct."

"Yes, that's right. It was a long time ago—the expedition, that is."

"The things that Mayhew talked about, did it strike you that he was speaking from experience?"

"There's little doubt. In my opinion, everything he said would seem to confirm that he had indeed been on an expedition. The mention of herbarium specimens, field notes, seeds—they're all key indicators."

"And China's a popular destination for plant hunting, I take it?"

Kingston smiled at Sheffield's choice of words. He certainly wasn't a gardener, that was for sure. "It is, and has been for many centuries," Kingston replied, biting his tongue.

One of those awkward pauses followed where each waited for the other to speak.

"On the tape, Mayhew mentioned *Rosa chin* something," said Kingston. "That's even more significant."

"Why is that?"

"He's almost certainly referring to *Rosa chinensis* var. *spontanea*. It's an ancient species of wild rose. Its age is unknown, but could date from at least the eleventh century B.C. One of the ancestors of most of today's rose cultivars—certainly the hybrid teas and floribundas. It may well have been the reason for the expedition in the first place. By all indications, an expedition that went wrong."

"It certainly looks that way." Sheffield paused, then said, "Mayhew mentioned an 'accident.'"

"Yes. Banks and I discussed that. Because of the hardships, the often-inhospitable terrain, plus the awful weather, accidents are not uncommon, particularly late in the year, in that treacherous mountainous region."

"I see. Anything more you can think of?"

"Not really. No."

"Well, Doctor, thanks for your input. Let's hope Attenborough can track down whose expedition it was and who else was on it. Obviously, that information could be extremely helpful."

"Oh, they'll track it down, all right. You couldn't mount a plant-hunting expedition to China without leaving a paper trail. If Kew draws a blank in Britain, they'll contact the relevant authorities in China: immigration, botanical organizations, universities, people who act as guides and drivers. I understand that they keep meticulous records. These trips require a lot of planning and liaison with officials in the country concerned."

"I can well understand."

Sheffield's mention of the word "accident" reminded Kingston of what Dr. Banks had said about the motorcycle accident. "I hope you don't mind my asking, Inspector," he said, "but Dr. Banks told me that you had more information about the motorcycle accident— that another vehicle was involved."

"That's correct. Forensics confirmed that there was another vehicle. It's going to be hard to track it down, though. The bike had saddlebags, which probably explains why we don't have any cross transfer of paint on the bike parts. Otherwise, we might be able to identify the make, model, color, and year of the vehicle from the manufacturer's paint layers. Though the accident seems suspicious, we can't assume that it was attempted vehicular homicide—which is a bit rare, I might add, because there's usually no guarantee that the victim will be killed. Frankly, it's much more likely that it was a simple case of hit-and-run."

"What about family, next of kin?"

Sheffield chuckled. "I'm the one who's supposed to be asking the questions, Doctor. But to answer your question, we're doing just that: trying to locate relatives, friends, and neighbors, anyone who knew him."

A few moments later, the conversation ended.

Kingston sat on the sofa thinking about what Sheffield had

said. Other than the vehicle that was involved in Mayhew's accident, the police apparently knew little more than he did. He went into the kitchen to make a pot of tea.

It wasn't until the end of the afternoon that Kingston finally managed to reach Clifford Attenborough. As it turned out, Inspector Sheffield had beaten him to the punch, so there was nothing for Kingston to report that Clifford didn't know already. The sixty-four-thousand-dollar question—who sponsored the expedition to China and who was on it?—remained unanswered. Clifford said that thus far they had been unsuccessful in tracking down any information about the expedition in Britain. That led them to believe that the project might have been initiated outside the UK. Because the search was now central to a murder investigation, it had been given top priority, and a multiteam task force had been set up at Kew to come up with answers. Currently one team was working full-time contacting all listed botanical organizations and arboretums abroad, particularly those in the United States. Another team was working with counterpart authorities in China. It could take time, Clifford said.

That day, the *Oxford Mail* carried a page-two story about the suspected murder at the hospital and the motorcycle accident. The report identified Peter Mayhew as the victim but made no mention of a plant-hunting expedition.

Midmorning, two days later, a cherry-red Mini Cooper S pulled up outside Kingston's flat. Andrew got out, bounded up the steps, and rang the doorbell. Kingston emerged seconds later and went through the now accustomed exercise of squeezing his six-foot-three-inch frame into a space the size of a small fridge. At least it was easier in the new Mini than in the old one.

As they drove off, Andrew said cheerily, "You're going to love this place, old chap. Word has it that Jamie Oliver practically lives there these days." Kingston knew, of course, that they were going to lunch, but not where. Andrew always liked the element of surprise. Not that it bothered Kingston, as long as Andrew was picking up the tab. From his modest stature and unassuming build, one would be hard-pressed to know that he was such an epicurean athlete. Why he didn't weigh 250 pounds by now was a small miracle. Kingston figured the only explanation was Andrew's partiality for the much-ballyhooed French diet, coupled with an astonishing capacity for mostly Bordeaux and Burgundy red wines—either that or something to do with his genes.

Forty minutes later, they were seated at a white-clothed table at Skate, a recently opened fish restaurant in Chalfont St. Giles in Buckinghamshire, thirty miles west of London. Andrew was quick to point out the obvious: There were only eleven other tables, all filled with well-dressed diners, each jam-packed with plates, cutlery, wine bottles, and enough wineglasses to stock the Ritz. By the subdued decibel level alone, it was evident that those who lunched and dined at Skate were serious about their food. Rich, too, going by the Jags, BMWs, and Mercedes in the dinky car park.

"Superb" was the only word Kingston could come up with to describe the lunch and the 1995 Pomerol that Andrew had selected to "match" the food. Regretfully, one embarrassing incident marred the experience. Midmeal, Kingston's mobile started ringing. He could have sworn that he'd turned it off, but there it was, sounding off in the middle of the main course. Instantly, a steely silence fell over the convivial scene. Forks, wineglasses, and voices were lowered. Heads swiveled, and withering looks zapped in Kingston's direction like poisoned darts. What made matters worse was that his ring tone was the "Colonel Bogey March." In no time, everyone in the restaurant, save Kingston and Andrew, was whistling—derisively.

Afterward, in the car park, Kingston checked the missed-call message. It was from Clifford Attenborough. As Andrew drove off, Kingston turned down the volume of the concerto on the radio and thumbed in Clifford's number. After a lengthy wait he was put through.

"Hello, Lawrence. Sorry to keep you waiting."

"No problem. Anything more on the plant-hunting expedition?"

"Not yet, I'm afraid. It's taking much longer than I'd anticipated. The good news is that we're pretty sure it didn't originate in the UK. The bad news, as you know, is that we have no idea when it took place. That's what's slowing us down. Don't worry, though, we'll have an answer soon."

"Let me know when you do. I'm curious."

"Of course I will."

In the following pause, Kingston was wondering why Clifford had called. Apparently it wasn't about the expedition. His question was answered without his having to ask.

"That wasn't why I called, Lawrence. I just got a phone call from Inspector Sheffield, and I thought you might want to know that there's been a new development in the case of that poor chap who was killed in the hospital. His name escapes me."

"Peter Mayhew."

"Right."

"Well, that's good news. What did Sheffield say?"

"Yesterday morning, Thames Valley Police received a phone call from a woman named Sally Mayhew saying that she was Peter Mayhew's half sister." Kingston was about to ask how she had learned about her brother's death but before he could, Clifford saved him the breath.

"It seems that a friend of hers who lives in Oxford saw the report in the *Mail* and read it to her over the phone."

"That must have been a nasty shock."

"In more ways than one, apparently."

"How come?"

"Well, about a minute into the conversation with the officer who took the call, the woman dropped a bombshell. She said that her brother had gone missing eight months ago on a plant-hunting expedition, and that though his body was never recovered, he was presumed dead. An inquest was held some months later."

"Good Lord."

"That's not all, Lawrence. This morning, she drove up to Oxford from Harrow—where she lives—for an interview with Sheffield and to identify the body."

"And did she—identify it, I mean?"

"Apparently not."

"I'm not sure that I follow you. Are you saying—?"

"That's right. The man in the city morgue is not Peter Mayhew."

SIX

W ell I'll be damned," Kingston murmured, closing the phone.

Andrew glanced at him, frowning. "What was all that about?"

"It was Clifford Attenborough."

"Your friend at Kew?"

"Right. He just got a call from Thames Valley Police. A woman called them claiming to be Peter Mayhew's sister—half sister, actually."

"Good."

Kingston shook his head. "Not really."

"Why?"

"She says that the body in the morgue is not her brother."

"Bloody hell!"

Kingston gave him a hesitant look and reached to turn off the radio. " 'Bloody hell' is right."

A short silence followed, each weighing the implications. Then Andrew spoke. "Are you saying that they killed the wrong man?"

"That's what it looks like. There's no other explanation. Whoever entered the ward that night, intent on murder, had to believe that his victim was Mayhew."

"The hospital thought so, too, and the paper reported it. Why would he—or she, I suppose—think differently?"

"Good question." Kingston gazed at the road ahead, thinking.

"What else did he say? You were talking for a good two minutes."

Kingston leaned back and told him everything Clifford had said. For a change—unlike when Kingston was describing his two-day Oxford experience over lunch—Andrew listened without butting in every ten seconds.

"That's the end of it, then?" said Andrew, his eyes watchful of the bumper-to-bumper traffic ahead. "I mean, as far as you're concerned?"

Kingston didn't answer right away. As he was thinking, he mumbled a grudging, "I suppose so."

He knew that Andrew was probably right. It was no longer just a question of trying to establish what had happened on an ill-fated plant expedition. It was now a murder case, and unless Clifford or the police were to ask him to collaborate further, he had no choice but to forget about it. The more he thought on it, the more he decided that it was probably a good thing. He looked at Andrew. "But if the police should ask me to help, I can hardly refuse to cooperate, can I?"

Andrew shot him a quick glance. "What kind of question is that? If you want my opinion—and you probably don't—let the police handle it. That's what they do. Before you know it you could easily find yourself in another mess, like the last time."

Kingston nodded but said nothing. Andrew was referring to

another murder case in which Kingston had become innocently embroiled. Three years ago, a former botanist colleague of his, Stewart Halliday, had gone missing and Kingston had promised the man's wife to help in the search. Before he knew it, he too was targeted by the people responsible for the kidnapping, narrowly escaping an ignominious end in a far-off land. Though it had a favorable outcome—for some, anyway—he preferred not being reminded of it.

Andrew continued in a lighter vein, eyes still on the road. "This is just an observation, so take it for what it's worth. I realize that it may come off as sounding a bit rich coming from me, but . . . well . . . don't you think the time may have come for you to, shall we say, have another woman in your life? Or at least consider it."

Kingston smiled. "Did you have anybody in mind?"

"Of course not. The idea only just occurred to me." After a pause he said, "Well, to be honest, the idea has crossed my mind a couple of times recently."

Kingston looked at the road ahead. "You think I've become a misogynist?"

"Lord no!"

"Look, Andrew, we've talked about this before. I realize that you mean well, but I've come to accept that I'll probably remain a bachelor, like you. In fact, though it's taken me a long time, I've learned to enjoy being single. That shouldn't be too hard for you, of all people, to understand."

"I wasn't necessarily suggesting marriage, Lawrence."

"Even so, a relationship is a big commitment. Mind you, I'm not saying that I'd rule it out entirely—companionship, that is. That said, I find the idea of actually looking for someone not appealing but appalling. Out of the question. If you think I'm going to go online and join one of those god-awful dating or matching services, you can forget it, Andrew."

"I'm sorry I brought it up, old chap."

Kingston looked at him and smiled. "If it *were* to happen, and I hit it off with some femme fatale, has it occurred to you that you could lose out, too? You wouldn't have my scintillating company for lunch and dinner so often, and no one to help you in your garden. Not to mention your having to find a new tennis partner."

Andrew shrugged and shook his head. "I worry about you sometimes. That's all."

They were crossing the river at Kew, close to home now, and had arrived at an unspoken meeting of the minds that there was nothing to be gained by further flogging to death either the subject of Kingston's bachelorhood or the mystery surrounding Peter Mayhew. For his part, Kingston was content to remain mostly silent, retreating into his own thoughts. Andrew turned the radio back on, tweaked the volume up, and the joyful strains of Vivaldi burst forth from the Mini's six speakers, drowning all other sounds.

In no time at all, it seemed, Kingston was back at his flat, more confused than ever about the nefarious goings-on that had taken place in Oxford.

In the days following, neither Clifford Attenborough nor Inspector Sheffield called. At first Kingston's nose was out of joint, but he soon became reconciled to the fact that his job was done. His participation, short-lived and negligible as it had been, was no longer needed. No doubt he would hear from Clifford sooner or later and learn about the expedition—when it was, where it originated, and who was on it—but that most likely would be the end of it. The best he could do was to keep a weather eye on the telly and the *Oxford Mail* Web site, hoping to catch newsbreaks about the case.

So it came as a surprise when a man named Trevor Williams

called late one morning saying that he was a reporter for the *Mail* and was Kingston willing to be interviewed about his role in the Peter Mayhew case? With barely a blink, Kingston agreed.

Williams asked where Kingston would like the interview to take place. He was coming down to London anyway, he said, to interview Sally Mayhew, Peter Mayhew's sister, and for obvious reasons he would like to do both interviews on the same day. Kingston saw the opening immediately. "Would you have any objection to interviewing us together?" he asked. Williams was agreeable and they made a tentative date to meet at Kingston's flat the coming Saturday at eleven A.M. Williams would call Sally Mayhew and let Kingston know if that suited her. An hour later he called back, saying he'd talked with her, and that it was a go.

Kingston went to the window, looking out onto parklike Cadogan Square. He smiled. Maybe he wasn't off the case after all—at least not for a while. He couldn't wait to hear Sally Mayhew's side of the story.

On Saturday morning, Williams arrived first. He was of average height, forty-something, and didn't fit Kingston's mental picture of a reporter. To him, newspapermen and schoolteachers were expected to look tweedy, even a little down-at-the-heels, and be generally mild mannered. Williams was fashionably dressed, outgoing, and by most standards would be considered good-looking. Just as he and Kingston had finished their introductions, Sally Mayhew arrived.

Kingston was off base with her, too. He had been expecting a considerably younger woman, assuming wrongly that Peter Mayhew would be the older sibling—and forgetting for the moment that the man he'd seen in the hospital wasn't Peter. He shook her hand, surprised at the firmness of her grip, making him wonder what she did for a living; Clifford hadn't mentioned that. She had hazel eyes, wrinkled at the corners, shoulder-length auburn hair, and save for a smudge of lip gloss wore hardly any makeup. A little might have helped, Kingston thought, as she and Williams shook hands.

The two visitors spent a few moments admiring Kingston's flat, complimenting him on how it was decorated and on his eye for antiques. Williams, who did most of the talking, was clearly bowled over by the eighteenth- and nineteenth-century English furniture; the Constable, the John Sell Cotman watercolor, and other fine paintings; the book-lined walls and overabundance of artifacts and bibelots. Collectively, they were a fitting metaphor for Kingston's refined taste, his eye for design, and his well-traveled life.

It was agreed that tea or coffee could come later, and they all took a seat.

"Okay if we start with you, Doctor?" asked Williams.

Kingston nodded. "Certainly."

Over the next several minutes Kingston related his experience, starting from the first phone call from Clifford Attenborough asking him to act as their proxy at St. George's Hospital, up to Clifford's recent call with the news that the body in the Oxford morgue was not Peter Mayhew. Williams listened intently, with few questions, making notes on the pad in his lap.

When finished, Kingston went to the kitchen, where he put the kettle on low heat and returned immediately. Next it was Sally Mayhew's turn. Kingston leaned back in his chair, trying not to make it too obvious that he was studying her. If she took a little more care over her appearance, she could be quite attractive, he thought.

"It must have been an awful shock to learn that your brother was a suspected murder victim," said Williams reverentially. "I'm sorry you had to go through that ordeal."

Sally Mayhew pursed her lips. "Accepting his death once was heartache enough. But to be told that he had been alive all this time and then, on top of that, had just been murdered—there are no words to describe how I felt." She made an anemic attempt to smile, then said, "I've gotten over it now, though."

"Tell me about your brother. What line of work was he in? How did he come to be on this plant-hunting expedition?"

"Peter worked at Melbury Botanical Gardens. It's a small place down in West Sussex, not too far from Arundel. I'm not exactly sure what his position was. Fairly important, I think."

"He was a gardener, a horticulturist?"

"Yes. Early on, he took a course at Hadlow College in Kent, liked it a lot, and went on to get a BSc in commercial horticulture." She looked at Williams tentatively. "You do know that he was my half brother?"

"Yes, the police told me."

"Growing up, we spent a lot of time together, but in later years we didn't see each other that often. In recent years, we lost touch altogether, sad to say. It happens with a lot of families, I suppose. It's a shame, really, because I was very fond of Peter. He was one of those people who go out of their way to help others. Thoughtful, always upbeat, everyone took a shine to him." She paused, as if talking about him had aroused memories that had lain dormant for too long. "That's why I can't tell you too much about what he did."

"When did you learn about the expedition?" asked Williams.

"I learned about it after the fact."

"Peter never discussed it with you before he went?"

"He didn't, no. That didn't surprise me, though. One of the men who'd been on the expedition phoned me and told me what had happened. At that time, it wasn't certain if Peter was alive or not."

"You received the phone call soon after they returned, then?" said Kingston.

Sally nodded.

"When was this, Sally? When did the expedition take place?" asked Williams.

"October, last year," she replied. "The man who called was Julian Bell. He said that he'd just returned from an expedition in China that was aborted because of a terrible accident, and that it was almost certain that Peter, who was a member of the group, had lost his life in the accident. He'd fallen into a gorge that plunged hundreds of feet into a river. He said that they'd reported the accident to the Chinese authorities on their satellite radio and that he'd tried unsuccessfully to reach me from a nearby village when they came down off the mountain." She gestured, as if to say that was about it.

"I can just imagine what a blow that must have been," said Williams. To his credit, he didn't press Sally with more questions, instead giving her breathing time before continuing. Williams made more notes then looked at her again. "I take it that Peter's body was never recovered?"

"No. I was told later that they'd conducted an exhaustive land and helicopter search but called it off after two weeks. They said that his body was most likely washed away in the fast-flowing river."

"Let me know whenever you want to take a break," said Kingston diplomatically. The whistle of the teakettle was barely audible.

Williams looked at Sally. "It's entirely up to you."

"I'm fine. Let's continue."

"Very well," said Williams, clearing his throat. "The police said that you'd given them the names of the other members of the expedition." He consulted his notepad. "Six all told. Is that right?"

"Not counting the Chinese men, yes. Julian Bell told me that, in addition to him and Peter, there were three other botanists, all men: Spenser Graves, David Jenkins—from Cornwall, I believe—and the third—" She looked up to the ceiling for a moment. "An American, Todd something-or-other. I don't recall his surname."

"That's only five."

"You're right. Bell said the sixth man was a photographer who was also proficient in Mandarin and knew some Chinese-Tibetan. I don't recall his name. Come to think of it, I'm not even sure Bell mentioned it." She looked aside briefly, then said, "I believe he was recommended by Peter."

Kingston was tempted to interrupt, to ask Sally more questions about the botanists, such as whether Bell had told her who had initiated the expedition. But he held his tongue. Why stick his oar in when Williams was off to such a good start? So far he had handled the interview patiently and competently, building a profile of Peter Mayhew and starting to shape a picture of what had happened on the ill-fated expedition.

The reporter continued. "I understand there was an inquest. I haven't had time to obtain copies of the notes of evidence yet. What were the findings, Sally?"

"Accidental death. But we have to wait another six years for a death certificate."

"I read that the government may be reducing the wait to three years, as a result of the hundreds of British subjects who went missing in the great tsunami," said Kingston.

"Seven years *is* a damned long time to wait," said Williams. He looked at Sally again. "Were any of the expedition members present at the inquest?"

"Only Julian Bell. It surprised me. I believe the others were told about it. I didn't expect the American to come, of course, but I'd have liked to have talked to the others."

Williams put aside his pad and pencil. "Anything that you want to ask Sally before we take a break, Doctor?"

"There is, if that's all right." Kingston shifted his position so that he was facing Sally. "In addition to that first phone call, did this Julian Bell fellow tell you more about the expedition—at the inquest, perhaps?"

"Yes, he did, but very little, really. When we first met, about ten minutes before the inquest started, he came off as self-important. He's a large man, with a bushy beard, a bit fierce-looking. We chatted again after the inquest, and this time he was very solicitous and kind. He suggested we go to a tea shop in the village so we could talk about it some more."

"The least he could do one would think, under the circumstances," said Williams.

Sally nodded, then continued. "He said that, in addition to the six members of the expedition, there were two Chinese guides and a botanist from a local institute. They'd collected quite a few specimens, seeds—or whatever it was they were looking for—during the first days. As I recall, he said that it was planned as a two-week trip but was aborted after the accident, on the ninth day. I remember his saying that the weather turned very nasty, too."

"By chance did he mention who organized the trip? Who funded it?"

Sally shook her head.

"What about the accident itself? Did he describe how it happened?"

"Briefly, yes. He said that they were on a narrow trail, near the summit of a high mountain. A bad storm had blown in and it was raining. The rocky trail was cut from the side of the mountain, leaving a steep gorge on one side. Peter started to complain of vertigo and stumbled." She closed her eyes for a moment, then looked back at Kingston. "It makes me dizzy even to think about it."

"I know what it can be like," Kingston said softly.

"Apparently, he insisted that he was all right and they continued. A short distance later, he stumbled again, falling to the ground. As he did so, the guide behind him lost his footing, too, and fell into the wall side of the trail, pushing Peter closer to the edge of the gorge. Before any of them could reach him, Peter got to his feet again. Bell thought he was okay, had gotten over it.

Then suddenly—probably looking down into the gorge—Peter lost his balance and fell over the edge." She pursed her lips again. "That was all," she said, a slight tremor in her voice.

A respectful silence followed. Reliving the tragedy, as recounted by Bell, was still painful to her. "I've read about Julian Bell," said Kingston, recognizing that a change of subject was called for. "There was a story about him in one of the garden magazines a couple of years ago—big chap, as you say, with a full beard. Doesn't he own a big farm somewhere in Dorset? Used to be a doctor?"

"Yes. He spent quite a bit of time talking about the place. He describes himself as strictly an amateur horticulturist, but you could tell that he's very knowledgeable and passionate about plants and collecting them."

"Thank you, Sally," said Kingston. "I'm sorry all this had to be resurrected. You've been very patient and understanding." He looked at Williams. "That's all I have," he said.

Williams nodded, then addressed Sally. "A couple more questions, then we'll wrap it up. What about the man in the morgue? He was riding your brother's motorcycle."

"I know."

"You didn't know who he was, I take it?"

"No. I didn't. He looked a little older than Peter, not by much, though. I'd never seen him before."

"This is probably a redundant question, but I'll ask it anyway. Do you know of anyone who might have had it in for Peter? Wanted to harm him?"

"No, I don't," she answered emphatically.

Shortly thereafter, the meeting was adjourned and Kingston served tea in china cups accompanied by scones from a local patisserie. Before leaving, Sally Mayhew and Kingston exchanged phone numbers, promising to keep in touch.

. . .

The much-anticipated call from Clifford Attenborough came the following morning. Kingston had just finished breakfast and had put aside the *Times*, having finally completed the Jumbo cryptic crossword. The very last clue had stumped him all yesterday: 8 down: *Round after round here?* (10,4). The answer was *nineteenth hole*.

"Sorry to call on a Sunday," Clifford said, "but I thought you'd like to know right away. It took longer than I'd hoped for, but we finally tracked down Mayhew's expedition."

"Good work." Kingston decided to wait before telling him what he'd learned from Sally Mayhew.

"There were six chaps," said Clifford. "Spenser Graves, from Audleigh Gardens up in Leicestershire, was one of them. I'm sure you must know him, Lawrence? The house has exceptional gardens and an impressive arboretum."

"I've met him on a couple of occasions, though I can't confess to knowing him personally. Bit of an eccentric, I recall."

"He's that all right. Did you ever visit his place?"

"No, but I've read about it. Big Victorian pile with the huge aviary and peacocks strutting the lawns."

"Right. Anyway, second on the trip was David Jenkins, who runs a tree farm–cum–nursery in Cornwall. Can't say that I know much about him, but apparently his place is known for its collection of dogwoods, Acers, and Stewartia. One of our chaps at Kew worked for him a few years back. Said Jenkins is a reclusive sort, collects Japanese sculptures."

"I don't know him, either."

"Third was our old friend Julian Bell."

"Yours, perhaps. I don't know him personally. I do know about him, of course."

"Fourth was an American, Todd Kavanagh. Interesting bloke, from all accounts. He runs Ravenscliff Botanical Garden in Mendocino County, in Northern California—quite a remarkable place, from the sound of it. A best-kept secret, carved out of the slopes of an old quarry. It's only twenty years old but their Web site lists it as the largest collection of temperate Asian plants in North America."

"I wonder why I've never heard of it."

"I have. He's been on expeditions with our people before." Attenborough paused. "The fifth man was Mayhew, of course."

"What was his background?"

"We don't have a lot on him yet. It seems that after grammar school he worked at a nursery for a couple of years, then took a three-year horticultural course at Hadlow, getting a bachelor's degree. Most recently he worked at Melbury Botanical Gardens, in Dorset."

"And the sixth chap?"

"A fellow named Jeremy Lester. Mayhew roped him in to document the trip on film and, if needs be, act as interpreter. He's fluent in Chinese. Not that they necessarily needed an interpreter; a botanist from the Kunming Institute was on the trip, along with two guides."

"Who organized the trip?"

"The Ravenscliff people, the Americans. That's why it took this long. I just got off the phone giving Inspector Sheffield the names. He said they've made no progress on the case. The expedition was October, last year."

"Yes, I know. Sally Mayhew told me."

"She did?"

"Yes. I should have told you sooner but I wanted to see if her account jibed with yours. Yesterday a reporter for the Oxford paper interviewed the two of us about Peter's death and the murder at the hospital."

"Really? How did she learn all this?"

"From Julian Bell. They met at the inquest, apparently—the inquest into Peter's death. Naturally the police have talked to her, too."

"We should get together and compare notes, Lawrence. It's certainly a rum affair."

"That it is."

"Anyway, I've got to run or I'll miss my tee-off time at Sunningdale this afternoon."

"Wouldn't want that to happen. I'll give you a call in the next few days, Clifford."

SEVEN

Kingston spent the rest of the day on the Internet. The first Web site he visited was Ravenscliff Botanical Garden. He was curious to find out more about their garden. The site was obviously professionally designed, providing a comprehensive picture and history of the garden with an extensive catalog of digital photographs documenting all the plants there.

Ravenscliff, he read, was in the foothills of the Mendocino Mountains on the southern border of Mendocino County where it adjoins Sonoma County, California. In 1967, Byron and Elizabeth Granger purchased seventy-five acres of the foothill land, planting vineyards in the valley floor section. Twenty years later, after her husband's death, Elizabeth began to create a garden on the rocky hillside above the vineyards. The remains of several old quarries dot the site. In the winter months, these excavations fill with water, eventually forming ponds and waterfalls. There is no better site for a botanical garden. The ravens that nested in the tall pines had given the garden its name.

Kingston scrolled down and continued to read: The slopes of Ravenscliff are home to one of the largest collections of scientifically documented, wild-origin Asian plants in North America. For twenty years Ravenscliff has participated in annual expeditions to China, Japan, India, Nepal, and Taiwan to collect seeds and herbarium specimens. Every last plant, shrub, and tree is sown from seeds collected in Asia. The garden boasts seed-started trees that are now fifty feet tall.

Next Kingston clicked on the Staff List button, where he found a biography of Ravenscliff's director, Todd Kavanagh. His credentials were impressive. Early in his career as a horticulturist he took a yearlong sabbatical to tour gardens in Asia and take treks into remote areas of China and Tibet. Returning to the United States, he and a partner opened a nursery and landscaping business in Mendocino County. Byron and Elizabeth Granger were among his first clients. Hired to take care of the one-acre ornamental garden surrounding the Grangers' home, Kavanagh's responsibilities were expanded considerably when he was asked to help create the new botanical garden. As a result he went to work full-time at Ravenscliff, eventually being promoted to director. His credentials listed him as a field associate of the Department of Botany, California Academy of Sciences, San Francisco, and an associate member of the Chinese Society for Horticultural Science. Kingston was impressed with the last line of Kavanagh's bio: He was also an accomplished classical pianist and transpacific sailor. He leaned back, thinking. It would be interesting to meet the man.

Next Kingston Googled Audleigh Hall, home of the enigmatic Spenser Graves. Scrolling down, he found that the house and arboretum were featured in various travel, stately homes, and garden sites but there was no individual Web site. Kingston didn't find this particularly unusual, knowing Graves's idiosyncratic nature and reputation as a recluse.

He sat looking at the screen and a small aerial picture of the rambling old redbrick-and-tile mansion, its gravel courtyard and sweeping lawns and formal gardens that featured some of the finest herbaceous borders in Britain. He noted that the revered Graham Stuart Thomas had designed the garden of old heirloom roses. Kingston went on to discover that parts of the estate's extensive collection of Asian art, portraits by Gainsborough and Reynolds, and works by Dutch and Flemish masters were on display to the public. After viewing more sites, seeing more pictures, and learning more about the Graveses' family seat and its "world-renowned" collection of plants from the temperate regions of the world, Kingston had convinced himself that a visit was a must. To see the arboretum was reason enough, but with the added attraction of the art and antiques, it was just too inviting to pass up. Even better, if Spenser Graves still remembered him—it had been some years since they'd met—perhaps he could wangle an invitation. It was certainly worth a try.

Two days later, Kingston double-locked the door of his rented garage, set the alarm system, and climbed into his TR4. After the break-in and theft of his prized Triumph sports car, two years earlier, he had taken measures to make sure that it couldn't happen again. With the top down on a bright, crisp morning, he slipped into first gear, quickly into second, and eased out of cobbled Waverley Mews into the rush-hour traffic on Belgrave Place. He was headed for the M1 Motorway and Leicestershire to visit Audleigh Hall, at the personal invitation of Spenser Graves.

When Kingston had phoned Graves two days earlier, he wasn't expecting such an outgoing reception. Eccentric or not, there was nothing wrong with Graves's memory. He remembered Kingston well, he insisted. Even recalled the place and occasion where they'd last met—a presentation dinner at the Savoy Hotel in the Strand, honoring the retirement of one of Kew Gardens' directors. By the time the conversation had ended, Kingston had not only been offered a personal tour of Audleigh Hall without asking, but had been invited to join Spenser for lunch.

Two hours later, Kingston passed through the impressive wrought-iron gated entrance to Audleigh Hall. Tires crunching on the sandy gravel, he proceeded up the long serpentine drive toward the house. It was several minutes before Audleigh Hall, in all its idiosyncratic splendor, came into view. As the house loomed closer, framed by a sky of seamless blue, Kingston scanned it with a critical eye. It had once been his ambition to follow in his father's footsteps and make architecture his career, before being swayed by botany. He could tell right away—confirming what he had read online—that the house had undergone many changes since it had been first built. Regardless, it was impressive.

Kingston pulled up in front of the house next to a mud-spattered older Land Rover. He got out and stretched. Suddenly the countryside quiet echoed with the cacophony of dogs barking. Before he could take a step toward the front door, two pony-sized Irish wolfhounds were at his feet, jostling and panting to be the first to welcome their new visitor. Temporarily rooted to the spot, he was encouraged to see that their tails were wagging. A shrill whistle sent them back to their master, standing on the front doorsteps. "Sorry about those two scallywags. Come on in, Lawrence," said Graves, beckoning. They shook hands and entered the house.

In appearance, Spenser Graves was a true-to-life country squire. He was lean and tall—an inch or so shorter than Kingston—and looked to be in his late fifties. There was no telling whether his ruddy, weathered face was as a result of time spent outdoors, or indoors in the company of Johnny Walker. Under bushy eyebrows flecked with gray, his blue eyes were pink-veined and watery. He wore a multipocketed Barbour jacket, tattersall shirt, and paisley silk scarf knotted casually at the neck. A battered felt hat completed the picture.

Graves led the way through a sparsely furnished entrance hall with massive gilt-framed portraits covering the dark-painted walls—ancestors, Kingston assumed. Their footsteps echoing off the black-and-white diamond-pattern tile floor, they continued along a hall, past several doors, and entered another large room. One of the most magnificent crystal chandeliers that Kingston had ever seen dominated the airspace. The comfortable seating, antique furniture, and elegant carpeting determined that it was a drawing room—maybe one of several, thought Kingston. Graves gestured to a chair and they both sat.

"Damned good to see you looking so well, Lawrence," said Graves, crossing his legs, exposing gaudy argyle socks. "So glad you could come up. I don't get too many visitors these days—well, the public, of course, but I try to avoid them as much as possible. Damned idiotic questions most of the time." He glanced at his watch. "How about a nip before lunch?"

Kingston smiled. "I don't see why not, if you're having one. A dry sherry, perhaps?"

Graves picked up the cordless phone on the table next to him and punched in two numbers. A pause followed while Graves stared up at the gilt-decorated coffered ceiling. Kingston hadn't noticed it when they entered. It was intricate and beautifully crafted. "Ah, there you are, Hobbs," said Graves. "Think you can rustle up a glass of dry sherry and the usual for me? We're in the drawing room. Thanks." Graves leaned back and turned his smiling attention to Kingston. "So, Lawrence, what have you been up to since we last met?" He frowned. "Must have been at least three or four years ago."

Kingston obliged, spending a minute or so telling him how it had taken a long time to come to grips with his wife's untimely death, but that he now found living in London well suited to his needs. "Couldn't wish for more," he said, wrapping up. Thankfully, there was no need for Kingston to dredge up the blue rose affair or the now-celebrated garden rehabilitation in Somerset and the architectural and art discoveries that resulted. Graves was well aware of Kingston's involvement. Not surprising, given the national news coverage.

Graves had just started to talk about the garden and arboretum when the graying-haired, bespectacled Hobbs, wearing an ill-fitting black jacket, arrived with their drinks. Kingston couldn't help thinking how much he resembled a taller Woody Allen. Lowering the small silver tray to the coffee table, Hobbs stepped back a pace. "Let me know when you would like lunch served, sir," he said obsequiously.

"I will," Graves replied, with a nod. "Thank you."

Hobbs turned and departed.

Kingston picked up his glass and took a sip of sherry. Now was as good a time as any, he figured, to do a little circumspect digging. "When we talked on the phone, Spenser, I believe I mentioned that I'd been involved in a small way with that strange case in Oxford. The one involving the expedition you were on."

"You did, yes," said Graves, picking up his highball glass containing a generous measure of what Kingston guessed to be scotch. "Said that our mutual friend Cliff Attenborough had asked you to sub for him, I believe?"

"Right. The hospital and the police wanted someone with knowledge and experience of plant hunting to observe and authenticate what the mystery patient was mumbling about. The whole thing was short-lived, as you probably know." He realized immediately his poor choice of words. "Anyway, as the saying goes, I'm no longer on the case."

"Yes, I read all about it, poor bugger. Murdered, of all things. Damned queer business, I must say. As a matter of fact, one of the local gendarmes paid me a visit not long after it happened. An inspector from Leicester." Graves glanced momentarily at the ceiling. "Name escapes me. Asked all the expected questions—what was the expedition about, who was on it, how Mayhew's accident had happened. Pleasant chap. Oddly enough, quite knowledgeable about Asian antiques. Collected Japanese swords."

A pause followed while Kingston took a purposeful sip of sherry, allowing him to frame his next words. "The reason I brought it up, Spenser, was that I happened to talk with Peter Mayhew's half sister, Sally, last week."

"I didn't know he had a sister. Not until I read the report in the newspaper."

Immediately, Kingston recalled what Sally Mayhew had said, that Bell had tried unsuccessfully to reach her by phone, right after the accident. He wondered if he should ask Graves why Bell hadn't mentioned that but decided it might be both premature and ill-mannered to start quizzing his host so soon after arriving.

"No reason you should, really," he replied. "She said they weren't close." Kingston put his glass on the table, then continued. "A few days ago, I agreed to an interview with a reporter from the *Oxford Mail.* He was doing a story on the case. As it turned out, to save time, he interviewed Sally and me at the same time."

Graves nodded. "I see."

"She said that after the inquest, she met briefly with Julian Bell, who had told her how the accident happened. It must have been devastating for all of you."

Graves was gripping his glass, which rested on the arm of his chair. After a pause, he took a healthy gulp of the amber liquid and pursed his lips. "It was, believe me. Damned rotten luck. In retrospect, Mayhew shouldn't have been on the trip. He wasn't in good physical shape. My opinion, of course, but shared by more than one of us, Bell, for one. Damned fool never told us he suffered from vertigo."

"Maybe, until that time, he wasn't aware."

"There's no saying now."

"Did you happen to see him fall, Spenser?"

"No. But I knew something was wrong when I heard scuffling sounds and realized that everyone behind me had stopped. When I turned, Peter was on the ground with David kneeling behind him."

"David Jenkins, right?"

Graves nodded. "As I walked back to ask what was happening, Peter got to his feet, insisting that he was all right and that we should continue. It was pissing with rain and windier than hell. We debated whether we should turn back, but we continued. You probably know the rest of the story. Less than a minute later, he fell again, this time over the bloody edge. Poor blighter." Graves downed his drink as if it were a metaphor for the finality of it.

Kingston finished his sherry, too, and shook his head. "As you say, 'rotten luck.'"

Graves nodded and took a deep sigh, as if he'd rather forget the incident.

"How many guides were there?"

"Three, if you include the Chinese botanist."

"I understand that one of them almost went over the edge, too."

Graves frowned and looked off into the distance for a moment. "Really," he said, looking back to Kingston. "As I recall, the guides were standing to one side right after it happened. I could be wrong, though. We were all in a state of shock, you know."

"I'm just going on what Bell told Sally Mayhew."

"And what was that?"

"He said one of the guides was last in line behind Peter. When

Peter went down, the guide lost his footing, too, and fell, shoving Peter close to the edge of the gorge."

Graves looked aside, thinking for a moment. "I suppose one of the guides could have been in back of Peter," he said at length. "Truthfully, I don't know. You have to understand, it was utter confusion."

"I can just imagine. I'm sorry to have dredged the whole thing up."

Graves rested his head on the back of his chair, a feigned smile on his face. After a measured pause he said, "I can see all this detective work has gone to your head, Lawrence. Besides, I thought you said you were off the case."

"You're right, Spenser, I am. I'm sure you'd prefer to forget the whole business."

A gentle knocking on the door interrupted them. They both turned to see the door partially open to reveal an attractive young woman in a fleece jacket and blue jeans. "Sorry to bother you, Daddy," she said. "Wanted to let you know I'm leaving now."

Graves rose, as did Kingston. "Come in, Alex. I want you to meet an old friend, Lawrence Kingston. My daughter, Alexandra," he said with obvious pride. With wavy chestnut hair, an English complexion, and intelligent gray eyes, she was right out of the pages of *Town & Country*. They talked only briefly, and in less than a minute she departed.

"You have a lovely daughter, Spenser. She appears to be around the same age as mine. As an only child, they become extraspecial, don't they?"

"Only natural, I suppose," Graves replied. "She's a wonderful person. Engaged to a fellow who's in the Diplomatic Corps. Getting married in Paris."

"Romantic."

Graves smiled and nodded. "Hungry?"

"Ready whenever you are."

They left the drawing room, Graves leading Kingston along a picture-lined hallway into another grand room, this one elegantly appointed with French antiques, mostly Louis XVI, a huge Aubusson carpet underfoot. On the walls, several large glass-fronted cabinets displayed Asian ceramics and other Oriental antiques. Kingston wished he could have paused to study them, but Graves was pressing on. They soon arrived at what had to be the dining room to end all dining rooms. The small picture he'd seen on Audleigh's Web site didn't do it justice—no mere photograph could capture the magnificent room.

The two stood in the middle of the room, Graves content to watch Kingston drink it all in. Kingston realized that most visitors' reactions—and Graves had doubtless escorted hundreds over the years—would likely be pretty much the same as his own at this moment: reverential awe and repose.

Graves broke the long silence. "Sadly, the room's not put to much use these days. I can't even remember the last dinner we served here. Must have been at least a couple of years ago. We'll lunch in the conservatory. You'll enjoy the view, Lawrence."

Two hours later, after a splendid meal of sorrel soup followed by roast guinea fowl with port gravy and celeriac, then ramekins of chilled gooseberry fool, all lubricated with a bottle of Vouvray and a grand cru Burgundy, Graves took Kingston on a tour of the gardens and arboretum.

The landscaping close to the house was quintessentially English in design and plantings. They walked the compact lawns and along wide herbaceous borders with a backdrop of climbing and rambling roses trained on ancient brick walls. Crossing a small Japanese bridge led them to a rose garden that Graves said was originally planted by his grandmother more than ninety years ago, and later redesigned by Graham Stuart Thomas. Planted among the profusion of scented heirloom roses was a white variety of campanula and blue-flowering catmint. A low clipped-boxwood hedge contained the breathtaking sight. Passing under a long arched tunnel of espaliered apple trees intertwined with clematis, they crossed a small orchard and were soon in what was clearly the woodland garden.

As they walked, Graves described how the arboretum was originally laid out and planted by his grandfather and later reconfigured to its present layout by his father. Over twelve thousand trees and shrubs—nearly seventeen hundred different species, he said, were growing within the fifty-five-acre hilly landscape, mostly grown from seed collected in the wild from various parts of the world.

A glossy detailed map that Graves had handed to Kingston before they left the house showed the arboretum divided into a dozen sections, each given a name, and each devoted principally to trees and shrubs of a specific country or geographic region, such as China, Japan, and North America. In some cases, sections or parts of sections were given to plants of a specific species, such as rhododendron. Graves also pointed out that every plant was labeled. A discreet metal tag gave the botanical name in Latin, its common name, the botanical family name, the plant collector's number and initials, an abbreviation denoting country of origin and province, and date collected. A database and location number were included for use by the arboretum's botanists and staff. Kingston was impressed.

For the next hour, they walked and talked along shady paths, across meadows dotted with wildflowers, by the side of riverbanks, over bridges, up steep banks off the main paths, crossed valleys— all the time discussing, admiring, and wondering at the extraordinary wealth of botanical riches that had been brought back from faraway lands over the last seventy-five years to create this one-of-a-kind garden in the heart of England.

All the hiking and climbing appeared to have had little effect on Graves, which didn't surprise Kingston. Anyone who has been on a plant-hunting expedition to China—not just once but several times, as had Graves—must be in top physical shape. Laboring up the perilous paths of twenty-thousand-foot-high snow-capped peaks requires the lungs, legs, and heart of an athlete.

"Follow me." Graves took off at a lively pace. Kingston hustled, falling in alongside. "We'll take a shortcut back to the house, along the ridge," said Graves. "You'll like the view."

Within a few minutes they were on a narrow grassy path that crossed the spine of a long ridge that stretched off into the distance. Now, high up out of the protection of the woodland's embrace, their trouser legs flapped in the stiff breeze. Off to their left, Kingston caught sight of a small village across the patchwork of fields. Graves stopped and looked out over the countryside, pointing. "That's Audleigh, way over there on the other side, between those dark stands of trees. Looks like a long way, but it isn't really." Before Kingston could say anything, Graves was off again, taking a small path to the right leading down the side of the ridge. "I want to show you something, Lawrence," he said. In less than a minute, a thatched cottage appeared. It stood alone in a green meadow, dwarfed by massive elm and copper beech. It even had the quintessential jumbled cottage garden behind its simple wooden gated fence.

Kingston was reminded of his childhood and his mother's collection of biscuit tins. Cottage gardens were popular among the Victorian images that were pictured on the tin lids. "Charming," said Kingston as they stopped by the gate. "Is it part of the estate?"

Graves nodded. "It was built by my grandfather. Whenever he tired of rattling around in the big house, he would come out here to read and paint. It has quite a well-stocked underground wine cellar. I do the same once in a while."

"Can't say as I blame you. I would, too."

"I'd show you the inside, but I didn't bring the key." He glanced at his watch. "Best get headed back, anyway," he said. "You've got a long drive ahead of you."

Standing on the wide front steps, the afternoon sun dipping beneath a lofty yew hedge along the side of the drive, Kingston and Spenser Graves shook hands. "You *must* come back, Lawrence." The emphasis gave Kingston reason to believe that Spenser really meant it. "Didn't even get a chance to show you some of my Asian antiques," he added, bringing a smile to Kingston's lips.

"I'd very much like to see them. It'll be a good excuse for me to return, Spenser. And thanks for a truly excellent lunch and the garden tour. I enjoyed it immensely."

Kingston eased into his TR4 and prepared to leave. "I'll keep in touch, Spenser," Kingston shouted over the rumbling of the sports car's engine. With a wave, he took off down the drive.

Heading south on the A508 toward the Motorway, Kingston was thinking back to their conversation and Graves's version of the fatal accident. It differed from Julian Bell's as told to Sally Mayhew—not a lot, but sufficiently so to be worrisome. Was one of them bending the truth, trying to cover something up, or did one of them just have a bad memory? On top of that, there was the business about the phone call. He recalled distinctly Sally saying that Julian Bell had tried to call her from China immediately after the accident. Graves, however, knew of no such thing. Given the gravity of the moment, it seemed highly unlikely that this was not discussed among all of the expedition members, that Bell had made the unsuccessful call without telling anyone.

EIGHT

On the drive back from Leicestershire, Kingston had plenty to think about. When he had told Spenser Graves how much he had enjoyed himself, he'd really meant it. Few things pleased him more—more now than ever, in fact—than to spend an hour or two wandering through someone else's garden. Over his lifetime, he had visited countless gardens in his travels, most of them, of course, in Britain. The long list included most of the noteworthy gardens and a great number that were small and privately owned. Along with all the obvious sensual rewards of spending time in these places of beauty, tranquillity, and seclusion, there was often the dividend of meeting the inspired gardeners responsible for creating these Edens on Earth. And Kingston had had the privilege of meeting many. Not surprisingly, each was as passionate as the next in a love of gardening, all unassuming in their creativity and achievements and steadfastly determined to keep going no matter what obstacles Mother Nature flung at them. Whether it was the humblest cottage garden or one-hundred-acre estate, he had long ago come to realize that their creators all shared the same challenges and ambitions. His writer and photographer friend Marina Schinz summed it up admirably: "Gardening is an exercise in optimism. Sometimes, it is a triumph of hope over experience."

But gardens were not what were on his mind right now. He was thinking of Julian Bell, trying to recall what he'd read about the man. It had to be at least a couple of years since he'd read the magazine article that featured Bell and his global peregrinations in search of undiscovered and vanishing plants. He could recall only fragments: that Bell was a retired doctor and bachelor divorcé, who lived alone on a farm in Dorset, and that the writer had found him as taciturn as his darkly bearded appearance would suggest. Kingston was starting to think about a way he could have a face-to-face with Bell and get his side of the expedition story.

As Kingston crossed the Chiswick Flyover, the last thin light of day was lingering over London's skyline. He checked his watch. It would be around eight by the time he garaged the car and could sit back and enjoy a wee drop of Macallan and watch some telly before retiring early. It had been a long day, with a lot of walking, parts of it uphill. He was reminded once again that he really must get back on his regular exercise regimen of walking at least three miles a day, five days a week. His overworked cocktail party quip, "I love long walks, especially when they're taken by people who annoy me," was not only wearing thin, it was becoming true. At least he wasn't hungry. With Spenser's hearty lunch, it was hardly surprising. If he got peckish later, the chunk of leftover Melton Mowbray pork pie in the refrigerator would have to make do.

Closing the door of his flat behind him, Kingston flicked on the hall light and picked up the post. A couple of minutes later, after having poured himself a drink and listened to his answerphone—

one message only, from Andrew, asking to call—he slumped on the sofa and took a sip of whisky as he flipped through the dozen or so bills and junk mail. He extracted a small white envelope. The address was handwritten in capital letters. Curious, he opened it and took out the folded single sheet of writing paper and read the note, also handwritten in black ink and in capitals.

DR. KINGSTON,

I HAVE INFORMATION ABOUT THE EXPEDITION YOU HAVE BEEN INQUIRING ABOUT. INFORMATION THAT MIGHT EXPLAIN HOW PETER MAYHEW MET HIS DEATH.

MEET ME ON WEDNESDAY AT 2 O'CLOCK P.M., JUNE 20, AT LYDIARD PARK IN WILTSHIRE. BEHIND LYDIARD HOUSE IS A SMALL CHURCH NAMED ST. MARY'S. I WILL FIND YOU OUTSIDE. DO NOT BRING ANYONE WITH YOU, OR TELL THE POLICE.

Kingston read the note a second time. Though there was nothing in it to suggest that the writer had been on the expedition, Kingston ran through the cast of players anyway. Ruling out the American chap for the moment, and Spenser Graves—who, for some reason, he seriously doubted wrote the letter—that left Bell, Jenkins, and the photographer chap, Jeremy Lester. If it wasn't one of those three it meant that the writer had been told about, or had come across, the information, probably from one of the three. He took another sip of whisky and gazed around the room, thinking of other possibilities. After a couple of minutes he could come up with only one other scenario: Whoever wrote the letter could still believe that it was Peter Mayhew who had been murdered at St. George's, as first reported in the paper. He or she may not have read the subsequent correction. But the letter had mentioned the "expedition," so it could mean only that Mayhew's fall was not an accident and that someone had helped him over the edge.

Why choose Lydiard Park? Was it because it was a convenient rendezvous for the writer? Was he—or she, perhaps—familiar with the grand estate and its Palladian house, or maybe lived nearby? He knew Bell lived somewhere in Dorset. But he could think of nothing that might connect Bell geographically with Lydiard Park, which was near the M4 and Swindon. He scratched his head trying to recall where Jenkins lived. Seconds later it came to him—Cornwall, Clifford had said. He found himself making a mental map of the fastest route from anywhere in Cornwall to London—from where Kingston would drive to meet the informer. It was grasping at straws, perhaps, but Swindon was close to the halfway point. If it were Jenkins, had he chosen it because it was convenient for both him and Kingston? There was little point in speculating further, he decided. Wednesday was tomorrow.

That night Kingston found it impossible to dismiss the letter from his mind. Despite the admonition at the end of the letter, should he tell Inspector Sheffield about it? This wasn't the first time he had faced this kind of dilemma. He knew that withholding information in an ongoing police investigation was a serious matter, subject to criminal charges. Regardless, he decided to put off talking with Sheffield until after the rendezvous. It made more sense that way, he rationalized, because he could have much more information by then. At least, that was his hope, and excuse.

Wednesday morning was clear and breezy. Barring unforeseen traffic problems, he figured he could make it to Lydiard Park in a shade under two hours. To be on the safe side, he was allowing an extra half hour. If he arrived early, he would visit the parish church. He had read in one of his reference books that, in addition to being one of England's finest small churches, it was "richly packed with monuments to the St. John family." Few would know, as did Kingston, that the name was pronounced "sin-jin"—yet another example of those nettlesome and often inexplicable English language eccentricities that had foreigners wringing their hands in exasperation, and rightfully so.

From his research, he had also learned that the interior of the thirteenth-century church held a rich collection of ecclesiastical treasures. The piece de resistance was the "Golden Cavalier, a life-size gilded effigy of Edward St. John emerging from his tent in full battledress." That alone could be worth the trip, he thought.

Kingston drove through the park gates at fifteen minutes before two. As he motored slowly along the wide carriageway, flanked by sweeping lawns studded with ancient cedars of Lebanon and shade trees, Lydiard's formal parkland came into view. Taking in the utopian surroundings, he wondered why he hadn't visited the park before. He arrived at the half-empty main car park a few minutes later, locked the TR4, and followed the signs toward Lydiard House and St. Mary's church.

Kingston could see why the church was considered so noteworthy. He stopped to admire it. Built of soft gray stone with a lichen-crusted tile roof, it was in Early English perpendicular style, faultless in its simplicity and proportions. Below the battlements, age-worn gargoyles peered down at him with leering faces. The clock on the bell tower read seven minutes before two. He was glad that he'd allowed the extra time.

There were few people outside the church. A family with two young children was off to one side, the father taking photographs. An elderly couple sat silently on a bench staring at nothing in particular. A clutch of youngsters—students by the looks of their backpacks and notebooks—huddled by the front door as if waiting for someone. Nowhere to be seen was a furtive man or woman wearing dark glasses and a trench coat with the collar turned up.

After waiting ten minutes, Kingston was starting to feel conspicuous, not that there were any park attendants or church staff around who might become suspicious of his obvious loitering. As much for something to do as anything, he decided to suss out the small graveyard on the south side of the church, still clearly visible from the entrance. Whomever he was to meet could still spot him there.

Church graveyards had always fascinated him and St. Mary's did not disappoint. Ancient headstones, crosses, and monuments jutted at tortured angles from the grassy sod, having come to rest after three-hundred-odd years of settling and weathering. Here and there a sprinkling of humble bouquets, a few limp and dying, added a touch of wistful color. Most of the epitaphs and markings were too worn to be decipherable. He was attempting to read a particularly elaborate inscription when he heard his name spoken.

It was the voice of a child.

Momentarily confused, he turned to see a freckle-faced boy no more than ten years old dressed in a school uniform: gray blazer with matching shorts, socks sagging to midshin, and a navy emblazoned cap. He held a white envelope in his hand. "Are you Mr. Kingston?" he mumbled.

Kingston looked down at him and nodded.

"I'm s'posed to give this to you," he said, offering the envelope at arm's length.

Kingston reached forward and took it. Before he could thank him, or ask the boy who had given it to him, the lad had sped away. Kingston watched, bewildered, as the boy disappeared into the park.

He sat down on a nearby bench, avoiding the bird droppings, and opened the plain white envelope, noting that it was identical to that in which the first letter had been delivered. Not coincidence, he thought. He pulled out a sheet of notepaper and placed the envelope on the bench. He recognized the printed handwriting immediately.

DOCTOR,

I AM SORRY THAT I COULDN'T MEET YOU AS PROMISED. I HAVE BEEN FOLLOWED, AND TO BE SEEN WITH YOU OR HAVING ANY KIND OF CONTACT WITH YOU COULD BE TROUBLE FOR BOTH OF US. BECAUSE OF THIS, I HAVE DECIDED NOT TO DIVULGE THE INFORMATION AS I HAD PLANNED. THE NEWSPAPER CLIPPING IS ALL I CAN OFFER RIGHT NOW.

What clipping? wondered Kingston. He picked up the envelope and looked inside. Lodged in the fold was a single-column clipping. He extracted it and read the headline.

GARDENER GETS OFF LIGHTLY IN DEATH OF TEENAGER
Dorchester, Dorset, May 22, 2003

A verdict was announced yesterday in the Weymouth & Dorchester County Court trial of Peter Mayhew. On trial for manslaughter in the motorcycle death of 17-year-old Samantha Bell, the 22-year-old Arundel resident was exonerated of four of the five charges, all except that of endangerment of a minor.

County Court Judge Raymond Iverson sentenced Mayhew to six months of community service to commence immediately. The case received countywide attention when Samantha Bell, the daughter of prominent Dorset farmer and horticulturist Julian Bell, was killed in an accident on the A352 when she was a passenger on Mayhew's motorcycle. Ten minutes prior to the fatal accident, the two were seen leaving the Fox & Hounds pub, in Little Wellminster. Blood alcohol level tests on both Mayhew and Miss Bell, performed at Dorchester General Hospital immediately following the accident, proved to be within legal limits.

Asked his opinion of the verdict, Julian Bell refused to comment.

Kingston stared at the church tower framed against the cloudless sky. There was no question that whoever had written the note had panicked. Though he or she had not come right out and said as much, the words suggested that the writer had good reason to think his or her life was threatened. With two murders already connected to the expedition, that wasn't an unreasonable assumption. "Trouble for both of us" made him feel uneasy, too. He folded the note, put it back into the envelope with the clipping, and started walking to the car park. Glancing about, he wondered if he was being watched, too.

The implication of the clipping was clear. It meant that there was indeed someone on the expedition who had reason to wish harm on Peter Mayhew. But would Julian Bell go that far? Would the grief of losing his daughter, due to Mayhew's recklessness and apparent licentious behavior, be enough for him to want to take the man's life? There was also the question of how much time had passed between the two events—four years. If Bell wanted revenge, why wait that long? Perhaps the most perplexing question: Given their history, why on earth would they both be on the same expedition? Surely Mayhew would have never agreed to that.

Approaching the car park, Kingston passed an unoccupied Park Police car parked alongside a small building, prompting yet another question: Was Inspector Sheffield aware of Samantha Bell's death? The police had interviewed Spenser Graves. Certainly they would have interviewed Bell and the others, including the American, he figured. For all he knew, Bell could now be a prime suspect. Calling Sheffield and telling him about the letters and the newspaper clipping was no longer a matter of choice. That was going to get him a good rollicking—for not only going to Lydiard Park but not having reported the first letter as well. The only thing in his defense was that the writer had cautioned him not to tell the police. He knew that, with Sheffield, that excuse wouldn't be worth the paper it was written on. If it wasn't too late by the time he returned home, he would call then. If not, he would make it the first order of the day tomorrow.

Kingston unlocked his TR4 and got in. Buckled up, he drove onto the carriageway, to see a line of uniformed schoolchildren being herded along the footpath by two teachers. He thought about stopping and asking one of the teachers if he could ask freckle face a couple of questions. He decided against it.

NINE

Two days later, at eleven thirty on a rainy Friday morning, Kingston walked into the police station on St. Aldates in the city of Oxford, well prepared for his meeting with Detective Inspector Sheffield. Crossing the threshold brought back fond memories of the fictional Inspector Morse, who, with his partner, the amiable Sergeant Lewis, had solved so many crimes out of this very police station.

Their phone conversation the morning before had been much shorter than Kingston had anticipated, hardly a conversation at all, in fact. He'd presumed, erroneously, that he would get a dressing down when he told the inspector about his trip to Lydiard Park, the letters, and the newspaper clipping. Kingston was surprised when he hadn't. Neither had Sheffield shown a great deal of interest in asking much about the incident—which he found odd—or offered, at the very least, a few crumbs of appreciation. As phlegmatic as ever, Sheffield had listened patiently to Kingston's story. Then, with not so much as a "thank you" or a question, had said, "I think it best if you come up to Oxford, Doctor, if it's not too much trouble—to make a proper statement, that is—and bring the letters."

Kingston had little choice. "Of course, no problem at all," he'd answered blithely, doubting that Sheffield would detect his salting of sarcasm.

It wasn't the first time he'd run into this kind of reaction when trying to cooperate with law enforcement. Here he was making a sincere effort to help the police in their investigation—in a murder case, of all things—but couldn't shake off the feeling that he was being humored. Though this time, to Sheffield's credit, he'd requested Kingston's help, even if it had been accompanied by sternly worded caveats—which Kingston had already violated.

When Kingston entered the inspector's office, a smiling Sheffield got up from his desk, leaned across, and shook Kingston's hand as they exchanged greetings.

In appearance, Sheffield bore no resemblance whatsoever to Morse. Sheffield was considerably younger, lanky, and sported a trim mustache. The only feature they shared was the gray hair; however, unlike Morse's, Sheffield's was closely cropped.

"I appreciate your coming all the way up here, Doctor," he said, sitting and picking up a yellow pencil that was on the desktop alongside a notepad. "Nasty morning, too."

"Not a problem. I always manage to find things to do in Oxford."

"Before I forget, before we get into the Mayhew business, I ran into someone a couple of weeks ago who said to say hello to you."

Kingston frowned, at a loss to think who it could be. "Really?"

"Another copper. Robbie Carmichael, Hampshire Constabulary. We were on a three-day course together, in London. Antiterrorism seminar. Told me a few stories about you. Said you'd make a good detective."

"Inspector Carmichael. How could I ever forget him?" Kingston smiled and leaned back. "What he actually said, if my memory serves me, was that he thought there might be a place in law enforcement for me. But then he added, don't look for employment in Hampshire, *please.*"

Sheffield chuckled. "Sounds like Robbie."

"He was being charitable. Truth be known, I probably gave him quite a few sleepless nights on that case with the water lilies. Nice chap. Good policeman."

"He is that." Sheffield stroked his chin. "So, did you bring those letters?"

"I did, yes." Kingston reached into his inside jacket pocket, pulled out the envelopes containing the two letters, and handed them to the inspector.

Sheffield read them carefully, then placed them side by side on the desk and looked at Kingston, twiddling his pencil with both hands. "A London postmark. Not much help there." He paused, frowning. "Someone on the expedition would seem to be a rather obvious candidate."

"Agreed. What do you make of the newspaper clipping?"

"We're already familiar with that case. Our chaps dug it up while they were researching Bell's background. We've gone back through all the trial transcripts."

"Doesn't it suggest that Bell could have had a motive for wanting to kill Mayhew?"

"It does, but waiting for four years to carry it out seems a bit much. Unless, that is, something else happened between him and Mayhew more recently. He vehemently denies any such thing, of course."

"I have to agree," said Kingston. "The time lapse does make it questionable. Also, surely Mayhew wouldn't have considered, even for one moment, spending three weeks, or however long the trip was, in the company of Julian Bell."

Sheffield nodded. "It would certainly be asking for trouble."
"It would."

"So what does this suggest?"

"Well, if someone on the expedition wrote the letters, then it narrows it down to five suspects—four, if you discount the American, unless he's over here now."

"We've been assured that he hasn't left the States since returning from the expedition."

"Okay." Kingston thought for a moment, then, using his index finger to count on the fingers of the other hand, named them. "Bell, Graves, Jenkins, and the photographer chap, Jeremy Lester." He hesitated. "If it's none of them, we can logically assume that the writer must have got the information secondhand from one of the five."

Sheffield put down the pencil and folded his arms. His demeanor had suddenly changed. He looked more serious, the muscles in his jaw flexing. "Unfortunately, Doctor, it's now *one of four*."

Kingston looked at him quizzically.

"We learned a few days ago that the man murdered at St. George's Hospital was also on the expedition. Jeremy Lester."

TEN

G od Lord." Kingston rubbed his forehead, nonplussed by
Sheffield's bombshell, scrambling to figure out how it dove-
tailed into everything else.

Sheffield paused, as if on purpose, to let the news sink in. "We
identified him from a thumbprint that matched a photo ID card.
Single, lived in Wallingford."

"I realize it's not my question to ask, but have you and your
people come up with any other ideas that would explain his murder? Any theories?"

"Nothing that points to a suspect or suspects, if that's what you're
asking. Until now—although we've never ruled out homicide—
we've been pursuing the line of argument that Peter Mayhew's death
was the result of an accident. Now, with Lester's murder coupled
with these letters here, that's all changed." He leaned back, massag-
ing his chin. "What about you, Doctor? You've had time to think
about it. Any bright ideas?"

The desk phone rang. Sheffield picked it up and swiveled his chair to face the window on his right. While the inspector was talking, Kingston mulled over this startling new development, trying to figure what it meant, how it fitted with what they already knew, and how to answer Sheffield's question.

After a minute, Sheffield ended the conversation and swiveled back to face Kingston. "Where were we?" he asked. "Right," he said with a nod. "Any theories, Doctor?"

"Not really. It would seem, as you said, that Mayhew was killed, for something he'd done either on or before the expedition—like that thing with Bell's daughter—or it's possible, I suppose, he could have discovered something on the trip that somebody wanted kept secret. Lord knows what that might have been, though. That part of the world is mostly wilderness."

Sheffield smiled. "A rare plant, perhaps?"

"Nothing worth killing for, I doubt," Kingston replied, returning the smile.

"What about Lester? He and Mayhew might have been friends."

"Could be. Clifford Attenborough at Kew said that it was Mayhew who suggested that Lester join them on the trip as photographer and interpreter. They were close in age, too, younger than the other members. And now we know it was Lester who was driving Mayhew's motorbike. I doubt he would have pinched it."

"Agreed."

"He had to get the bike somehow. Maybe Mayhew had just sold it to him."

"If he had, the DVLA would know about it, which they don't. Plus, there were no transfer of ownership papers, bill of sale, anything like that in Lester's flat. According to DVLA, the bike's still registered in Mayhew's name."

"So going back to what you said earlier, if Mayhew did stumble onto something, he could have confided in Lester. They could be conspirators."

"Possibly. But Lester's homicide perplexes me. If he weren't murdered mistakenly for Mayhew, why would someone want him dead? It's looking more and more as though Lester's motorcycle accident wasn't an accident after all."

Kingston frowned. "Maybe the same person who wanted Mayhew dead also wanted Lester out of the way."

"A possibility." Sheffield sighed. "Well, think about it, Doctor." He paused, then said, "I know you will."

Kingston was about to get up, thinking that their conversation was ended, when the inspector surprised him with an offhand remark that was more of a question than a statement. "Graves said you were up in Leicestershire to see him?"

"Yes, I was. I'd never seen the arboretum or Audleigh House before and decided it might be worth the trip, and to renew our acquaintance. We'd met years ago, but I must say, Spenser had no trouble recalling the occasion."

"Nothing to do with the expedition, then?"

The question was innocuous enough, but Kingston didn't miss the veiled smile in Sheffield's eyes as he posed it.

"Well, we talked about it, of course. Graves was quite up-front about it."

"Did you learn anything? Anything that could help us?"

Kingston was ready for the question. He was planning to tell Sheffield anyway. "I was coming to that, actually. Graves's recollection of Mayhew's accident—how he said it happened—differs from Julian Bell's."

Sheffield squinted at him. "You've talked with Bell, too?"

"No I haven't. Let me explain. Immediately after Peter Mayhew's inquest, Julian Bell spent some time chatting with Sally Mayhew, Peter's half sister. During their conversation at a tea shop, he recounted what had taken place on the mountain trail. According to her, he recalled it quite vividly, which doesn't surprise me. Not something you would forget very quickly."

"And you learned it from Sally Mayhew?"

"That's correct."

"When the chap from the *Mail* interviewed you and Miss Mayhew at your flat, right?"

"Also true," Kingston replied. He knew that Trevor Williams would have talked to the police, too, and more likely than not, that meant Inspector Sheffield. He looked more closely at the inspector, to see if he could detect anything in his expression to suggest that he was about to get a wigging for stepping out of line, both by seeing Graves and by going to Lydiard Park.

The inspector looked impassive, pursed his lips, and gave Kingston a long gaze. "Well," he said with a sniff, "perhaps we can get you back on the case. Not officially, of course, and not running around trying to solve things on your own. Whether you know it or not, you've earned yourself a bit of a reputation in that regard. And, frankly, it's not going to be tolerated."

Kingston knew that this was one of those situations when the less said, the better, so he simply nodded in agreement and waited for Sheffield to continue.

"I'll be up-front with you, Doctor. Much as I would have liked to, I haven't been able to conduct all the interviews we've done so far—not personally, that is. After the Cornwall police talked to him, I met with David Jenkins, the fellow from Cornwall—he came here for the interview—and I've conducted a phone interview with Julian Bell, who's just returned from a trip to Taiwan, of all places. As far as I can tell, their accounts of the accident jibe. I don't know if Graves told you, but it was our blokes up in Leicester who questioned him. They turned in their report to me, of course. An agent from the FBI field office in San Francisco is interviewing the American chap; we're not ruling him out. I expect to get their report any day now." He threw up a hand. "You see what I'm getting at, I'm sure?"

Kingston nodded. "I do. For one thing, you can only hope your other chaps are all asking the right questions. If they're not, it'll be impossible for them to pick up on small inconsistencies."

"Exactly. That's why I asked you up here. It's not often we ask a member of the public to do what I'm about to suggest, but in this case I'm making an exception. There's no question that your knowledge of these plant-hunting expeditions—all the ins and outs of how they're organized and conducted, what you go looking for—could be of great help in our investigation. As you pointed out, it's very often the little things—small mistakes that would otherwise go unnoticed—that eventually solve cases like these. However—"

Kingston waited for the caveat, already guessing what it might be.

"Everything you do will be under strict supervision by me. Under no circumstances—*none*—can you contact any persons involved in the case without my go-ahead or, heaven forbid, place yourself in any situation that might involve bodily harm to you or anyone else. Our job, Doctor, is to protect the public, and that includes you."

Kingston took a deep breath. "Anything I can do to help, I will, Inspector."

Sheffield nodded. "Good," he said, swiveling to one side, crossing his knees. He fixed his wrinkle-edged eyes on Kingston. "You said that you found a discrepancy in Graves's and Bell's accounts of the accident?"

"I did, yes. There's also the question of the phone call from China to Sally Mayhew that Bell claims he made. He told Sally that he was unable to reach her at the time. Graves wasn't aware of any such phone call. Given the tragic circumstances, one would surely think that they would all have known about it—if it took place, that is."

"That'll be enough reason to bring Bell in and have you sit in on the interview. We were going to talk to him again, anyway. We need to know where he was when Lester was murdered. Graves and Jenkins, too, for that matter."

Kingston pulled on his earlobe, thinking. "If we do that, Bell's going to have time to get his story straight——"

"If he's the one who's lying."

"Right. May I suggest another idea? I'm going to be in Dorset in the next few days anyway. I have a niece who lives near Sherborne. She's been at me for weeks about going down and giving her some ideas about a new garden she and her husband are putting in. Why don't I give Julian Bell a call, see if I can talk him into a short visit?" Kingston paused. "It worked with Graves."

Sheffield didn't answer right away, puckering his lips, pondering Kingston's suggestion. "It's highly irregular, but I don't see how it could pose a problem, as long as there's no mention of your working with us. I mean, I can't stop you from going, anyway. If you talk to Bell about the expedition, that's your business, right?"

Kingston nodded in agreement.

"Only one thing, Doctor, keep it all nice and pleasant-like. And a word of advice: Whatever you do, don't make it sound like you're grilling him. If he's got something to hide, he'll spot you right off. Lastly, don't say anything that might give him reason to think that we've sanctioned your visit or that you're still working with us."

Sheffield gave Kingston Bell's unlisted number, and the meeting broke up a few minutes later, Kingston promising to call the inspector to report on the outcome of his assignation with Julian Bell.

On the drive back to London, Kingston thought back on their conversation. With so many ambiguities and unresolved issues shrouding the case, he had forgotten to mention to Sheffield his theory as to why the letter writer had selected Lydiard Park as the rendezvous: that it was at the halfway point between London and Cornwall, where David Jenkins lived.

ELEVEN

Though he still knew little about Julian Bell, Kingston had gained the impression that he was not one to suffer fools lightly, nor, probably, out-of-the-blue phone calls from complete strangers. However, the real possibility did exist—and Kingston was counting on it—that Bell was aware of Kingston's credentials and would welcome a call from a fellow botanist. On the minus side, there was also the likelihood that Bell would know of Kingston's reputation as an amateur sleuth. Given the circumstances, and the fact that the police had already interviewed him, this might not sit too well with Bell. All that said and done, Kingston had to come up with a compelling reason for calling, or he could expect to suffer the same verbal thrashing that Bell might unleash on a time-share salesman. After much thought, he'd come up with a ploy that he was confident would simultaneously satisfy Bell's curiosity and intrigue him.

While researching Bell's background, Kingston had found that he was particularly interested in a vanishing species of Asian maple, *Acer pentaphyllum.* With five narrow leaflets, it is quite distinct from the 150 species and other maple cultivars. The rare maple was discovered in 1929 by the Austrian botanist and linguist Joseph Rock in southwestern Sichuan, near Tibet. The somewhat eccentric, gifted, and self-trained scientist spent almost thirty years in China's mountainous terrain collecting plant specimens and studying the cultures of the region's inhabitants. Even then he had noted in his journals that stands of *Acer pentaphyllum* were rare.

Kingston had also read a recent paper by one of America's foremost biologists who had contended that the world was in the midst of a sixth mass extinction that had enabled the global population to increase and eventually inhabit most of Earth. As the world's population continued to grow at an accelerating rate, so would the rate of extinction of plant and animal life, he predicted. In the treatise, *Acer pentaphyllum* was mentioned as an example.

Kingston hoped that if he confessed more than a mere scholarly interest in the rare maple, and proposed that an expedition be organized, with Bell as the leader, he would agree to meet. In the meantime, Kingston would read up on the maple.

Midmorning, a day later, he finally caught up with Julian Bell on the phone.

"The celebrated Lawrence Kingston. This is a surprise," said Bell.

Kingston wondered what he meant by "celebrated." He hoped it referred to his reputation in the field of botany. "Do you have a couple of minutes to chat? It's about a new project I'm working on. It concerns *Acer pentaphyllum.*"

"*Acer pentaphyllum,* eh? Sure. I've just returned from a trip to Taiwan. You know how that is. Still dragging a bit, but go ahead."

"I've read about your research on the species, which is impressive. Over the last year or so, I've been doing much the same. To cut to the chase, I'm exploring the idea of forming a committee, whose task it will be to start the process of preserving and encouraging regeneration of the species. It's a subject close to your heart, I know, and I'm calling to ask if you'll consider serving on the committee—perhaps head it up?"

"First task will be to convince the botanical, horticultural, agricultural, and land development authorities in China to commence immediately on an educational program. That could all take time, you know."

"All too well." Kingston now knew that Bell was most likely coming on board.

They talked for another five minutes, during which time Kingston artfully dropped a couple of important names in the botanical world and used his gift of the gab and powers of persuasion ultimately to convince Bell that they should meet to discuss the matter further.

"I have a niece who lives near Sherborne," said Kingston. "I was planning to see her soon, anyway. She wants me to take a look at her garden. It wouldn't be a bother for me to come down to meet you in Dorset."

Bell seemed to like that idea and it was agreed that they would meet on Thursday, five days hence.

Kingston was pleased with the morning's accomplishment and started getting ready for his one o'clock lunch with Andrew. Afterward, they planned to take a bus across the Thames to Lambeth for a long-overdue visit to the Museum of Garden History. Five years had passed since Kingston's last excursion. On that occasion, the museum was celebrating its twenty-fifth anniversary and he had been among the special guests.

After a two-hour lunch at a fancy West End seafood restaurant, fortified by several glasses of Vouvray—Andrew picking up the tab—they hopped on a number 3 bus headed for the museum on Lambeth Palace Road and climbed upstairs. Kingston had always enjoyed the surreptitious view of the palace gardens, possible only from the top of double-decker buses that passed along the Embankment, blocked from view at street level by an imposing stone wall. He mourned the impending demise of London's historic Roadmaster buses, recalling the innumerable times he had leaped on and off at the back.

Over lunch, Kingston had told Andrew a little about the small museum: It was founded in 1977, when the family tomb containing two seventeenth-century plant hunters, John Tradescant father and son, was discovered in the overgrown churchyard surrounding the derelict nine-hundred-year-old church of St. Mary-at-Lambeth. The parish records began noting burials in the 1530s, and since then more than twenty-six thousand people had been interred in the church, graveyard, and adjacent burial ground in Lambeth High Street. Andrew's interest perked up when Kingston told him that the tomb of Captain Bligh of *Bounty* fame was also in the churchyard.

They started their tour in the church's nave, which housed the main gallery. The exhibit there featured a tool and garden-related artifacts collection plus a paper archive exhibit. The displays included prints, photographs, bills, receipts, catalogs, and brochures, some dating back to the 1700s. Andrew showed great interest in the records, which not only gave an insight into garden history but also provided a social record of the times.

The highlight of the main gallery was the library, a repository of historical botanical and horticultural treasures. Included was a 1656 copy of *Musaeum Tradescantianum*, diarist John Evelyn's personal copy of the Tradescant museum catalog, and Fothergill's *Hortus siccus*, a mid-seventeenth-century herbarium. The book contains over six hundred remarkably well-preserved pressed plant specimens used to teach botany. Before leaving the gallery, Kingston pointed out a small Victorian sampler hanging on the wall. It read:

There is peace within a garden
A peace so deep and calm
That when the heart is troubled
It's like a soothing balm

There's life within a garden
A life that still goes on
Filling the empty places
When older plants have gone

There's glory in the garden
At every time of year
Spring summer autumn winter
To fill the heart with cheer

So ever tend your garden
Its beauty to increase
For in it you'll find solace
And in it you'll find peace

After an hour and a half in the museum, the two went outside for some fresh air and to explore the garden. As they strolled the path, Kingston explained that the garden was designed by the Dowager Marchioness of Salisbury of Hatfield House, in a style that would have been familiar to the plant-hunting John Tradescants, the elder of whom had been the head gardener at Hatfield from 1610 to 1615. She had designed the compact space to be historically authentic, he said: a mixture of shrubs, roses, herbaceous perennials, herbs, annuals, and bulbs planted in borders surrounding the central feature, the knot garden. The symmetrical knot pattern was created with low hedging of dwarf box, filled with plantings that changed with the seasons. Farther along, Kingston pointed out *Rosa* x. *alba "maxima," Rosa "De Meaux,"* and

Rosa gallica v. *officinalis*, the Apothecary rose, all blooming quite happily.

Before seeking out the tombs of the Tradescants, and Captain Bligh—Andrew expressing more interest in the latter—they took a break on a bench in a corner of the garden. With mention of Tradescants, the conversation turned to plant hunting. Never one to miss the chance to spin a good yarn, Kingston grabbed the opportunity to impress upon Andrew the dangers of plant hunting.

"We all grew up learning about the courageous Captain Cook and his voyages to the South Pacific and Australia, right, Andrew?"

"Sure."

"How about Joseph Banks? Have you heard of him?"

Andrew shook his head.

"Don't worry, few people have. When Cook set sail from Plymouth on an expedition that would cover nearly eight thousand miles and cross four continents, a young botanist by that name was aboard Cook's ship, a converted coal transporter renamed the *Endeavour*. Accompanying Banks was a team of nine assistants. Their objective was to study and catalog the natural history of the continent and search for new plants."

Andrew grinned. "I appreciate the history lesson, Lawrence, but why are you telling me this?"

"To give you an idea of how dangerous plant-hunting expeditions were in those days—and still are today."

"Very well."

Unfazed, Kingston continued. "Banks and the crew would suffer extreme hardships on the trip. In a snowstorm off the coast of South America, two of his team died of hypothermia, the remainder surviving after eating a raw vulture. Later, they ate dog, rat, kangaroo, and albatross."

Andrew made a face.

"Arriving in New Zealand, members of the crew were attacked by a war party of Maori. Much to Banks's regret, several of the natives were killed. Crossing the Great Barrier Reef, the *Endeavour* struck the coral and came within hours of sinking. Toward the end of the journey, scurvy, venereal disease, and fever were rampant among the crew. By the end of the voyage, the *Endeavour* had lost forty of her ninety-man crew."

"How about Banks's people?"

"Only he and two others survived."

"Good Lord."

"The good news is that, as a result of the expedition, Joseph Banks—later to be knighted for his work—described, cataloged, and named a staggering thirteen hundred new botanical species and a hundred and ten new genera."

"That's impressive, I must say."

"There's an interesting postscript to the account. Not many years later, Cook would select another officer for the position of sailing master on his third and fatal voyage to the Pacific. That naval officer's name was Bligh."

After visiting Bligh's tomb, and before leaving the garden, Kingston and Andrew took a moment to read the epitaph atop the ornately decorated Tradescants' tomb.

KNOW, STRANGER, ERE THOU PASS, BENEATH THIS STONE
LYE JOHN TRADESCANT, GRANDSIRE, FATHER, SON;
THE LAST DY'D IN HIS SPRING; THE OTHER TWO,
LIV'D TILL THEY HAD TRAVELL'D ORB AND NATURE
    THROUGH,
AS BY THEIR CHOICE COLLECTIONS MAY APPEAR,
OF WHAT IS RARE, IN LAND, IN SEA, IN AIR.
WHILST THEY (AS HOMER'S ILIAD IN A NUT)
A WORLD OF WONDERS IN ONE CLOSET SHUT,
THESE FAMOUS ANTIQUARIANS THAT HAD BEEN

BOTH GARDINERS TO THE ROSE AND LILY QUEEN,
TRANSPLANTED NOW THEMSELVES, SLEEP HERE & WHEN
ANGELS SHALL WITH THEIR TRUMPETS WAKEN MEN,
AND FIRE SHALL PURGE THE WORLD, THESE THREE SHALL
    RISE
AND CHANGE THIS GARDEN THEN FOR PARADISE.

"There's a legend that goes with it," said Kingston, breaking the silence. "Lambeth folklore states that if the tomb is danced around twelve times, as Big Ben strikes midnight, a ghost appears."

TWELVE

When his radio alarm woke him at six-thirty on Thursday morning, Kingston didn't need the weather forecaster to tell him that the day would be a sizzler. Pulling aside the curtain of his bedroom window facing Cadogan Square, he saw it was already squinting bright, though the sun had not yet cleared the rooftops.

Showered and dressed appropriately for his country spin, he turned his thoughts to Julian Bell, recalling how Sally Mayhew had described him, wondering how they would hit it off and what the day would bring. Unfortunately, he'd had to scotch the idea of seeing his niece, Miranda. When he had phoned to say that he was coming down to Dorset, the house sitter had answered, telling him that Miranda and her husband were away on holiday in Spain.

Kingston had spent part of the previous afternoon and evening poring through reference books from his considerable library, and on his iMac, boning up on *Acer pentaphyllum*. It was evident that Bell knew of Kingston's teaching credentials and reputation in botany, so convincing the man that he was an authority on the subject should not present a problem.

It had been several years since he'd had the pleasure of visiting Dorset. He was not only looking forward to the trip but also toying with the idea of making it a two- or even a three-day affair. His calendar was blank for the next several days—not that it was ever that full anymore. He worried sometimes that he was becoming a bit of a recluse. Were it not for Andrew, his renewed friendship with Desmond Scott, who owned the water plant nurseries, and good old Henrietta the "hussy," he would have no social life at all. Recently Andrew had been encouraging him to date Henrietta more often, but while Kingston enjoyed her intellect and could tolerate her flamboyant nature, he could take her only in small doses. After years of knowing her, he'd never managed to summon up the nerve to tell her that he found her overt sexuality a bit offputting.

If he were asked to choose which English county he would pick for a leisurely summer's drive in his TR4, with the top down, Dorset would likely top Kingston's list. Wild heath land, undulating dairy country, rolling chalk downs, patchwork fields, green valleys, one pretty thatch-roofed village after another: a gentle landscape that had doubtless saved the BBC trillions of pounds in set building over the years. Home to writers Thomas Hardy, Jane Austen, William Barnes, and T. E. Lawrence, little has changed in the countryside since their days. With village names like Toller Porcorum, Plush, Piddlehinton, and Up Sydling, it leaves no doubt that one is truly far from the madding crowd.

Now, after breakfast, having read the *Times* front to back—as he did daily—he set off for Dorset.

With Bell's directions on the passenger seat, now memorized, Kingston turned off the A350 a mile south of Shaftesbury onto the B road that crossed Cranborne Chase, headed for a village with the whimsical name of Sixpenny Handley. Exactly one mile and a quarter after passing through the village, a gravel road would lead to Magpie Farm. Bell had said that the fingerpost was small, so to keep an eye open for it. Kingston was already getting to appreciate one of Bell's character traits: a preference for privacy.

Five minutes later on the gravel road—really more cart track—the farm came into view. For home seekers in Britain, the word "farm" holds a certain cachet. The word, purloined by canny estate agents, is used to describe any attractive country property having sundry outbuildings. In many cases, the likelihood that the property had once been home to a plow, a tractor, or any farm animals was dubious and usually went unquestioned. So Kingston was pleasantly surprised to see what resembled a working farm. Ahead was a wide opening set in a drystone wall. On either side, sagging wooden gates were anchored permanently in a sprawl of periwinkle and ivy. Beyond, scattered around, were half a dozen outbuildings of various shapes, sizes, and age; some wooden, others built of what appeared to be local stone. These he took to be barns, stables, cowsheds, and storage buildings for supplies and farm equipment. The house, set apart from the rest, was a simple whitewashed structure with a steep thatched roof, redbrick chimneys, and a sturdy-looking plain wooden door. Late eighteenth century, Kingston judged.

He pulled into a grassy space beside the house, alongside a Jeep, got out of the TR4, and stretched. For several moments, he gazed around, the reason for his being there momentarily forgotten. He let the earthiness and simple beauty of the surroundings sink in: the fields, neatly subdivided by hedging, that sloped up to meet the woods in the summer-hazed distance; the small orchard on the other side of the house, the tree trunks painted white above the uncut grass; the spire of a far-off church breaking the line of trees. Any moment he expected to hear the distant chime of its bells. He wondered what kind of garden lay beyond the high stone wall surrounding the house. He inhaled deeply, taking in the wholesome sweet smells, glad to be back in the country—deep in the country. Walking up to the oak door, he rapped twice with the heavy iron knocker.

A few moments later the door swung open with a loud creak, to reveal a dumpy, silver-haired woman with shiny apple cheeks. She was smiling, ample of bosom, and wearing a frilly apron. Kingston noticed that her hand holding the door open was dusted with flour. Knowing that Bell was a bachelor, it was reasonable to conclude that the woman, who resembled the quintessential grandmother, must be the housekeeper or cook, or both.

"I'm Mrs. Hudson, Mr. Bell's housekeeper," she said, resolving the matter. "You must be Dr. Kingston," she added, stepping aside to let him enter. "Mr. Bell is expecting you. He's in the study. It's the second door down the hall on the right." Kingston thanked her and started down the hall. The aroma of whatever she was baking was ineluctable and tantalizingly good. He reached the study door, which was half open. He knocked anyway. "Come in," said a booming voice.

Bell, a blacksmith of a man, was standing in front of a floor-to-ceiling bookshelf occupying one entire wall—a wall at least twenty-five feet long. He held an open book, closing and replacing it on the shelf upon seeing Kingston. They crossed the room and shook hands. After exchanging greetings, Bell gestured for Kingston to be seated in an overstuffed easy chair on one side of a glass-topped coffee table strewn with magazines. Bell sat opposite, on a plaid-blanket-covered leather couch.

Observing Bell, Kingston was reminded of Sally Mayhew's description. He was an imposing man, neatly bearded, and Kingston could see why she had used the words "fierce-looking." What she had neglected to mention were his eyes. Under bushy eyebrows, they were deep set and, from where Kingston sat, appeared to be black, glinting when the angle of light caught them right. Though an inch or so shorter than Kingston, Bell appeared larger because of his strapping build. Unsmiling, he looked across at Kingston. "Welcome to Magpie Farm, Lawrence," he said, leaning back and crossing his legs. His voice matched his appearance, deep and resonant. "You brought good weather."

"Yes. I'd forgotten just how beautiful your part of the world is. Even more so on a day like today."

"Can I get you something to drink?"

"No thanks, I'm fine for now."

The small talk continued for a minute or so before Bell brought up the subject of *Acer pentaphyllum,* the reason for Kingston's visit, as he put it. For a time Bell talked about how he had become interested in the species, recounting three separate trips over a span of ten years to the mountainous regions of Yunnan, Sichuan, and Gansu, where he'd had the opportunity to study them in the wild. On each successive expedition, the stands became fewer and farther between, he said. Over decades, subsistence farmers and locals had ravaged the maples, burning them for fuel. They had been further decimated by the onslaught of bulldozers and mechanical equipment employed in road building and ever-increasing construction projects that were pushing farther and farther into wilderness areas. Unless action was taken to halt the destruction, he was convinced that the rare maple would become extinct within a few years.

Kingston commiserated, slipping smoothly, and with convincing authority, into his prepared commentary, lasting four or five minutes, not a problem for someone with his silver tongue. As they went on to discuss what steps would be required to create the exploratory committee, Bell's body language began to betray subtle signs of impatience. Kingston noticed that his expression had hardened somewhat, the beginnings of a frown starting to wrinkle his brow. His next comment caught Kingston off balance.

"Let's be frank with each other, Doctor. Is the *Acer* the real reason you came here? Or did you really want to talk about the expedition? About Mayhew's death?"

"No, that's not the reason I'm here," Kingston replied, shaking his head, trying to sound offended by Bell's question, but mildly so. "I thought that was all resolved."

"You were working on the case with the police, were you not?"

"I was, yes." Kingston wondered how Bell knew. Had he learned it from Graves? Sally Mayhew, perhaps? He need not have given it thought.

"Spenser Graves told me." His eyes narrowed. "You know, the police have questioned both of us about Mayhew's accident."

Although it was rhetorical, Kingston sidestepped the question. "You know I went up to see his arboretum last week, then?"

"I do."

Kingston was starting to feel uncomfortable with Bell's shift in attitude and his confrontational stare. It was time to move off the subject, but Bell was having none of that.

"Mayhew's death was accidental, plain and simple. And if you're proposing that it was anything else, you're barking up the wrong tree."

Kingston was thinking fast. Telling Bell that he had talked with Sally Mayhew and that, according to her, his recollection of the accident differed from Graves's was not only pointless but liable to get Bell riled up. That was definitely not something he wanted to witness. Anyway, it no longer mattered. Graves had told Bell of Kingston's visit and their having discussed the expedition. If, indeed, either or both were lying, they'd had plenty of time to compare notes and get their stories straight. Kingston was already thinking of making a graceful exit, but to his surprise, Bell didn't drop the subject.

"Vertigo, most likely, or the altitude. You've been in those mountains, Kingston, you know damned well what it's like."

Kingston nodded and was about to speak, but Bell continued

as if he didn't want his train of thought deflected. "I heard a noise and turned round to see Mayhew on the ground with David and one of the guides kneeling beside him. After a few seconds, he got up, saying that he was okay, so we set off again. We'd only gone a few more steps up the trail when Mayhew fell again. He looked wobbly but managed to get to his feet. Then suddenly, before anyone could get to him, to grab him, he lost his balance, tottered a couple of steps, and went over the damned edge. That was it. Exactly as I reported it to the police."

Kingston shook his head. "Bloody awful thing to happen."

"Irony is, we'd just been talking about turning back. The weather was wretched and we were all dog tired."

Kingston wanted to ask about the other guide and if he had also fallen, but that would confirm Bell's suspicion of the real reason for his visit. He had a feeling that he'd learned all that he was going to learn. Unless Bell was going to volunteer more about the expedition—which was unlikely—then the meeting was essentially over.

But Bell went on. "Did the police tell you about my daughter and Mayhew?" he asked, his dark eyes never leaving Kingston's.

"They did, yes."

"Let me tell you something, Doctor. If I'd wanted to kill Peter Mayhew for what he did to Samantha, I'd have done it long ago, not waited four bloody years."

Kingston knew he was treading on eggshells. "That's what the police have more or less concluded," he said.

"They didn't tell me that."

"I'm surprised that you agreed to go on the expedition in the first place—knowing the bad blood between you and Mayhew."

"I hadn't planned to."

Now that they were on the subject, Kingston wanted to keep it going. "What changed your mind?" he asked nonchalantly.

"Graves, and Kavanagh. They insisted on it. Graves said that the others knew damned little about ancestral roses, which I found odd. It was my understanding that roses were the principal reason for the trip. That, and because the American wanted a doctor on the trip."

"*Rosa chinensis spontanea* and *odorata gigantea*, the two wild ancestors of the China rose?"

"Mostly, yes."

"Weren't you worried that Mayhew could be . . . troublesome?"

"He would have far more to worry about than I, don't you think?"

"I suppose so."

Bell shrugged. "As it was, we needn't have worried. I'm not saying that there weren't some awkward moments, but most of the time Mayhew kept pretty much to himself, except for Lester, whom I think he knew fairly well."

A ponderous silence fell. Kingston saw his cue to leave and started to get up. Bell followed suit and for a moment the two of them stood awkwardly on each side of the coffee table.

Bell broke the stalemate. "I don't think we have much more to talk about, Doctor. If you were hoping to discuss the aborted plant expedition in detail, I'm sorry to have disappointed you. It seems that your coming down here has been mostly a waste of time—yours and mine." He started toward the door, then paused with one hand resting on the back of the sofa. "Should you decide to pursue the *Acer pentaphyllum* project, keep me informed. I may become involved. I'm not making any promises, mind you."

"I will," Kingston replied, following Bell into the hallway.

Few words were said at the front door. As Kingston got into his car and started the engine, he made a halfhearted wave, which Bell returned in like manner. Then Kingston drove off.

Heading north on the B road for Shaftesbury, Kingston glanced at his watch. It was still early, not yet one o'clock. Whether or not it had to do with the aroma that had wafted from Bell's kitchen, he was suddenly hungry. When he got to Shaftesbury, he would leaf through his Egon Ronay guide and decide on a pub for lunch and a much-needed beer.

Sitting at a window table in the Rose & Crown, a pretty black-and-white timbered pub in the village of Compton St. Andrew, Kingston sipped his lager. He looked out at the attractive garden with a backdrop of climbing roses and clematis and took stock of things. On the drive from Magpie Farm, he'd had time to think about his all-too-brief encounter with Julian Bell. Perhaps "skirmish" might be more apt, he thought. In addition to the purpose of the trip—to extract a firsthand account of the accident from Bell—Kingston had hoped to make a positive impression on him, establish rapport, and learn more about the man. As it was, he'd achieved none of the latter. As far as Graves's and Bell's conflicting stories were concerned, Kingston was just as confused as before. On one hand it appeared that Graves and Bell might have got together to get their stories straight. Bell had said that when he turned to see Mayhew on the ground, David Jenkins and one of the guides were beside him. That pretty much meshed with Graves's account but certainly not with the version Bell had told Sally Mayhew. The mention of the guides raised another unanswered question. Surely they and the Chinese botanist must have been interviewed about the accident by the Chinese authorities. If so, Inspector Sheffield should have received that report. Kingston made a mental note to ask the inspector the next time they spoke. One way to straighten out the inconsistencies, perhaps, would be for him to talk to Sally again, to determine if her recollection of Bell's account was still the same.

Kingston's muddled train of thought was interrupted by the arrival of the young, personable waitress who lowered his plate gracefully to the table, positioning it as if she'd cooked it herself.

For her benefit mostly, he gave it his visual and olfactory approval. She departed with a smile and an "Enjoy."

The perfectly baked Scottish salmon fillet, confit of fennel and locally grown new potatoes and lemon butter lived up to the menu description and more. Having forgotten to bring the *Times* with him to continue where he'd left off with the crossword, he spent the duration of the meal thinking about the expedition and Lester's murder.

When he returned, he would have to call Sheffield and tell him that the meeting with Bell was a bust. He would use a more ambiguous phrase, of course—something like "relatively unproductive." Before calling the inspector, however, it might be a good idea to contact Sally Mayhew, to see just how good her memory was.

Downing the last of his beer, he started to wonder if he wasn't making too much of the conflicting stories, trying to make something out of nothing. Perhaps it was asking too much to expect that everybody's recollection of such a traumatic incident would be identical. The only other avenue of investigation he could think of was to dig a little into David Jenkins's background. Maybe something there had been overlooked. Inspector Sheffield had said that he'd interviewed Jenkins, and his story agreed with Graves's. But that didn't necessarily count him out as a suspect. As for the American, being out of the country, he would appear the least likely to have a motive for wanting to do away with Mayhew—if indeed he was murdered—or Jeremy Lester, for that matter. As things stood, he wouldn't worry about Kavanagh until Sheffield had received a report from the FBI.

For the first time since he'd become involved, ripples of doubt were starting to undermine Kingston's usually steadfast confidence. Sheffield or no Sheffield, he was now questioning whether he should become further involved. The maddening thing was that, even taking into account the claim in the anonymous letter he'd received at Lydiard Park, the cause of Mayhew's death was still a question mark. Suppose it *had* been an accident. Then what? The answer—much as it didn't sit well with him—was that he'd wasted an awful lot of time for nothing. On the other hand there was no question whatsoever about Jeremy Lester's demise. It was premeditated murder.

By the time the bill arrived, he had made a decision. Despite his insatiable curiosity and his promise to Sheffield, he was going to forget the whole business—for a while, anyway. It was starting to take over his life. He'd faced similar situations before and knew how his good intentions often got the better of him. These things always started innocently—as this one had—with him playing the good citizen, offering help. Whereas most rational people would recognize when they were getting in over their heads, or would realize that they had promised something they couldn't deliver, and would admit it and politely retract the offer—not so him. It never failed. Before knowing it, he stumbled inadvertently across an illusory line into a no-man's-land of uncertainty and, more often than not, trouble. While he'd been known to quote Sod's law that "every good deed deserves its just punishment," it was paradoxical that when it came to his own good deeds, he was the first to flout it. No more, he promised himself.

He glanced over the bill. It was amazing how often he found mistakes; not this time, though. He slipped his credit card into the faux leather folder, then leaned back, satisfied with his decision. What should he do with the rest of his life? he wondered. A complete break might not be a bad idea—a trip to Seattle to see his daughter, Julie? It had been five years since his last visit. What else? Perhaps when he got back home, he would call his friends Kate and Alex Sheppard in Wiltshire. He hadn't spoken with them in months. His musings were interrupted as the waitress returned, with a dimpled smile and his bill. Kingston signed it, adding a decent tip, got up, and left.

A veil of gray clouds was appearing on the horizon, not that it mattered. With Miranda off sipping Cava by a pool somewhere on the Costa Brava, Kingston had abandoned his earlier idea of making his Dorset junket a two- or three-day affair. He got into the TR4 and turned on his mobile, noting that there was one missed call. Few people had his mobile number, so he usually recognized the phone numbers of those who did. This missed call number wasn't familiar. He decided he would wait until he got home before returning it. He'd had enough for one day.

THIRTEEN

After a late, light supper, accompanied by a glass of Pemerol, Kingston hashed over his fruitless trip to Magpie Farm. Bell had been halfway convincing when he had explained why Peter Mayhew's being on the expedition was of little concern to him. Kingston wondered how he would feel, placed in the same situation. Even with the passing of time, would he be able to forgive a man who'd been implicated in the death of *his* daughter?

Kingston thought back to an expedition he'd been on ten years ago. Roses had been the main reason for that trip, too. Sipping the last of his wine, he got to thinking about roses in general and how little the average person knew about them: where they came from and what they had come to represent in the hearts and minds of people in every part of the world and for so long.

Faced with the prodigious and ever-growing selection of rose hybrids offered by today's nurseries and garden centers, and the seductive blooms displayed in countless catalogs and on the Internet, it is understandable that today's rose buyers might prefer not to spend even more time delving into the history of the rose. Should they do so, however, they would be undertaking an awe-inspiring journey back to prehistoric time embracing myth, legend, archaeology, discovery, world history, literature, and art.

From rose fossils found in rocks of the Oligocene epoch in North America, Europe, and Asia, there is indisputable evidence that roses existed at least thirty-five million years ago. As evidenced by archaeological excavations in ancient cities, settlements, and burial sites throughout the world, the rose as a symbolic image extends far back into the mists of time. Rose remnants found in an Egyptian tomb are thought to date from A.D. 170. Roman coins from 500 B.C., unearthed in Rhodes, bear imprints of roses. The oldest known painting of a rose is on a fresco that decorated the walls of a palace at Knossos, in northern Crete, thought to date from 1450 B.C. As far as Asia is concerned, there is no doubt that the roses had existed there for thousands of years. References to Chinese floriculture go back as far as the eleventh century B.C. Numerous records reveal medicinal use of the plant, and written lists indicate that large numbers of roses were planted in the imperial gardens.

In his teachings at the University of Edinburgh, Kingston had enjoyed the luxury of weeks, even months, plotting the complex evolution of the rose up to the present day. However, for talks and slide shows he presented to various garden clubs and horticultural and botanical organizations, he had developed a less complex, concise explanation that took no more than an hour to deliver and could be readily understood by the average gardener or neophyte.

As he had in the past, but this time without the help of slides and a family tree chart, of course, Kingston began to trace the evolution of the genus *Rosa* in his mind. It all came back so quickly and effortlessly. He could have easily been back in the classroom in Scotland.

To begin, long before the time of man, various parts of the planet were populated with wild roses, what scientists now term species roses. It is generally agreed that as many as two hundred such species exist today.

To simplify matters, Kingston had divided the rose family into two main groups: those that originated in the Far East and those from various parts of the Western world, principally Europe and the Middle East. Two of the earliest wild roses from the latter group are *Rosa gallica* and *Rosa moschata*. While their origin may never be determined, it is generally agreed that they are ancestors of many of today's cultivars. Over centuries, with natural cross-hybridization, new species developed and roses continued to thrive.

It wasn't until the Renaissance, when botanists and herbalists began exploring plant forms, that it was discovered that variations in these ancient roses might occur by harvesting the seeds in the hips and replanting them. Soon, roses were widely cultivated and used for personal adornment, in cosmetics, and in cooking. The rose as a symbol became increasingly secularized. It became a symbol not only of love but also of monarchal power: During the Wars of the Roses, the white rose was associated with the House of York and the red rose with the House of Lancaster.

Botanists labeled these hybrids as Antique roses and began to classify them. Five families of Antique roses resulted. Gallicas are the oldest of the group, of which there are now about fifty hybrids in general cultivation. Damasks are thought to have reached Europe with the help of the Crusaders and believed to be a natural hybrid between a Gallica rose and a Persian rose. Albas are a cross between a Damask and the European dog rose. Grown by the Romans, Albas are usually white or off-white. Centifolias—also known as cabbage roses—are so called because they have up to one hundred petals. The Dutch are credited with developing Centifolia roses in the seventeenth century. Last is the Moss rose family, first observed in France in the 1600s. Mosses are distinguished by mosslike growth on their stems, calyxes, and sepals.

At this point in his presentation, Kingston usually turned off the projector for a while and talked about roses from the East, specifically the history of the China rose, a subject dear to his heart. The China rose is actually a complex of natural and cultivated hybrids that have evolved over more than a thousand years in Chinese gardens. China has an unparalleled richness in biodiversity, and its roses are no exception: 93 species and 144 varieties are native, with 80 percent occurring naturally, mainly in Yunnan and Sichuan provinces.

Of all the many species of rose found exclusively within the subtropical and temperate northern latitudes, two have contributed uniquely to our rose heritage. They are *Rosa chinensis* var. *spontanea* and *Rosa odorata* var. *gigantea*. These two wild roses have provided the world with traits highly prized in modern rose culture, thanks to centuries of domestication in China and subsequent hybridizing in Europe. Up until the mid-sixteenth century, the Chinese had been obsessively suspicious of foreigners, allowing few to visit the country's interior. As a result, little is known about rose culture prior to that time. The first person to introduce a Chinese rose to Europe was Peter Osbeck, a pupil of Carl Linnaeus, the famous Swedish botanist, responsible for the present day system of naming, ranking, and classifying organisms. The small pink rose Osbeck brought back in 1752 later became known in England as Old Blush, Parsons' Pink China. It was to become the first of the four garden roses to be known as the Four Stud Chinas.

The second Stud rose, Slater's Crimson China, arrived in Britain in 1792. A low-growing shrub, it became the parent of the Portland rose and subsequently grandparent of the Hybrid Perpetuals. The next Stud rose to arrive in Europe was Hume's Blush Tea-Scented China. It was brought back in 1810 by Sir Abraham

Hume, oddly enough a specialist in chrysanthemums. Following, in 1824, came the climber, Park's Yellow Tea-Scented China. This rose was important because it introduced yellow into breeding lines.

The introduction of the China roses to Europe changed rose culture forevermore. Chinese roses offered several distinct traits that had been lacking in European roses of the eighteenth century: repeat, or perpetual blooming, usually from early or mid-summer to late autumn; true crimson red coloring that did not fade with age; and a lower, dwarf, bushy habit. Along with Chinese roses came a new range of yellows and new fragrances, some described as tea scented, others as fruity and peppery.

Of all the patrons of horticulture and the arts at the beginning of the nineteenth century, none was more charismatic and influential than the Empress Josephine, wife of Napoleon Bonaparte. After their marriage, the couple acquired the Château de Malmaison outside of Paris, and while her husband was away on military matters, she happily went about spending his money, beautifying the house and the garden. She assembled what would become, at the time, the greatest rose collection in the world. In its heyday, Malmaison boasted roses in the hundreds, including 167 Gallicas, 27 Centifolias, many Damasks and Albas, and more than 20 species roses.

In 1810, at the height of the Napoleonic Wars, extraordinary measures were taken by the French and British navies to ensure the safe passage of the newly discovered Hume's Blush Tea-Scented China from England to Malmaison. Nurseryman John Kennedy received a special passport to take the rose and other plants from an English nursery to Josephine's garden. Such is the power of the rose.

The elucidation of both ancient and modern rose genealogies was greatly advanced in the mid-twentieth century by the pioneering genetic research of Dr. C. C. Hurst. His studies, though performed at the infancy of genetic science in the 1930s, have not been significantly challenged to this day. Were it not for the introduction of China roses to Europe, our gardens and parks would not be graced with Tea roses, Bourbons, Hybrid Perpetuals, Hybrid Teas, Floribundas, Polyanthas, Noisettes, or any of the new hybrids from breeders the likes of David Austin, Poulsen, and Meilland.

Kingston thought back to the garden he and his wife, Megan, had created at their home in Edinburgh. It wasn't large, but it contained an amazing variety of plants and several mature trees. Chief among them were his favorites: roses, clematis, hardy geraniums, and hellebores. Exhausting the horizontal space, he had trained many of the roses to climb into the trees. In early summer, when the old climbers and ramblers came into bloom, the effect was breathtaking. When he had first moved to London, he had missed the garden terribly, yearning to be able to walk out through the French doors into its enclosed beauty and inhale the heady fragrance. At least nowadays he had Andrew's garden to visit on pleasant days. Not only that, there were all the hundreds, if not thousands, of public and private gardens scattered throughout Britain to satisfy his passion. He smiled, recalling the aphorism: He who smells the flowers, owns the garden.

Kingston took his empty wineglass into the kitchen, turned out the lights in the living room, and made for the upstairs bedroom. He was at the top of the staircase when he remembered the message on his mobile. He went back down to the hall closet and retrieved the phone from his jacket pocket. He was always hunting for the damned thing, but this time he remembered where he'd left it. Back in the living room, he sat down and punched in the number. After half a dozen rings, a woman's voice: "Hello."

"This is Lawrence Kingston. Sorry to ring you so late. I'm returning your call."

"Yes, thank you. How are you?"

Her voice wasn't familiar, but she clearly knew him or she wouldn't be inquiring after his well-being. Not unless she was making a friendly sales pitch.

"I'm fine, thank you," he mumbled. Still, he couldn't place the voice.

"This is Sally Mayhew."

"Well, uh, what a nice surprise. And how are *you?*"

"Me? I'm doing okay, thanks." Her tone suggested otherwise.

"Have you spoken with Inspector Sheffield recently?" he asked, mostly for something to say, not wanting to be impolite by asking outright why she was calling.

"Not recently, no. Early on, he told me that you were helping them on the case. I was going to call him, but I thought I'd call you first, to see what you thought."

"Is it about your brother?"

"Yes. It's about some things I found in his belongings, in with his books. They could have a bearing on his accident." She paused, then continued in a lackluster voice. "You are still concerned with trying to find out what happened to Peter, aren't you?"

"I am, very much so."

She explained that after she learned of Peter's death, she'd gone down to Arundel to meet with the owner of the cottage Peter had been renting, to pick up his personal belongings and arrange to have what little furniture, books, and paintings he owned shipped to her. "I had a feeling that he wouldn't have much in the way of possessions," she said, "and I was right. The place would've made a monk look like a pack rat. Peter was one of those people who place little value on material things. As long as he had a roof over his head, three meals a day, and a steady supply of books, he was perfectly happy. I suppose that's why he took to horticulture the way he did."

"What kind of things are you referring to, Sally? The things you found in your brother's belongings?"

"Some court documents and a letter."

"Really?"

"The court documents are about a trial in which Peter was the defendant. It seems that, some years ago, he was implicated in the death of Julian Bell's daughter. She was killed in a motor-cycle accident—on the back of Peter's bike." After a little pause she continued, her tone even more forlorn. "He never told me about it."

"I imagine that he wanted to save you the grief. He had enough of his own at the time, I'm sure. All the charges were dismissed, you know. All except one."

"You know about it, then?"

"Yes. Inspector Sheffield told me," he fibbed. He wasn't going to tell her over the phone that he'd received a letter suggesting that Peter's death might not have been the result of an accident. Or that he'd met with Bell, who'd insisted that it *had* been an accident.

"It doesn't look too good for Julian, though, does it? The police could think that it might be revenge for his daughter's death."

"That's true. But as the police have pointed out, why would he have waited four years?"

The silence that followed was hardly surprising. Kingston could picture her struggling not only with the upsetting revelation about Samantha's death and how it might provide a possible motive for Peter's murder, but at the same time undoubtedly flustered that the police and Kingston were already aware of it.

"You mentioned a letter?" said Kingston at last.

"Yes. It was from David Jenkins, one of the men on the expedition. It was still in the envelope addressed to Peter. The letter was to inform Peter that Julian Bell was going to join them on the trip and urging Peter to reconsider going."

"Was it dated?"

"Yes. It was postmarked and dated two weeks before the expedition departure."

"So this could have been a last minute decision on Bell's part?"

"Could have been, I suppose."

"What else was in the letter? Did Jenkins explain why he thought it wasn't such a good idea?"

"No. That was about it."

"We'll need to see the letter, Sally."

"Of course."

"Make a copy for yourself and then send me the original by special delivery. I'll forward it to the police."

"I'll send it tomorrow morning."

"Good. I'll call you after I've had a chance to look it over."

There was another pause, this one shorter.

"Do you ever get up to town?" Kingston asked before she could speak.

"Occasionally. I have a friend who lives by Regent's Park."

"Good. Next time you come up, give me a call and perhaps we can have lunch at Fortnum's or the Ivy. At the least, a glass of wine."

"I'd like that."

They said goodbye and rang off. What on earth had gotten into him, asking her to lunch? For some inexplicable reason, the words had just popped right out. He shook his head and headed for the kitchen to get a glass of water. Maybe he'd been listening to Andrew too much.

Lying awake in bed, Kingston thought about the letter and David Jenkins, and why he would want to urge Mayhew not to go on the expedition. Was it simply because Jenkins knew about Samantha's death and thought it politic that Bell and Mayhew shouldn't be put in a situation where they would be living in each other's pockets, day and night, for so long? Or was there more to it? Kingston had to admit that—considering the circumstances and knowing what expeditions were like—Jenkins had a good point. It could be asking for trouble. Kingston was beginning to realize how little he knew about Jenkins. Hadn't Clifford Attenborough said that one of the chaps from Kew Gardens had worked with him once? He would call Clifford in the morning to find out. Another thing bothered him. What had taken Sally so long to mention the letter? She, or someone, must have known about it for months. He must remember to ask her when they next talked—if they ever did.

Drifting off to sleep, he gave one last thought to Sally Mayhew, thinking about his impetuous invitation. He hoped she didn't get the wrong idea. What did it matter, he told himself. She's not going to call anyway.

The next morning, before calling Clifford Attenborough, Kingston tried to reach Alex and Kate Sheppard, his friends in Wiltshire. The phone was answered by Peg, a close friend of Kate's. Alex and Kate were on holiday in America, she said, and wouldn't be back for another two weeks. They chatted for a few minutes, with Peg promising to tell the Sheppards that Kingston had called. Next he called Clifford.

There was nothing wrong with Clifford's memory. When Kingston asked about the man at Kew Gardens who had once worked with David Jenkins, he remembered his name right off the bat. It was Oliver Wilkins. Wilkins had recently retired but Clifford was certain that Kew would have a forwarding address and phone number. Explaining that he wasn't permitted to provide the number, he said that he would call Wilkins personally and, without going into a song and dance as to why, have him phone Kingston. Knowing that Clifford was a man of his word, he wasn't surprised when Wilkins called later that afternoon.

"Of course I remember David," was Wilkins's answer to Kingston's first question. "Nice enough bloke, once you got to know him. I heard he's down in Cornwall now. What would you like to know about him?"

"Sort of a character reference, I suppose you'd call it. What he was like to work with, his personality, his habits, what he does in his spare time—that sort of thing?"

"Are you thinking of hiring him, then?"

"No. Not at all," Kingston replied. "I take it Attenborough didn't tell you why I wanted to talk with you?"

"He didn't. No."

Good, thought Kingston. He offered a cobbled-up version of what had happened on the plant-hunting expedition, carefully omitting any mention of homicide or police involvement. He was going to meet Jenkins, he said, and simply wanted to get a general idea of what he was like.

"Well, let's see, David was intelligent, quiet, soft-spoken. I believe his father was in the diplomatic corps, so I assume he had a good education. He kept pretty much to himself mostly. Introverted, I suppose would describe him. As far as women were concerned, he didn't have much time for them. I don't think there were any in his life to speak of—other than his mother, of course." He paused but Kingston didn't interrupt.

"He liked to watch cricket, whenever he could, particularly the test matches. He didn't drink or smoke and was always in good physical condition, though, to the best of my knowledge, he didn't exercise or participate in any kind of sports."

"What about hobbies?"

"None that I know of. Wait—he collected those little Japanese ivory carvings, I forget what they're called. He showed me a couple once that were erotic."

"Netsuke. They were functional as well as aesthetic, you know." Kingston knew he was running the risk of sounding like a know-it-all, but went on regardless. "They acted as a toggle at the end of a silk cord suspended from an obi—kimono sash—to prevent items like tobacco pouches, pipes, and small purses, called *sage-mono*, from slipping through. Some of the early ones fetch a pretty penny. I have a couple myself."

"Really?" said Wilkins, in a tone that suggested that Kingston might as well have been holding forth about the Great Plague. Kingston wished now that he hadn't gone to the trouble of sharing this nugget of antiquarian wisdom.

"Getting back to Jenkins, did he participate in any plant expeditions when you worked together?"

"I don't think so, because he talked about wanting to do it."

"Do you know about any of his other jobs, before you met?"

There was a momentary silence while Wilkins considered the question. "I know that, after grammar school, he took a course at the Wellington School of Garden Design. After that he got a job with a landscape design company. Not sure where that was." Another pause. "That's right, he worked at a wholesale nursery at one time. In Surrey, I think it was. He was very good at propagating. Oh yes, and Lydiard Park. He was—"

"He worked at Lydiard Park?"

"Yes. As a gardener."

"Interesting. How long is it since you last saw him?"

"Hmm, has to be at least five years. Maybe more."

"By chance, do you have an address or phone number?"

"Sorry, I don't. We weren't what you'd call chums."

"Well, I appreciate your phoning me. If I think of anything I've overlooked, perhaps I could call you back?"

"Not a problem. Give David my regards when you see him. Tell him to drop me a note sometime."

Wilkins gave Kingston his phone number and address and the conversation ended.

Kingston went to the window and looked out on Cadogan Square. Rain was hammering the ink-slick pavement, mostly hidden by the colorful parade of umbrellas, black predominant, of course. But it wasn't the weather that he was thinking about. It was that David Jenkins had once worked at Lydiard Park. It was too much of a coincidence, leaving little doubt that Jenkins had written the anonymous letters. What had he planned to divulge at the aborted meeting? Kingston wondered. Was it just to disclose that Mayhew was implicated in Samantha Bell's death, thereby providing a motive for her father, or was there more? What else did Jenkins know? Kingston went into the kitchen to put the kettle on.

With his second cup of tea, Kingston finished his third McVities' digestive biscuit. Usually he rationed himself to two, but today was a day for breaking petty rules, including the one he'd made rather impetuously a few days ago, about suspending his inquiries into the Mayhew affair. By the time he'd taken his last sip of tea, he had decided that if the stalled investigation was to be jump-started, a face-to-face meeting with David Jenkins was imperative. But even if he were to get Jenkins's phone number—he could hardly ask Sheffield for it—a call to him could result in his denying any knowledge of the letters. Not only that, it could slam the door shut on future conversations. Somehow Kingston had to find a way to confront him, whether Jenkins was agreeable or not. Buoyed by his decision, he was reminded that before driving all the way to Cornwall—which would require an overnight stay—he had to be certain that David Jenkins would be home or at his place of business. It was starting to look as if another foray to the country was in the offing. This time, to the land of ancient legends and myths: Celts, druids, King Arthur, pasties, and piskies—the county of Cornwall.

FOURTEEN

Since his chin-wag with Oliver Wilkins, Kingston had made several phone calls to various friends and acquaintances in the horticultural world, trying to find an address for David Jenkins, but without success. None of them knew of his whereabouts.

It was the Internet that came to the rescue once again. All Kingston had to go on was "Jenkins" and "Cornwall," which is what he typed into the search bar. Testing the mettle of the search engine's gazillion-page memory bank managed to dredge up two Cornwall B and Bs run by folks called Jenkins, a retired county council recycling director, a Cornish smuggler of yore, authors of *Ironmaking in the 14th Century* and *Local Sightings of the Little Egret*—all Jenkins—plus umpteen hundred pages of Cornish Jenkins's genealogy. No Jenkins with horticultural connections.

Not one to give up easily, Kingston typed in "Cornish gardens." Again, he scrolled through page after page on specific gardens, tourist information, accommodations, garden blogs, on and on. About to try another tack he almost missed the listing: <u>Trevassick Tree Farm Celebrates Third Year</u>. He clicked on it and read the item culled from the *Cornish Courier*.

Fowey

The Annual Trevassick Tree Farm and Nursery Sale will take place on Saturday and Sunday, July 7 & 8. Bargains aplenty can be had with price reductions on all trees and shrubs in stock, ranging from 20% to 35%.

Owner David Jenkins and nursery staff will be on hand to answer all questions concerning the selection, planting, and care of your purchases.

Complimentary tea and a variety of baked goods will be served and drawings will take place every three hours for prizes of dogwoods, Japanese maples, and other specimen trees. Delivery is available, with charges based on distance.

Trevassick Farm is located at the end of Badgers Lane, Lostwithiel. Hours: 9:30 A.M. to 6:00 P.M. on both days.

He was pleased and energized. The coming weekend he could motor off to the West Country, knowing that a meeting with the reclusive David Jenkins was all but guaranteed. And Sally's package containing Jenkins's letter certainly would arrive before then.

Kingston's phone conversation with Inspector Sheffield lasted only a couple of minutes. The inspector was clearly not in one of his chatty moods and listened patiently to Kingston's report of his meeting with Julian Bell. Nor was he overly surprised when

Kingston told him that Bell was emphatic that Mayhew's death was an accident, that there was no friction between the two of them on the expedition, and that Graves's and Bell's versions of the accident were now the same. He agreed that it would be a good idea to question Sally Mayhew again, to see if she would stick to the description of her brother's accident as told to her earlier by Julian Bell. While on the subject, Kingston raised the question of the guides.

"Yes," Sheffield replied. "We did receive copies of statements from the Chinese Bureau. One, I recall, was from a Chinese botanist who was on the trip, the other, from one of the guides. I can't remember the exact details of the transmission without digging it out, but their versions of the accident support those given by the other members—Graves, Bell, Jenkins, and Kavanagh."

"Only one guide?"

"Apparently they've yet to locate the second. It seems he returned to Tibet."

Kingston couldn't help but notice that Sheffield's answers were unnecessarily terse. "You received Kavanagh's statement, then?"

"We did, yes. The FBI, San Francisco office, sent us a transcript of their interview with Todd Kavanagh."

"That's it?"

"I'm afraid so. The bottom line is that Kavanagh's account of Mayhew's accident jibed with the others." He paused. "I know it's probably not what you wanted to hear, Doctor, but it appears that all of them are in the clear. It looks like Mayhew's death was accidental after all."

After putting down the phone, Kingston couldn't help thinking that Sheffield's ambivalence gave strength to what had become a worrisome concern of Kingston's: Sheffield's shuffling him off to see Julian Bell had been simply to placate him, make him feel he was making a worthwhile contribution to the case. On further thought, he dismissed the idea as being crabbedness on his part. Surely Sheffield—and the police generally, for that matter—were above that sort of pettiness. Thinking back, perhaps he should have told Sheffield about his upcoming Cornwall trip. He should have also mentioned the letter that Jenkins had written to Peter Mayhew. It was too late now. As far as the letter was concerned, since he hadn't received it yet, he felt somewhat less guilty about not having brought it up. He would probably be calling Sheffield again within the next several days, anyway, and he could tell him then.

Sally Mayhew's package arrived Monday afternoon. Sitting on the sofa, he opened the letter-size manila envelope and withdrew another, smaller manila envelope, bearing a white label addressed to Peter Mayhew. He noted the date stamp, September 26. Just as Sally had said, approximately two weeks before the six men left on the expedition. He withdrew Jenkins's letter, noting that there was no return address.

Monday, September 25

Dear Peter,

This week I heard from Todd Kavanagh that Julian Bell will be joining us on the China expedition. Apparently this was a last-minute decision on Bell's part, agreed to by Todd, who was eager to have him on board because of his experience in the field with species roses and as a doctor. There was nothing I could do to forestall it.

I and the other members of the expedition are aware of the tragic circumstances that brought you and Bell together as antagonists three years ago. For that reason alone, we feel that it is in everybody's interest, yours in particular, that the two of you not be placed unfairly in a close-quarters situation that could well become uncomfortable, possibly confrontational.

Much as I have been looking forward to having you with us on the trip and making your acquaintance, I am reluctantly recommending that you withdraw. I do this with regret but earnestly feel that this is for the good. I trust you will do the right thing by calling Todd and informing him of your decision.

> *Cordially,*
> *David Jenkins*

Kingston read the letter a second time, set it aside, leaned back into the cushions, hands clasped behind his head, and stared at the ceiling, ignoring a couple of stray cobwebs. Why had Jenkins taken it upon himself to suggest that Mayhew quit? he wondered. It certainly appeared that the letter was composed without consulting the others. If, as Clifford Attenborough had said, the American was the organizer, shouldn't such a request have come direct from him? Had Jenkins really spoken with Kavanagh? It was all very equivocal. His list of questions for Jenkins was growing.

Kingston's decision to drive to Cornwall on Saturday created a problem that he had to deal with right away. He'd promised Andrew that he would spend a couple of days this week at Andrew's garden in Bourne End, helping tidy it up for a garden open house—Andrew's first—taking place the coming Sunday. He still planned to do this but he knew Andrew wouldn't be chuffed to learn that Kingston might not make it back in time for Sunday's main event, particularly since he had persuaded Andrew to accept the invitation from the Chalfont St. Peter Garden Club in the first place. It was too bad because Kingston had been looking forward to it also. Nothing pleased him more than sauntering through a garden on a sunny day, a Pimms in hand, politely answering questions from little old ladies. Nevertheless, he couldn't pass up the chance to meet Jenkins face-to-face. He might not get another opportunity like this for some time. He picked up the phone to call Andrew.

Midafternoon Saturday, under a blue sky daubed with fleecy white clouds, Kingston drove onto the Torpoint Ferry at Devonport. On the other side of the river was Cornwall. He had a special place in his heart for England's farthest-flung county. For many centuries it had remained isolated from the rest of England, both in customs and in language. It was a Hobbit-like land of ancient lore and legend, fertile with tales of shipwrecks, smuggling, and strange happenings from the not-so-distant past when copper and tin miners toiled their way to early graves in narrow tunnels under the sea. Many was the time he'd sat in pubs listening to locals talk about the pagan rituals and mores that were still very much alive and well in that particular village and other parts.

Though it was much slower, he'd chosen to take the coastal route, the smaller roads that, once in a while, offered views of the craggy shoreline, sheltered coves, and picture-postcard fishing villages that hugged the rocks like barnacles. Whimsical place names were also part of the Cornish charm, villages like Portwrinkle, Budge's Shop, Mevagissey, Mousehole, and Fowey. To make it even more confusing, the last two were pronounced Mowzle and Foy. It was the town of Fowey where Kingston was headed. Another twenty miles and he would be there.

Now the lanes were barely wide enough for two passing cars, on some stretches, not. Winding and sunken, with impenetrable hedges of hawthorn, dog roses, and brambles pressing in on both sides, they made driving for the uninitiated a heart-thumping adventure. He'd toured the West Country on several occasions, so this was nothing new to Kingston. He navigated the spidery roads like one of the locals. Half an hour later, on a downhill slope, he saw three cars stopped ahead, water beyond. He was almost at Fowey. The cars were waiting for the Bodinnick–Fowey car ferry. He was in luck. The ferry, not much more than a floating dock, carried only six cars. On weekends and holidays the line of waiting cars could be backed up for almost a quarter mile.

On the Fowey side, he drove through the squeaky-narrow streets flanked by medieval and Tudor cottages, cobbled walkways, and attractive shops festooned with hanging baskets spilling with bright flowers. Now and again, through gaps in the buildings, he caught a glimpse of the shimmering estuary: the naked masts of sailboats with flags snapping in the offshore breeze, the sun burnishing the portholes and windows of an armada of schooners, yachts, and motor launches moored in the harbor.

For a moment, at a traffic stop, he was transported through time to twenty-five years earlier, when he and Megan had spent a month touring the West Country. They had stayed two days in Fowey, and the memory of those golden days flooded back. The never-to-be-forgotten weekend at Padstow on May Day, when the entire fishing village—kids and dogs included—plus a jostling army of onlookers, turn out in force to celebrate the pre-Christian festival of the "'Obby 'Oss," as it is spelled and pronounced by the locals. The pagan ritual defies description, and spending time to figure out what it's all about is pointless, because the Beltane rite reaches so far back in time that its origins are so hopelessly blurred even the village elders can't explain it in full.

To outward appearances the celebration is an excuse for an annual round-the-clock surfeit of singing, dancing, chanting, and drumming—with white-shirted locals wearing either blue or red sashes, and visitors parading through the jam-packed village behind a man wearing a bizarre black hobbyhorse costume, bearing no resemblance whatsoever to a horse. All of this revelry places a severe strain on the thirst, which is happily alleviated by the several pubs in the village. The incessant chanting and drum beating, which can be heard for miles around, goes on late into the night, by which time, the villagers, along with the remaining stragglers— mostly die-hard tourists—are too weary or inebriated to go on. To this day, Kingston remembered the first verse of the "Morning Song." It wasn't surprising, since he'd sung it countless times on their two trips.

> *Rise up, Mr. Hawken and joy to you beside,*
> *For summer is acome unto day*
> *And bright is your bride that lies down by your side,*
> *In the merry morning of May.*

One week later, they had lodged at a B and B for a couple of days to see the Furry, or Floral Dance, at the market town of Helston. Like Padstow, the streets had been thronged with thousands of visitors taking in the day-into-night carnival that celebrates the coming of spring and the passing of winter. The Furry Dance itself is not so much a dance but another, albeit more dignified, procession through the town's narrow streets. The gentlemen wear morning dress with gray top hats and tails, the ladies full-length dresses and ball gowns. An added attraction is the Hal-an-Tow— an ancient Celtic song sung to a costumed performance in which St. George and St. Michael slay the dragon and the devil, cheered on by a crowd wearing Elizabethan dress.

A toot from the car behind jogged Kingston back to the present. He shook his head and smiled. Those had been wonderful times. A minute later, he pulled up outside the Old Quay House Hotel, where he dropped off his bag and picked up a prepaid permit for a nearby car park. In ten minutes he was back at the hotel, checked in and enjoying a glass of wine on the sun terrace overlooking the estuary. His plan for the evening was to take a stroll through the town, which had several art galleries, and afterward, dine in the hotel's restaurant, which he'd already sussed out, sold on the mouthwatering menu that described the fare as a "blend of seafood, using local produce with Mediterranean flavors." An early night, then off in the morning to meet David Jenkins at his tree farm in Lostwithiel, which, according to the concierge, who had given him directions, was little more than a ten-minute drive from the hotel.

Next morning at eight, Kingston picked up a *Sunday Telegraph* from the front desk—the *Times* were all spoken for—and sat on the terrace for a breakfast of kippers, toast with marmalade, and a pot of Earl Grey tea.

It is a little-known fact—but known to Kingston, of course—that Howick Hall, famous for its magnificent arboretum and gardens, is also the home of Earl Grey tea. In the mid-1800s, Charles, the second Earl Grey, had the tea specially blended by a Chinese mandarin, formulated to suit the water at Howick, using bergamot to offset the chalky taste of lime in the local water. Soon after, Lady Grey, who entertained frequently in London, started serving it at many of her social and political gatherings. The tea became so popular that she was asked if it could be sold to others. It is now sold worldwide, but unfortunately the Greys were not businesslike and failed to register the trademark. As a result, they have never received a penny.

Taking his last sip of tea, Kingston finished reading the sports page and was about to fold the paper when, for some inexplicable reason—he'd rarely done it in all his many years of newspaper reading—he glanced down at the horoscopes. What would today bring? he wondered. He smiled as he read it.

SAGITTARIUS
November 23–December 21

This week, travel could bring unexpected surprises. Thursday's powerful link between the sun and your ruler, Jupiter, could bring greater understanding and help solve a problem that's been plaguing you for some time. It could also bring, as travel is wont to do, a new friendship of the opposite sex. A surprise visit could bring unexpected repercussions. Tread carefully, Sag. All is not as it appears.

Signing the check, he wondered if perchance a ravishing young divorcée, who was rolling in it and had a thing for older men, might be staying at the hotel. What would Andrew say to that?

Kingston left the Old Quay House and set off for the car park and Lostwithiel. Hands stuffed in the pockets of his peacoat, he walked briskly, enjoying the gray morning and muffled quiet. A cool veil of sea mist embraced the houses and yet-to-open shops along Fore Street, the town's daytime bustle and squealing chorus of gulls conspicuously absent.

Kingston cleaned the TR's windscreen and windows with his squeegee and soon was on his way to Trevassick Tree Farm. He was looking forward to catching up with Jenkins at long last, hoping that the meeting would be more congenial and revealing than that with Bell.

Ten minutes later, Kingston turned off the Lostwithiel road onto Badgers Lane, which led to the tree farm. After about a quarter mile, rounding a curve, he saw the farm's sign alongside a wide steel gate. He pulled up in front of the gate, surprised to see that it was padlocked. Then he saw the makeshift sign attached to the gate. He got out and read it.

THE SALE HAS BEEN CANCELED DUE TO AN URGENT
FAMILY MATTER. WE APOLOGIZE FOR THE INCONVENIENCE.
PLEASE WATCH THE NEWSPAPERS FOR NEW SALE DATES.

His first reaction was anger. He'd spent all this bloody time and money to meet Jenkins, and it had come down to this. He stared at the sign. "An urgent family matter" could mean many things. The first that came to mind was that Jenkins had been called away suddenly, a sickness in the family, something like that. "Sod it," he said, averting his eyes from the sign, debating what next. As he was about to get back in the car and return to the hotel—the only idea he could come up with on the spot—a short-haired young woman on a bicycle and wearing a yellow anorak and corduroy trousers approached the gate from the other side. "Good morning," she said as she reached the gate, got off the bike, and unlocked the padlock. By the way she had said it, coupled with the look on her face, it was anything but a good morning as far as she was concerned. "I guess you read the sign," she added, now on Kingston's side of the gate. She was short and pretty but looked as if she'd lost a pound and found a penny.

"I did, yes. Quite a disappointment," Kingston replied. "I came all the way from London for the sale. You work here, I take it?"

She nodded. "Yep."

"Do you know if David Jenkins is here?"

She bit her lip and looked as if she might start weeping at any moment.

"I'm afraid not." She put a hand up to her mouth. "He's dead."

FIFTEEN

Kingston's jaw dropped.

She remained silent, trying to avoid his gaze. It was clear that she'd learned about it recently, was still in a state of shock herself, and didn't want to talk about it.

Scores of questions raced through Kingston's mind, but this was not the time to dump them on her. "I'm awfully sorry," he said solemnly. "I'll be on my way, then."

"Was he a friend?" she asked, getting on her bike.

"No." The question was innocent enough, but it threw Kingston off guard. He paused. "A friend of a friend, you might say."

His last words seemed to strike a sympathetic chord with the young woman. As their glances met, he could see that the whites of her eyes were veined with red, from crying and lack of sleep, no doubt. "I must go," she said with a sigh. "You've come such a long way. Why don't you go up to the house? As far as I know, the police are still there. Perhaps you should talk to them."

"Police?"

She nodded one more time.

"Where is it? The house, I mean."

"Go back the way you came in. About a hundred yards, you'll see a small lane off to your right. That'll take you to Larkfield—the house." She released the brakes, stepped on the pedal, and took off down the lane without looking back. Kingston watched her until she disappeared, thinking about the grim news.

He drove out Badgers Lane and followed her directions. Rounding a bend, he spotted redbrick chimneys poking up from a tall holly hedge. In less than a minute the house came into view. It was a pleasant-looking structure of modest proportions, built of local stone, no doubt, with a gray slate roof and white painted trim. The plantings around the house were abundant and mature, particularly the trees. Like a well-chosen frame on a so-so painting, they made the house appear more appealing and important.

A stretch of blue-and-white crime-scene tape spanning the entire front of the house was a jarring incongruity to the otherwise inviting scene. A multicolored panda car and three other cars were parked out front. Kingston took the last parking space, got out of the TR4, ducked under the tape, and walked to the front door, which was open. He knocked and went in.

Passing through a tiled entry hall with the obligatory mirror, coat rack, and umbrella stand, he entered the living room. A young, sandy-haired uniformed policeman who was sitting at a table, writing, stood to face Kingston. He wasn't smiling.

"Hello. I'm PC Truscott. Can I help you, sir?"

"Perhaps," said Kingston, looking around the room, which had all the earmarks of having been recently ransacked. He wondered if he should tell the policeman, right off the bat, that he was working with the Thames Valley Police but decided not to. First he would try to find out how David Jenkins had died and why the police were involved.

"Are you a family member? A friend?"

"Neither. I drove down from London hoping to meet Mr. Jenkins, only to discover a few minutes ago that he'd just died."

"How did you learn that, sir?"

"From the young woman at the tree farm. I just talked to her, and she suggested I see you."

"Well, I'm sorry, sir. Unless you have information concerning Mr. Jenkins's death, I'm afraid you must leave. This is a crime scene. You've already broken the law by entering this house. Why do you think we put up the tape?"

Kingston realized that if he was to gain the policeman's confidence and learn more, he would have to play his only trump card and explain the true reason for his being there. This would certainly result, sooner or later, in a phone call from the Cornwall police to Inspector Sheffield. He was not only going to be surprised to learn that Kingston was in Fowey but also ticked off—to put it mildly—that he was investigating Jenkins's demise, flying in the face of everything the inspector had warned him not to do.

"I'm sorry," said Kingston, careful not to adopt a superior attitude, an impression that—because of his physical stature and silken way with words, should he choose—was often misinterpreted. "I should have told you right away. I'm consulting with Detective Inspector Sheffield of the Thames Valley Police on a murder case. Jenkins was implicated. That's the reason I'm here. I came down from London yesterday to talk to him about it."

"Jenkins?" The PC recoiled, looking more confused. "A murder case?" he mumbled, frowning.

"Right." Kingston reached in his pocket and took out his wallet, withdrawing his card and handing it to the policeman. "Name's Kingston. Dr. Lawrence Kingston."

The constable looked at him as if he'd said "Bond, James Bond," then glanced at the card, appearing suitably impressed. "I'm afraid I'm not the one you need to talk with, Doctor," he said, apparently warming to the idea that Kingston wasn't some thrill seeker who'd just wandered in off the street. "A detective inspector's on his way from St. Austell as we speak. I was informed that he'd be here sometime around the middle of the day."

"Can you tell me briefly what happened?"

"I think you'd best wait for the inspector, sir."

Kingston nodded. "If you wish." He drew himself up to his full six feet three inches and looked down at the policeman. "I don't wish to appear obstreperous, Constable, but surely the inspector will be unable to brief me on what took place here. Not until he first hears it from you—your people. Isn't that correct?"

It was as if the frown had never left Truscott's brow. "I see what you're getting at—"

"Look, I don't need a full-blown report, just the sequence of events. Who found him? Where? When? That's all."

Truscott thought about it for a moment, pursing his lips like a little boy being forced to admit to scrumping. "We got a call yesterday morning," he said at last. "From Jenkins's partner, who said that for some time he'd been trying to reach Jenkins on his home phone and his mobile, without success."

"Partner?"

"Business partner, I believe. Not the other kind."

Kingston nodded. "Sorry to interrupt, go on."

"According to the report, he became concerned because Jenkins had told him that he would be at home that morning up until about nine or so, sorting out last-minute things before going to the sale. Not only that, but Jenkins was expecting his call."

"Was Jenkins alone?"

"It's believed so. Yes."

"So this partner decided to look in on Jenkins?"

"Right. He said he got here a few minutes after eight thirty to find the place ransacked and the subject slumped on a chair in the library, dead."

"Any signs of a break-in?"

The young policeman didn't answer. Instead, he took another look at Kingston's card, as if hoping to find something he'd missed earlier that would later justify to his superior why he had permitted a total stranger to enter a crime scene—and of all things, a homicide. In a way Kingston could appreciate the PC's dilemma. Murders were hardly two a penny in Fowey. The last had probably been long before the lad was even born.

"One last question," said Kingston. "Have you questioned any of the neighbors?"

"Just one—the only one, actually—the farm at the corner of Badgers Lane. The farmer's wife reported hearing a motorcycle sometime after midnight, early Saturday morning. She didn't know the exact time."

"Hmm. Do we know if Jenkins had a motorbike?"

Truscott looked anxious. "Look, sir. I've got to get these reports finished before the inspector arrives. So I think you'd best leave and come back when he's here."

"I understand perfectly well, Constable. Mind if I look around outside while I wait—the garden?"

Truscott shrugged. "I suppose not. But for Christ's sake, don't touch or move anything. You do, and you can be charged with tampering with a crime scene."

"Don't worry, I won't," Kingston assured him, smiling. Actually, the only reason he'd asked Truscott for permission to stay on the property was so that he could wait until the inspector showed up.

He left the house and walked to the gravel parking area, wondering what to do until the inspector arrived. Only then did it occur to him that he hadn't asked Truscott what was the cause of death. He hoped he would get the chance to ask the inspector. The sea mist had evaporated, and every now and then the sun nudged its way through the gauze of cirrus. From where Kingston stood, looking at the front of the house, there was no evidence of a garden. But surely someone like Jenkins would have one. It would probably be in the back. A walk about would give him a chance to do some serious thinking. There was certainly enough to think about. Was this a classic case of an intruder—a would-be burglar—disturbing Jenkins and killing him to avoid recognition or possible capture? Had he been killed during a struggle? Or was it premeditated murder disguised to look like a break-in?

Kingston walked to the side of the house and unlatched the simple wooden gate set in a yew hedge. Closing it behind him, he walked down a shallow flight of stone steps that ended on the edge of a wide Yorkstone terrace that stretched across the back of the house. Above the French doors, a white canvas awning provided shade for a weathered teak table and half a dozen white-cushioned chairs. Carefully composed groupings of terra-cotta and glazed pots were spotted about, some containing polyantha roses, others plump with mixed white annuals laced with gray helichrysum and ivy. Beyond the terrace a freshly mown lawn the size of a tennis court was edged with deep herbaceous borders and backed by a high privet hedge. Two arched openings in the hedge hinted that another or other gardens lay beyond. Kingston was impressed.

Passing through one of the openings, he followed a narrow grass path into a vegetable garden large enough to provide sustenance for the family and staff of a large manor house. Net-covered soft fruit cages stretched for thirty feet down one side. On the opposite side, rows of apple, pear, peach, and plum trees were showing fruit. At the rear of the garden a large barnlike stone structure was partially concealed by trees.

Sauntering along the paths between the raised beds, he took his time poking and peering absently at the crop of vegetables, many ready for picking. As he did so, more questions about Jenkins's untimely end kept tumbling into his mind. What *was* the cause of death? If it happened, conveniently, to be lidocaine, it would prove, almost beyond doubt, that Jenkins's murderer was the same person who dispatched Jeremy Lester in St. George's Hospital. That would be too much to expect, though. Besides, premeditated homicide was yet to be established. PC Truscott had said that Jenkins was slumped in his chair. That could mean anything, from a heart attack to repeated blows to the head. Had it been the latter, or if there had been a lot of blood, surely the constable would have mentioned it. Not for the first time, he wondered if his coming down to Cornwall to meet Jenkins could have anything to do with his death. If, indeed, Jenkins had written the letter proposing that they meet at Lydiard Park, he was taking a calculated risk. The subsequent letter, delivered by the boy, implied that he was no longer willing to take that risk, that it was too dangerous. So if someone—for example, one or more of the other expedition members—had found out that Jenkins was about to snitch on them, what possible reason could there be to justify silencing Jenkins? It had to be something almighty serious to resort to murder.

Coming to the end of a row of courgettes and beets, Kingston found himself facing the stone barn, about thirty feet from where he stood. The timing was good, because at that moment, the skies opened up with a typical unheralded summer shower. Jacket over his head, he ran toward the barn, hoping to find temporary shelter under its eaves. He was surprised to find the door ajar. A heavy-duty open padlock dangled from the hasp. He noted a sturdy dead bolt, too. He could only conclude that the police had opened it, otherwise why the security? Lowering his jacket, he pushed the door open partway and peeked in. With only two small windows, both barred, it took a few seconds for his eyes to adjust to the dim light. He opened the door wider and stepped in.

SIXTEEN

Kingston's eyes soon adjusted to the meager light. The room was about thirty feet wide and fifteen deep, with open rafters and workbenches built into two of the walls. The benches were partially covered with boxes, cartons, and miscellaneous files and folders. The place was unusually tidy—not a tool in sight and a clean floor—more storage than workspace. Evenly spaced shelves covered the two walls above the benches, most of them lined with bottles, jars, and packages of gardening supplies: herbicides, fertilizers, seeds, and so on. Other shelves stored paint, garden pots, and cleaning supplies. He was about to turn away when he spotted some items on a lower shelf that appeared out of place. It was pottery of various shapes and sizes. Not garden pottery but decorative pieces. The majority was small pots and bowls. Some were plain terra-cotta, others painted, and a few painted and fired, with a soft glaze discernible in the low light. The finished pieces were painted blue and white. Not the classic blue-and-white striping of Cornish ware. Kingston was all too familiar with that, as anyone who had spent time in Cornwall would be. The pottery on the shelf was Asian blue-and-white, as it is referred to in the antiques trade. He recalled Wilkins saying that Jenkins collected Japanese netsuke, but he'd made no mention of ceramics. Staring at the pottery, he realized he was trying to make something out of nothing. There could be any number of explanations for the ceramics: Jenkins renting the barn to someone else, for one.

Kingston picked up one of the small bowls. He placed it carefully on the bench and studied it. Asian ceramics was not one of his areas of expertise, but he knew a little about blue-and-white transferware, a decorative technique developed in England in the mid-1700s. These were not transferware. In his judgment they'd been hand-painted.

He stared at the bowl. Something was not right about it. He picked it up, surprised at the lightness and the superior craftsmanship. Under the thin and transparent glaze was the design of swift-scrolling flowers in elegant cobalt blue against the white background. The brushwork was masterfully executed. Among the refined Asian ceramics he'd seen, nothing compared to this one so far. He turned it over. The underside bore six small Chinese character marks in a double circle. Even with the signs of slight wear, the bowl was in excellent condition. Not that he was a divvy, but he knew enough about antiques generally to recognize that the bowl, if genuine, was of considerable value. In the antiques trade, a divvy is a dealer who physically reacts in the presence of a bona fide antique as opposed to a forgery. Like a truffle dog, a divvy knows instinctively when an object has collectible or antique value.

He took another bowl from the shelf. At first glance it looked the same, but it wasn't. It bore no character marks and the design was subtly different, but still the same dark cobalt blue on a white background. He put it back on the shelf and gazed around the room. Were they real? If so, he could be looking at a small fortune in Asian ceramics. If they were forgeries—many of the bowls were neither painted nor glazed, which indicated that was likely the case—it suggested that Jenkins, or someone, was having them manufactured and palming them off as the real thing. This was obviously a storage room and they were being made elsewhere. It explained the barred windows and locks. Cornwall and Devon, he knew, had countless small potteries and individual artisans turning out highly desirable work. He was tempted to put one in his jacket pocket—purely for research, mind you—but resisted.

He was about to leave when an idea struck him. He could take a picture with his mobile. He'd done it before, and it was easy. He took down the same bowl he'd looked at originally, picked up a cardboard box from the bench, and carried them outside, where the light was better. Under the shelter of the eave, he placed the bowl on the box, took out his mobile, and clicked off three shots, each from a different angle and focus. He replaced the bowl and box and left the barn, careful to leave the door ajar, as it was when he arrived. While he'd been inside, the shower had passed.

Back at the house, Kingston saw a gray Rover parked outside and assumed that the inspector had arrived. Entering the living room, he saw two men talking to the constable. Not wanting to interrupt, he stood by the door. After a brief wait, Truscott spotted him, waved him over, and introduced him to Detective Inspector Hannaford and Sergeant Pascoe of Devon & Cornwall Constabulary. Both were relatively young—to Kingston's eye, barely over forty—and casually dressed; the inspector in a brown leather jacket and tan slacks, the sergeant in a black Windbreaker and washed blue jeans. Truscott spent a minute telling the DI that Kingston had shown up unexpectedly, claiming that he was associated with the Mayhew murders case and was collaborating with Inspector Sheffield.

"I insisted that he wait for you," said Truscott, with a fleeting glance at Kingston.

"That's correct," Kingston interjected. Truscott looked visibly relieved.

The DI glanced at Kingston's card, still in his hand. "Truscott says you're a doctor? Would that be a medical doctor?"

"No. My field's academic—botany."

Hannaford looked perplexed and changed the subject. "Thames Valley, eh?"

Kingston nodded. "Inspector Sheffield."

"We're familiar with the Mayhew case, of course."

"Who wouldn't be?" said the sergeant.

Hannaford ignored the comment. "Jenkins was on the expedition. As a matter of fact, it was one of our chaps at St. Austell who interviewed him—some time ago."

"Yes, Sheffield mentioned at the time that you were cooperating."

"So how come you happened to be here today, of all days, Doctor?"

Kingston had anticipated the question. "I came down to see David Jenkins about a letter he wrote me. It could have had some bearing on the case."

"I see."

Kingston figured this was as good a time as any to ask. "Does it appear to be a homicide?"

"That's for forensics to determine. We'll know the answer when we get the postmortem results from the Home Office. We'll inform Sheffield, of course."

"Of course."

"Anything else, Doctor?"

"There is, yes. I found some Chinese pottery in one of the barns. A couple of the pieces could well be of some value."

"Is that so?"

Hannaford glanced at Constable Truscott. The look implied that he wasn't too happy that Kingston had been allowed to trample all over the property. "Any particular reason you mention them—other than security?"

"Two reasons, actually. First, given the Chinese angle to the Mayhew murders, and the fact that they could be forgeries, it's possible, albeit remote, that there could be some connection."

"And the other?"

"If burglary was the motive, those are the kind of things they might have been looking for—providing they're genuine, of course. I'm told that Jenkins also had a collection of Japanese netsuke. They're jade, ivory, stone, and wood carvings—quite valuable."

"I know what they are. No need to worry, though, we'll be going through the house from top to bottom. And as of now, we'll be conducting round-the-clock surveillance."

Kingston nodded his approval.

"Are you staying in Cornwall?"

"Not much point now," Kingston replied. "I'll go back to London later today."

"Where are you staying? Just in case we need to reach you."

"At the Old Quay."

"Nice."

The DI took one last glance at Kingston's card. "Well, we know where to find you. There's no point in your hanging around here, Doctor. You're free to go."

Kingston left Larkfield and headed back to Fowey and the hotel. He wondered how long it would take for Inspector Sheffield to call. That wasn't a worry right now, though. His mobile was off, and he would probably keep it off—for a while, anyway.

In the hotel room, Kingston sat at a desk by the window overlooking the estuary. He was thinking about the bowls. What was it about them that bothered him? Hard as he tried, he couldn't figure what it was. With the telephone directory and a notepad in front of him, he started making phone calls to antiques stores and potteries. His objective: first, to find out if any dealers had been offered antique Asian ceramics for purchase recently and, second, to determine if there was an organization or an individual who had extensive knowledge of the region's potteries—the type of work each produced, and which potteries, if any, were known to take on custom assignments.

Half an hour later, he knew it was a futile exercise. None of the seven antiques dealers he had spoken with had seen nor heard of any Asian ceramics being shopped around or put up for auction. Furthermore, his idea of tracking down someone who might be able to provide information or answers about the ceramics also produced zero results. The man he had talked with at Cornwall Artisans, an association that represented a fair number of the county's ceramicists, was polite but of little help. All their craftspeople produced contemporary works, he said. Pressed by Kingston on the matter of reproductions, the man's answer was deferential, but as much as he tried, he couldn't disguise his true thoughts: Even to suggest the very idea that any of his craftspeople might be culpable of reproducing works of antiquity was tantamount to implying that one of his local artists might be knocking out the occasional Renoir for sale.

Calls to a few local potteries elicited similar sentiments. As he thought about it, the more he realized that if Jenkins had commissioned someone to forge the antiques, he would have made damned sure that whoever was making them, and where, would be a tightly kept secret. Even if he lucked out and managed to find the pottery, those involved would certainly have covered their tracks by now, or done a bunk.

Kingston went out to the balcony. He watched the sailboats tacking across the estuary, thinking about poor David Jenkins and the grisly fact that three of the men who were on the ill-fated plant-hunting expedition were now dead—one known to have been murdered, and the deaths of the other two highly suspicious.

There was no point in hanging around Fowey any longer. He would have to get the results of the postmortem from Sheffield. Not that it mattered much anymore. It was up to the police now. He packed his few clothes and toiletries, surveyed the room to see if he'd forgotten anything, then went down to the desk to check out.

The next day Sheffield called, as if on cue. Kingston had just got out of bed when the phone rang at eight o'clock. He had slept later than usual, having returned from Cornwall after midnight. Wearing his dressing gown, he took the call in the kitchen while waiting for the kettle to boil.

Not unexpectedly, Sheffield started by saying that he'd received a phone call from Inspector Hannaford, followed by the portentous words, "I'm sure you know the reason why I'm calling." Kingston was fully prepared—though still not quite awake, and perhaps it was just as well—to be read the riot act. So he was both surprised and relieved that Sheffield had apparently chosen not to castigate him, at least not yet. In a tone measured to the gravity of the subject, the inspector expressed his regret and concern over Jenkins's death. Hannaford had told him it that it was homicide, he said, and that the postmortem results were being forwarded.

Kingston knew damned well that the inspector hadn't called to tell him how upset he was about the business in Cornwall, and that the ball would bounce quickly into his court. He was right.

"So tell me, Doctor," asked Sheffield, "how come you just happened to be in Fowey a few hours after Jenkins died?"

Kingston told him how he'd spotted the squib on the Internet announcing the sale, and that, secure in the knowledge that Jenkins was going to be there in person, he decided, on an impulse, to drive to Cornwall to meet him.

Sheffield either accepted this explanation or chose not to question what he doubtlessly thought was not only an ill-advised idea on Kingston's part but also one that flew in the face of everything the inspector had cautioned. Sheffield's next question was not unexpected. "Anything to connect this to the Mayhew case?"

"Not that I can tell."

"This Asian pottery Hannaford mentioned. You found it in a barn, he said. What's that all about?"

"I'm not quite sure. It may have no bearing whatsoever on why Jenkins was killed."

"What about burglary? In your estimation, were any worth stealing?"

Kingston thought for a moment. "Let me put it this way. While I'm no expert on Chinese ceramics, there was one bowl among them that showed a patina consistent with considerable age and bore marks to suggest that it could be an original early piece. Just what the value would be if it were, I haven't the foggiest idea. Then again, for all I know, they could all be forgeries."

"Hannaford didn't say anything about forgeries."

"Perhaps he misconstrued what I said."

"Which was?"

"I believe I told him that I wasn't sure if they were genuine or not."

"We seem to be going around in circles, Doctor."

"If they are forgeries, then the question is not only why, but also what were they doing in Jenkins's barn?"

"You tell me. Maybe he was flogging them as the real thing, and some unhappy camper wanted his money back. Argument follows—struggle—Jenkins bangs his head on a hard object. Easy as that."

"A reasonable supposition, I guess. But why Chinese antiques—pottery? I know that Jenkins collected Japanese ivory pieces called netsuke. I suggested that DI Hannaford search the house for them.

If it does turn out to be a robbery gone wrong, they might have been stolen, too. They're quite valuable and would be relatively easy to peddle."

"I must confess that antiques, generally, are not my cup of tea. But considering Jenkins was always running off to China looking for plants, what would be so unusual about his collecting Chinese antiques?"

"Good point. Nothing at all."

"Well, we've got two homicides now, plus Peter Mayhew's death, and not one suspect. This damned case is going nowhere fast and I'm starting to get rumbles from upstairs. If you come up with any bright ideas, Doctor, let's have 'em."

"I will, of course."

"By the way, Mayhew's sister called me a couple of days ago. Wanted to know if we'd made any headway. I've told her that we have every reason to believe that her brother's death was an accident, but she wants definitive answers. Can't say as I blame her."

"You'll be questioning Graves and Bell again?"

"We will. Among other things, to ask where they both were at the time of Jenkins's murder. Up 'til now they've been cooperative, but this will be the third time, I believe."

"I never did ask, Inspector, but I assume that they both had alibis for Lester's murder."

"I'll be up-front with you, Doctor. There's no reason you shouldn't be told. Over the last weeks, as you know, we've conducted interviews with the four remaining members of the expedition. All have given sworn statements concerning Mayhew's death—their versions of what happened on that mountain in China. I conducted two of them. The first was with Bell—who had just got back from a trip to Taiwan—and then Jenkins. Graves, I believe, already told you he was interviewed by our chaps up in Leicestershire, and an agent from the FBI field office in San Francisco talked to Kavanagh at some length. The upshot is that all their accounts jibe."

"They all told the same story?"

"I know what you're thinking. If Mayhew's death was not accidental, whoever might have reason to withhold information—to cover something up—has had time to get his story straight."

"Or *their* stories."

"Right."

"What about Lester's murder?"

"They were all questioned about it, except the American. The FBI has reassured us that he hasn't left the States since returning from the expedition."

"Alibis?"

The long pause that followed had Kingston wondering if he was asking too many questions. Then the inspector answered.

"Graves was in London for two days, attending a Sotheby's antiques auction. He bought two pieces. He also had receipts from his hotel and for a purchase he made at Austin Reed. One evening, he had dinner with a former colleague and his wife. It all checked out. As for Bell and Jenkins, they were together at the time of Lester's death."

"Really? How . . . convenient." Immediately, Kingston regretted his skeptical remark, wishing that he could take it back. It didn't appear to have bothered Sheffield, though.

"That's what I thought at first. Expedient. According to their separate statements, the day before Lester was murdered, Bell drove down to Cornwall to meet with Jenkins to discuss a project that he'd been working on—something to do with saving some rare trees from extinction. They were also in the early stages of planning a future trip."

"And the next day?" The tree comment had validity, he knew.

"I'll get to that. Bell said he stayed at Jenkins's place overnight, and they went out to dinner that evening at a local pub—the Lighthouse, I believe it was. Bell paid for the dinner and has the receipt to prove it."

"Credit card?"

"Yes, with Bell's signature. The waitress remembered serving Jenkins—she said he'd dined there before—and that he was with another man. Unfortunately she couldn't provide a description. They were busier than usual that night, she recalled, something to do with a local regatta. It was a trifle flimsy, you might say, so we asked ourselves if there was any other way his story could be corroborated. One of our chaps pointed out that it was a decent drive from where Bell lived in Dorset to Cornwall and back, and that he'd have had to stop for petrol sooner or later. He drives one of those big Jeeps, and even if he'd filled it up before leaving Dorset, he couldn't have made it there and back without refueling. We asked him about this: if he'd stopped for petrol, and if he had, where? He remembered right off. Just outside Plymouth on the way back the next day, near Buckfastleigh, he thought. We did a calculation based on the tank capacity and the fuel consumption, and determined that, if he'd started with a full tank, that's just about where he'd have had to refuel. Give or take, about thirty miles east of Plymouth. Not only that, turns out that he'd kept the credit card receipt, which he sent us two days later."

"Hard to argue with that."

"Right. But to make doubly sure, we obtained the closed-circuit TV tapes from the station. A black Jeep was shown to be there at three twenty-four P.M. It had Bell's license plate number. Seems conclusive to us."

With little more to be said, the conversation ended just as the kettle had come to a boil and switched off. Kingston got up to fetch the *Times* and make a pot of tea. While waiting for it to steep, he thought about Bell's and Jenkins's alibis. Listening to Sheffield, he had detected an underlying tone of disappointment and frustration. There had been no progress whatsoever, and he, too, was starting to question his own failure to come up with any ideas or new avenues of investigation. The mention of Sally Mayhew had reminded him of his hasty lunch invitation. Thankfully, nothing had come of that, at least not yet.

With Kingston, bringing up superstition, spirit manifestation, channeling, crop circles, or any form of psychic phenomenon would likely be met with good-humored ridicule. He was, after all, a man of science, and most scientists, by schooling and nature, are skeptics. He would tell you that skepticism, not to be confused with cynicism, is the application of reason to any and all ideas. It is critical thinking, diligence, and inquisitiveness, the need to see compelling evidence before believing, a stock-in-trade that might explain why he had become so good at solving problems and crimes. Thus he found it uncanny, embarrassingly so, to receive a phone call only a couple of hours after he'd hung up on Sheffield from none other than Sally Mayhew.

"It's Sally," she said, pausing. "Sally Mayhew."

"Well, how nice to hear from you. You're not going to believe this, but Inspector Sheffield and I were just talking about you earlier this morning."

"Yes, I called him to see if there was any more news on Peter's death."

"He told me."

"I'm beginning to wonder if we'll ever learn what happened on that trip. Too much time has passed now."

"You may be right." He was wondering if she knew about Jenkins. How could she? Sheffield had said she'd called two days ago. He decided not to bring it up, just for now. Why give her more to worry about? "How have you been?" he asked cheerfully.

"I can't complain, I suppose."

"Well, that's good to know."

"Actually, the reason I'm calling is that I'm in London this week. I'm house-sitting for a friend of mine who has a nice place near Regent's Park. She has two Siamese cats."

Kingston had little choice—unless he lied, saying he would be gone for the rest of the week. "How nice," he said after a pause. "Why don't we have the lunch we talked about?"

"I'd like that, if we can do it before Saturday."

"How about tomorrow?"

"That's fine. Where shall I meet you?"

Kingston thought for a moment. One good thing about having Andrew as a friend was that he was never stumped when it came to picking a restaurant. He was like a walking Egon Ronay. "There's a charming place on Chiltern Street, off Marylebone Road. It's called La Chaumière. Can't be much more than a five-minute walk from where you are. I'll make a reservation for eleven forty-five; that way we'll beat the crowd. If there's a problem, I'll call you back. Give me your phone number."

She gave him the number and he repeated the time, name of the restaurant, and the street.

After hanging up, Kingston wondered why he wasn't feeling pleased that she'd called. Maybe Andrew was right. Maybe he was becoming a misogynist. He smiled at the thought. What the heck, he said to himself. What could be so tough about having lunch in a fashionable French restaurant, accompanied by an intelligent and fairly attractive woman several years younger than he? Thinking back to his first, and only, meeting with her, he couldn't help wondering if she would take a little more care about her appearance this time. After all, he was taking her to a three-star restaurant. Dismissing the thought as vanity on his part and sexist, he picked up the phone book and leafed through the yellow pages to Museums. He had an idea. It might not lead anywhere, but it would be interesting to pursue.

SEVENTEEN

Kingston found the listing he was looking for and, with one hand, entered the numbers on the phone with his thumb, a practice he'd learned from his daughter when she presented him with his first mobile five years ago. Lacking in digital dexterity, he'd found it cumbersome at first, but with his latest phone—why they needed to change them every six months or so it seemed was beyond him—it was much easier.

He was calling the Percival David Foundation of Chinese Art in Bloomsbury. Earlier, he'd read that the collection began in 1912 when Indian-born Percival David started collecting Chinese art. Later, when he inherited his father's baronetcy, Sir Percival embarked on what would become a lifetime study and a connoisseurship of Chinese art as practiced at the highest level—that of the Imperial Collection, housed in the Forbidden City, Beijing. In the 1920s, using his own money, he staged an impressive display of some of the collection's treasures in smaller pavilions within the Forbidden City. The exhibition was a huge success, and his reputation as a connoisseur and collector of Chinese art was on the ascent.

Over the ensuing decades, Sir Percival was able to purchase many pieces from the Imperial Collection, exporting them to the United States and eventually England. The foundation's collection now numbers over one thousand seven hundred pieces and is the finest collection of Chinese ceramics outside China.

The polite woman who answered, transferred his call, and in a few seconds he was talking with an assistant curator. In as few words as possible—a discipline that Kingston had never quite mastered—he told the curator, who sounded like a younger woman, how he had found the blue-and-white bowls and had photographed one of them with his mobile. Though they had Chinese character marks, he suspected—mostly because there were so many—that they might be fakes. Without mentioning that the bowls might end up being evidence in a homicide case, he asked if the foundation might take a look the photos.

The answer was an immediate yes. If he would submit the photographs, she would be happy to have a staff member look at them and give an opinion. He went on to tell her a white lie about their having to be moved from the barn in the next few days and that a quick response would be appreciated. She promised to do what she could.

Kingston hadn't the slightest idea how to obtain photo prints from an image on a mobile. Up until now, he'd not even thought about it. Andrew came to the rescue. As former owner of an IT company, he knew all about that kind of stuff. Next morning, Kingston dropped off the photo prints, together with a note on his personal stationery, at the foundation's gallery on Gordon Square in Bloomsbury.

. . .

Kingston made a point of getting to La Chaumière fifteen minutes early. It was less to do with punctuality, more a question of good manners: not wanting Sally to have to wait alone in the restaurant. Long ago, he had come to the sad realization that common courtesy and good manners were gratuitous, that the enduring hallmarks of a cultivated life were slipping away, and that the scrap heap of things good and decent was mounting daily—all casualties in a world gone mad with political correctness. He smiled—a smile of resignation tinged with regret. Perhaps the time had come to expunge the word "manliness" from the *OED* and *Webster's*.

He had been careful not to overdress for the occasion: navy double-breasted blazer, open-neck sport shirt, and tan slacks. After all, he didn't know if she would turn up dressed to kill or looking like a throwback to the '60s. It was beyond his grasp, as it was with many men of his generation, to comprehend what passed for "fashion" these days.

Kingston need not have worried. Sitting at a table against the wall, sipping his mineral water, he noticed a woman enter who he thought might be Sally. Having met her only once, he couldn't be sure. The maître d' greeted her and then escorted her through the restaurant toward where he was seated. It wasn't until they were almost at the table that he recognized her. Even then he wasn't totally convinced, because she looked so different from their first encounter. As he stood to meet her, she smiled and said, "Hello, Lawrence." The voice, too, was somehow different from the one he remembered.

She wore a cream blouse under a lightweight jacket, and a camel-colored skirt. The single strand of pearls at her neck looked like the real thing. As the maître d' helped her into her chair, Kingston was struck by her attractiveness compared to their last meeting. He was no judge of makeup, far from it, but he wondered if a beauty salon and stylist might have had a hand in her makeover. He smiled inwardly, recalling his earlier thoughts about her appearance.

"You're looking very well," he said, as Sally shifted in her chair to get comfortable.

"Thank you," she said demurely, her eyes taking in the room. "It's a lovely restaurant."

"The food is as good as the decor. It's one of my favorites."

With Kingston doing most of the listening, the small talk continued through the first course of salade Niçoise, accompanied by a bottle of Vouvray. On the way over in the taxi, he had decided, for his part, to keep the conversation light and amusing at the start, at least until he could sense her mood and receptiveness. Unless he felt it relevant or appropriate, he would avoid any mention of the plant-hunting expedition or his recent activities at Lydiard Park and in Cornwall.

Waiting for their main course, Sally sipped her wine. "Tell me about plant hunting," she said. "Why these men risk their lives looking for plants and collecting seeds. What's the point?"

Kingston was surprised. It wasn't the attitude he was expecting. He thought that by now she would have at least a little understanding of what, for three centuries, had driven men to far-flung parts of the world in the pursuit of new and rare plants. Surely, with her having a horticulturist brother, there should be no need for such a fundamental question. Nevertheless, he was more than happy to accommodate her. Asking him to talk about anything connected with plants was like asking Billy Graham to say a few words about the Bible.

"Where to begin," he said, pausing. "I suppose as good a place to start as any would be to accept the fact that all life on Earth depends on plants. Without plants we would cease to exist. They are basic to our ecosystems, our most precious resource that provides shelter, food, medicines, and many of the materials we use in everyday life."

"I'd never really thought of plants in that way."

"Most people don't. Why would they? But just think of all the products made from wood. There's rubber; many fabrics, like cotton and flax; musical instruments; sports equipment; rope and yarns; fragrances and cosmetics. And what about paper? Even our money comes from plants. And let's not forget fossil fuels—one of our principal sources of energy, unfortunately. Coal was once living plants."

Sally smiled. "Now, that I do know. Plants and dinosaurs, right?"

"Right." Kingston held up a finger. "Medical science. Some of the most remarkable new medicines and cures come from plants and trees. Plants maintain our atmosphere, purify wastes, protect topsoil, and on and on." He paused to take a sip of wine. "As for plant hunting, it has endured for centuries, Sally. A gardener named John Tradescant was hunting abroad in the early 1600s. At the time, he was head gardener at Hatfield House in Hertfordshire, where Queen Elizabeth I spent much of her childhood. The gardens there are extraordinary. You should go there sometime."

"I'd like to." She smiled coyly. "Perhaps you'll take me there."

Kingston nodded. "Not a bad idea."

Sally thought for a moment. "So what exactly do you hunt for?"

"Many things. New species of plants; rare plants; plants that are facing extinction; for propagation and research; to share plant material and data with other botanical gardens, and to stock seed banks like Kew's global Millenium Seed Bank Project at Ardingly, in Sussex. Despite our reliance on plants, we're losing them at an alarming rate. The last time I checked, as many as a hundred thousand plant species are threatened." He smiled briefly. "I'm sure you don't want me to go into the many reasons why."

"I don't think so," she said politely.

Still, Kingston wasn't quite finished. "Kew's seed bank is extraordinary," he said. "It's the largest plant conservation project ever conceived, with more than thirty countries participating. Last year they banked their billionth seed in the underground cold-storage vaults. Norway has recently developed one, too."

Sally smiled. "You're a veritable mine of information, Lawrence."

"You forget, I used to teach this stuff."

"I can tell."

Kingston frowned. "Let me see, what else can I tell you about plant hunting?" He looked up briefly at the ceiling. "Well, we take a lot of equipment with us. That's where horses and mules sometimes come in handy. On top of all the obvious things, like luggage and backpacks, sleeping bags, clothing, and personal items, the list includes tents, a GPS device, botanical books, plant presses, herbarium tags, satellite phone . . . let's see, pruning poles, saws and shears, torches, cameras, binoculars. One needs a checklist before packing."

"So when you find a plant or a tree of interest, what do you do? Gather seeds, cut off twigs?"

Kingston smiled. "The first, definitely, but rarely the latter. In fact, on most expeditions seed collection is the principal purpose, the reason most trips take place in autumn. But we also collect what we call herbarium specimens—ideally, a manageable branch complete with stems, leaves, and, where possible, some reproductive aspect of the plant, which could be flower or fruit. These are dried in small plant presses. Later they will be identified and cataloged by research botanists. We usually know what most of them are, of course."

"You also photograph them and make notes, I take it?"

"Yes. Each person on the expedition is usually assigned a job. One of the jobs, an important one, is to make field notes. Each plant or tree specimen is not only described, but its location is pinpointed with a GPS coordinate. Notes are then made detailing its location, habitat, and aspect. This will include whether it's growing in sun or shade; what kind of terrain—for example, alpine, hillside, or valley; flat ground, steep, or vertical—if it's found in forest, woodland, et cetera; what type soil; and so on."

During a lull in the conversation that followed, Kingston sensed that further talk about plant hunting would risk losing her interest. Pausing to take a sip of wine, he decided to sum up. "So now, Sally, you know a little more about what Peter was doing and why. Plant hunting has been going on for centuries, and were it not for all those adventuresome and inquisitive souls, our nurseries and garden centers would be sadly lacking. Many, many of the plants we enjoy today we owe to plant hunters—and to hybridizers, of course."

"Plant breeders?"

"Right. Another fascinating world that's little understood by most people, sad to say." Kingston was about to stop there, but because he knew that he could make this part more entertaining, he continued. "For most of the general public—particularly the couch potatoes—pollen means allergies and bees mean stings. They don't realize that for at least one out of every three bites of what they eat, they should thank a bee, wasp, butterfly, bird, or one of the many other pollinators."

It was now clear from the look on Sally's face that she was trying hard to feign interest. But Kingston knew that she was close to the point where she would start examining her fingernails. He'd seen the look on students' faces too many times in the past not to recognize it. "Let me tell you one last little plant story, Sally," he said. "A short one, I promise."

"All right," she said, clearly glad that she wouldn't have to sit through two more courses and coffee while he rambled on about bugs, pests, and ravaging plant diseases.

"Do you like chocolate?" asked Kingston.

"Of course."

"Well, chocolate comes from cocoa trees, *Theobroma cacao.*

They grow in the tropics and look different from most other trees. This is because they have their flowers on the trunk and lower branches. The flowers are small and inconspicuous, since they face downward. There's good reason, though. They attract only midges. Midges are ordinarily attracted by fungus, and because the cocoa flowers smell like mushrooms, they feed on them, too. So for the cocoa tree to bear fruit, first it has to be pollinated by midges." Kingston smiled. "So the next time you open that box of Godiva and take a bite of chocolate, pause for a moment to thank a midge."

Sally chuckled. "I like that."

Kingston glanced sideways, to see that their main courses were about to arrive. A short interval followed while the waiter placed the plates on the table, fussed with the cutlery, and topped up their water glasses.

Silence fell as they started their meal, then Sally spoke. What she said took Kingston by surprise.

"Are you still helping the police?"

"Not as much, but yes. I believe you already know that the Thames Valley Police enlisted me right after the motorcycle accident—the man who was at St. George's Hospital, the one they thought was your brother." Kingston paused, resting his knife and fork, dabbing his mouth with his napkin, just long enough to observe her surreptitiously. He saw nothing in her eyes or body language to suggest that talking about her brother's death still unsettled her. "I still talk to Inspector Sheffield from time to time."

"Have there been any breaks at all?" she asked hesitantly, with a wan smile. "It's a silly question, I suppose. If there had been, I'm sure the police would have told me."

"No, I'm afraid it's still much of a mystery. You do know that they identified the man in the hospital, don't you?"

"Yes. I forget his name, though."

"Jeremy Lester."

"That's right. The inspector said it was Peter's motorcycle he was riding."

"It was. That's why, at first, they thought it was Peter who was injured in the accident. But you already know all this."

"Yes."

"What about Jeremy Lester? Do you know anything about him?" Kingston asked offhandedly, slicing into his medium rare entrecôte.

"No." She shook her head.

"One would conclude that they were fairly close friends. Apparently, it was Peter's idea that Lester be included on the trip."

"They might have been, though Peter never mentioned him. Not that he would, necessarily. Maybe they met more recently."

Kingston looked into her mascara-rimmed hazel eyes. "This is none of my business, but did Peter leave a will?"

"One was never found, no. But it's not too surprising, considering how little he owned."

"Did you know he had a motorcycle?"

She smiled briefly. "Of course. Peter's always had motorcycles, ever since he was old enough for a license."

"I know the answer to the question, but I'll ask it anyway. Did you find DVLA papers or a bill of sale indicating that Peter might have sold his bike?"

Sally shook her head. "No, nothing like that."

Kingston stopped eating and stared briefly into space. "Then we can only assume that there was either some kind of arrangement whereby Jeremy Lester had permission to use the bike, or Peter had lent it to him," he said, looking back at her.

Sally shook her head. "I've no idea."

A few moments of silence followed, as they turned their attention to their lunch. Kingston felt good, having invited her, pleased that she seemed to be enjoying his company, even though they were discussing the unexplained death of her brother. He couldn't help admiring her openness and sangfroid. She spoke, interrupting his thoughts.

"What did you think of that letter? The one I found in Peter's belongings, the letter that David Jenkins wrote warning Peter off the trip—that, and the newspaper clipping. You did get them, didn't you?"

Kingston nodded. "I did, yes. I passed them on to the police. They said to thank you."

"You said you were going to get back to me."

"I was, and I apologize." He sipped his wine, all the time looking into her eyes. "I'm curious, Sally. Jenkins sent the letter in September, right? And you went to Arundel to get Peter's things in December or thereabouts. How come you've waited all this time before bringing it up?"

"When I brought his stuff home, I put the boxes of books in my spare bedroom, under the bed. I already knew that none of them were of interest to me. I kept putting off going through them until a couple of weeks ago. I was going to give them to the library. That's when I found the letter and the court papers. They were tucked inside a book. A book about China."

"I knew there must be a simple explanation."

"What did you think of the letter?" she asked, taking a sip of wine.

Kingston wondered how he should reply. He might as well tell her about Jenkins. She would learn sooner or later. "I'm sorry to say that David Jenkins died a few days ago," he said as delicately as he could.

"Good Lord!" She paled and put down her glass. "I thought you said there hadn't been any breaks in the case—that you only talk to the police occasionally. What happened?"

"I'm sorry. I thought you meant breaks that might shed some light on Peter's accident." He proceeded to tell her how he had gone to Cornwall to meet Jenkins, and what he'd encountered at the tree farm and at Jenkins's house. "Inspector Sheffield is now collaborating with the Devon & Cornwall Constabulary," he added. He was about to mention the Chinese ceramics but decided against it at the last moment. It was irrelevant. There was nothing yet to connect them with Jenkins's death.

"Are you saying he was murdered?"

Her question surprised him. When describing what had happened at Larkfield House, to make it easier on her, he'd purposely avoided any mention of foul play. He took his time answering. "I'm afraid it looks that way," he said soberly. "It won't be confirmed until they get the postmortem results, of course."

By the time dessert had arrived—strawberries with Jersey cream—there was little or nothing left to say in the matter of David Jenkins's untimely demise. The letter was forgotten and the talk drifted to everyday matters. The conversation appeared to be winding down when she made a statement that took Kingston by surprise.

"I should tell you that I've been toying with the idea of getting out of Harrow and London and living elsewhere."

"Really?" said Kingston, eyebrows raised. "What made you decide that?"

"City life and I no longer agree. It took me a long time to figure it out, but I came to realize that it was a bigger part of my problems than I realized—the reason for my apathy, my growing dissatisfaction with life in general."

"You've no doubt given it considerable thought?"

"I have. Yes. On top of everything else, the horrible crowding, the cost of living, I no longer feel safe in London. I should explain—"

Kingston was about to interrupt, but she continued.

"It was my bad luck to have been at the Edgware Road tube station when the terrorists set off those bombs." She pursed her lips. "It was ghastly. I'll never forget it."

"I'm sorry to hear that, and I can understand why you feel the way you do. These are dangerous times we live in."

She nodded.

"What about your job? That's of no consequence, I take it?"

"Not really. I work for a pharmaceutical company. Accounts manager. I like the work and it pays well, but I can get by on less, which I'll probably have to."

"Where would you go?"

"With Peter gone and no other family ties, I'm thinking about living abroad for while, to see if I like it."

"Europe?"

"Yes. I'm looking into what's required in the way of EU work permits et cetera."

"I have to admit, there's a lot to be said for it, not the least being the weather. And you can always come back if it doesn't work out."

She smiled. "My French is atrocious and I only speak about ten words of Italian. I'm not going to worry about that, though."

"I hope you'll let me know, if and when it comes about. And I trust you'll give me a forwarding address."

"Of course," she replied cheerfully.

Half an hour later, their shared cab dropped Sally off at her friend's house on York Terrace, facing Regent's Park. Kingston wished her well with her plans for living abroad, she promising to keep in touch. On the cab ride back home, he mused about their lunch. He had enjoyed himself and was left with the impression that she had, too. He would be sorry if she were to move away.

Back at his flat, Kingston played back his one phone message: Andrew had tickets for Royal Ascot the coming Friday, and would Kingston be his guest? Andrew went on to say that he had made a reservation for lunch in the Panoramic Restaurant. It was a brilliant five-course job, and if Kingston had never been there, he'd be knocked for six. Kingston had, but not lately.

No need to check his calendar; he would go regardless. A day out with Andrew was always an adventure. There was no telling what might happen before the clock struck midnight. He smiled, recalling one such bout of serious eating and drinking. What had started as an innocent lunch in Hampstead had ended up in the small hours at a raucous houseboat party on the river at Kew. The next day, all he could remember was dancing—gyrating, more like it—on the towpath to live trad jazz. Neither could recall who had invited them, what the occasion was, or who owned the boat. It was all lost in an alcohol-induced fog. That was the only time Kingston could ever remember having suffered a headache that lasted two days.

He sat on the sofa, debating what to do with the rest of the afternoon: whether he should go food shopping, do laundry, or clean up the flat. None had much appeal. He glanced to the sideboard, where the manila envelope containing David Jenkins's letter sat atop a stack of books. He reached over and picked it up, deciding, for no particular reason, to reread it. He was about to open the envelope when the phone rang.

"Hello, this is Kingston," he said.

"Well, I've some news for you, Doctor."

He recognized Sheffield's regional accent right away. "About David Jenkins?"

"Right. I heard from Hannaford this morning. Postmortem results showed burns around the mouth. It looks as though the assailant used chloroform to put him out, then finished him off with multiple blows to the head."

"Interesting. First, we have Lester and lidocaine, and now Jenkins and chloroform. If it's the same person, it has to be someone who has access to drugs and knows how to administer them—in Lester's case, with a dose intended to kill, perhaps. A pharmacist, lab technician, or—"

"A doctor."

"And Julian Bell is a doctor. Or practiced, at one time."

"Right."

"You're going to interview him again, I take it?"

"We are. Without question."

"What about the Chinese pottery in the barn? Did Inspector Hannaford say anything more about that?"

"He did indeed. As a matter of fact, we've talked about it since. If Jenkins was mixed up somehow in a scheme to sell phony Chinese antiques, then who else might be in cahoots with him? Another collector?"

"Spenser Graves," Kingston replied after a pause. Not wanting to come off sounding smart-alecky, he wasn't about to tell the inspector that he had also made that connection—some time ago.

"None other. Maybe, just maybe, we're starting to get to the bottom of this damned affair."

"I hope so."

"We're bringing Graves and Bell in for questioning."

"Good. Perhaps you'll let me know how it goes?"

"I will. It may take a few days, though."

Kingston put down the phone and leaned back into the sofa, trying to decide what to make of this latest development. From the beginning, he'd suspected that Jenkins's death would turn out to be a homicide. Thinking back on Sheffield's call, he'd forgotten to ask—now that robbery was ruled out—whether they'd found the netsuke, if Jenkins still had them.

As he pondered Jenkins's murder, trying to connect it with Lester's, it struck him that both might have been killed for the same reason: Both had known something that posed a serious threat to the murderer. What's more, there was little doubt left that the "something" had to do with the plant-hunting expedition.

As he was thinking, he had been staring at the manila envelope. He picked it up again. He examined the white address label, to study the handwriting. He noticed that the edge of another label showed under the top one. It wasn't much more than a fraction of a millimeter, but it was there, as if someone had gone to the trouble to conceal it with the top label. He tried to lift the corner of the top label with his little fingernail, but it was firmly affixed. He took it to the kitchen, where he poured a modest amount of water in the kettle, plugged it in, and flicked on the switch. A minute of careful steaming, and the top label peeled off clean as a whistle. The label underneath was addressed to David Jenkins, PO Box 196, Fowey, Cornwall PL23.

Kingston leaned on the kitchen counter, looking at the envelope, trying to figure out what to make of it. His immediate thought was that Jenkins must have a little Scottish in him. But recycling envelopes wasn't such a bad idea. For all he knew, maybe a lot of people did it. But this was taking "green" a little too far for his liking. Since the kettle had boiled, he decided he might as well make a cup of tea.

Five minutes later, he was sitting at the kitchen table with his tea, munching on a digestive biscuit. He had just set aside the *Times* crossword after finally solving the last clue, 12 down: *Memento Japanese bar will do?* (8). Of course—*keepsake*! He looked at the envelope again. It was the postmark date that finally helped him figure out a plausible reason why David Jenkins had reused the envelope. The letter inside was dated before the expedition took place, as was the St. Austell postmark. This made sense because in the letter Jenkins urged Mayhew not to go on the trip. To outward appearances, it was all in order. But, for the sake of argument, Kingston asked himself, what if Jenkins had written and dated the letter *after* the expedition? How could he make it look otherwise? Kingston figured that he had reused the envelope of an old letter or document that had been addressed to him *prior* to the expedition—hence the first label and the early date stamp. All he had to do after the expedition was to use an identical label, address it to Mayhew, and carefully place it over the old one. This time, rather than post it—because it was already postmarked—he had to hand-deliver it. This was easy, because by now Mayhew was a missing person, presumed dead. Jenkins only had to slip it through the postal slot in Mayhew's door for the new tenants or the landlord to find, and for one of them to put it in with Mayhew's belongings that were waiting for Sally to pick up. Nobody would question the St. Austell postmark. If Kingston's fanciful theory was correct, it meant that Jenkins had gone out of his way to prove, falsely, that he had warned Mayhew not to go on the plant-hunting trip *before* it took place. If Kingston was right, the question was why?

EIGHTEEN

Friday's outing to Ascot turned out to be a slap-up affair all round. The weather couldn't have been better for a day at the races, nothing but blue skies with a lingering white cloud here and there, the "going" good to firm. Observing the dress code required for Premier Admission badge holders, both Kingston and Andrew wore summer blazers, shirts and ties, and straw hats. Kingston sported a wide-brimmed Panama from the venerable Lock & Co., the St. James's Street hatters founded in 1676, as the label attested. He had splurged on it for his honeymoon many moons ago. Each time he took it down from the dark upper recesses of his wardrobe, he admired its superb quality and timeless style. It also conjured tender memories and never failed to bring compliments.

The five-course Epicurean Lunch in the Panoramic Restaurant, with wines suitably paired by Andrew, far exceeded

Kingston's expectations. They had a window table with an unimpeded view of the emerald green racecourse, the winning post directly below them. The vantage point also offered a far-reaching panorama across Windsor Great Park to the London skyline in the hazy distance. As if all this wasn't enough, both of them came out on the winning side, with Kingston making a bundle on the twenty-to-one outsider that won the Coronation Stakes, the third race on the card. The name of the horse: Saucy Sally.

Arriving back in Chelsea, with full stomachs and wallets, they decided that a celebratory drink at the Antelope was in order before going home. With Andrew, there was no such thing as "a drink" singular. "Drink" existed only as a verb in his mind. Thus, it was past eight o'clock before Kingston got to kick off his shoes and plonk down on the sofa to go through the day's mail. An envelope bearing the logo and address of the Percival David Foundation of Chinese Art caught his attention. He opened it with his bone-handled letter knife and took out the one-page letter.

Dear Dr. Kingston,

We have examined the photographs of the Chinese bowl that you provided and are able to offer the following opinion accordingly.

Visually, the ceramic appears to be a Ming Dynasty Palace bowl of Chenghua period (1465–87). It bears the correct Chinese character reign marks, scrollwork, and shows modest wear, as would be expected.

Without examining the bowl itself, to study the glaze and determine the weight, etc., we are unable to confirm if it is a genuine work or a reasonable copy.

Few examples of such Palace bowls exist today and we are fortunate to possess several of them. If judged authentic, it would be considered extremely rare.

If you are able to bring the bowl to our offices, we would be happy to provide a more accurate opinion. To facilitate this, please make an appointment with one of our curators by phoning the number below.

> *Yours truly,*
> *Warren Yee*
> *Curator*

Kingston was pleased. He hadn't expected the bowl to be authenticated from a photograph. Anyone who knew anything about antiques would know that it was not possible. What was encouraging was the information about the period and its rarity. He would have to do more research, but from what little he'd read, the bowl, if genuine, would be of considerable value—in the £1–2 million–plus range. That said, he doubted it was the real McCoy. Given the dubious circumstances, it was looking more and more to him as if the bowl was a good fake, indicating that Jenkins had been involved in a scheme to produce counterfeit Chinese ceramics.

He put the letter on the coffee table. Something that Inspector Sheffield had said came back to him: "Jenkins was always running off to China looking for plants, what would be so unusual about his collecting Chinese antiques?" Collecting authentic antiques was one thing, but forging them on a grand scale was another entirely. Clearly Jenkins hadn't been alone in the venture. Whoever had made the bowls was unquestionably a skilled craftsman or woman. Another thing: To reproduce any antique so perfectly as to be virtually indistinguishable from the real thing required that the artisan possess the original. So where had the original or originals come from? China? Not necessarily. Chinese antiques were now in much demand worldwide, not only by collectors but also by investors. Ancient Chinese ceramics now appeared regularly for sale at Christie's, Sotheby's, and Bonham's auctions in London and abroad. Kingston had read that when China entered the World Trade Organization in 2001, many of the tight controls on the trade and export of antiquities were lifted. No longer was it illegal to sell such relics. As a result, antiques markets and auction houses dealing in Chinese antiquities sprang up all over the country, and the price of the ancient works of art, many once held in private collections, started to rise dramatically.

If Jenkins had been acquiring antique ceramics on his expeditions to China, could Graves, Bell, or any of the others be in on it with him? Another problem bothered Kingston. Why produce so many bowls? Conservatively, there had to be at least two dozen on the shelf at the barn, all the same size and shape. To flood the market with so many would seem to be not only illogical and counterproductive, but would also invite the risk of discovery.

With so many questions spinning in his head on top of the day's wine and spirits—far beyond his normal intake—he decided to give up worrying about it for now. A phone call in the morning to Sheffield, telling him about the Percival David letter, should result in permission being granted to release one of the glazed bowls sitting in Cornwall and have it delivered to the Percival David curator for authentication. After that, its pedigree would be known, once and for all. He thought about making a cup of coffee but changed his mind. He got up, turned off the lights, and headed for the stairs. After a long and lively excursion, an hour's reading—if he could keep his eyes open—then an early night would be a welcome and fitting end to a memorable day.

The weekend passed uneventfully, which was a welcome change for Kingston. No important phone calls and little contact with the outside world, save for a visit to his barber in Kensington and a trip to Sainsbury's, where he stocked up on essentials for the pantry and food for only the next couple of days. Shopping for anything, except books, paintings, and antiques, was about as appealing to Kingston as watching paint dry. By and large, he shopped for food much the same way as the French and Italians: buying only enough fresh fish, meats, and vegetables in season to cover the next two or three days' meals, versus the next several weeks, which, by the appearance of some of the supermarket shopping carts, had become the prevailing practice of today's younger families.

The morning after he'd received the Percival David letter, he had called Sheffield, telling him about his earlier conversation with the foundation and his submitting the digital photos. Then he had read aloud their reply. Sheffield had agreed that it was significant and assured Kingston that he would call Inspector Hannaford that afternoon and arrange to have one of the glazed bowls sent off immediately.

With time on his hands, a rare indulgence of late, he caught up with his e-mails and correspondence, finishing a letter to his daughter, Julie, embarrassed to discover that he'd started it two weeks ago. Having now had plenty of time to mull over the events of the last weeks, it seemed clear, like it or not, that if there were to be any kind of break at all in solving Mayhew's death and the two murders, it would come after Sheffield had interviewed Julian Bell and Spenser Graves. They had to be mixed up in it all, somehow. Who else was left? Kingston would dearly love to sit in on those interviews, but from experience he knew that such a request would fall on very deaf lawful ears. There was little he could do for now—perhaps until the case was solved—other than to sit and wait patiently until Sheffield felt the need to call him.

It was *Country Life* that broke the stalemate. Kingston might have been sitting around his flat until the cows came home but for an item at the end of the Art Market Review pages that caught his eye. He read it twice, chuffed at his good fortune.

ASIAN ART EXHIBIT AT AUDLEIGH HALL

Visitors to Audleigh Hall Gardens and Arboretum in Leicestershire will enjoy an additional attraction from July 16–21. For the first time, Spenser Graves, Audleigh's owner, connoisseur and collector of fine Asian art, will be exhibiting his entire collection of Asian antiquities. Included in the display of over 500 objects are several 15th-century Imperial jade beaker vases; a number of 19th-century hanging scrolls; and a fine selection of 18th-century Qianlong jade carvings, cloisonné enamel jars and bowls, and Gue yue xuan porcelains. Highlight of the show is an exceptionally rare 14th-century Yuan Dynasty jar set. Hours of the exhibit are from 10 A.M. to 4 P.M. every day. Admission is free. Audleigh Hall is located on the A6, five miles north of Market Harborough, Leicestershire.

Kingston slapped his thigh. What a stroke of luck. The 16th was only two days away. Now he didn't need an excuse to pay a visit to Spenser Graves. Not only that, he had a legitimate reason for going should Sheffield chew him out later for unnecessary meddling. He thought about calling Graves first but decided against it. Graves already knew that Kingston was collaborating with the police. If, as it now appeared, Graves was mixed up with the fake Chinese ceramics—let alone the murders—he wouldn't want Kingston snooping around, far from it. There was also the remote possibility that Graves would not be in residence, though with such an important exhibit, that seemed unlikely. Even knowing Graves as little as he did, Kingston was sure that he would be on hand to oversee things. From what Sheffield had said, the interviews with Graves and Bell should have taken place by now. It would help if he knew the outcome. For all he knew, Graves or Bell or both of them could be under lock and key. Somehow, he doubted it.

Graves or no Graves, he was going to take a run up to Leicestershire and play it by ear. It would be worth the drive, anyway, just to see the art collection. Would there be a blue-and-white Ming Dynasty Palace bowl among the exhibits? He would soon find out.

NINETEEN

Rain was tattooing the canvas top of the TR4 as Kingston drove through the iron gates of Audleigh Hall. From the moment he'd left London, the weather had been wretched. This time, when the house came into view through the blurry arcs of the wipers, it looked bleak and inhospitable. What a difference from his first visit, he thought. That time, he had driven right up to the front door, now the road was roped off and all traffic was directed to a car park. This, he discovered, was two hundred yards from the house. Several minutes later, Kingston locked the car, zipped up his Barbour jacket to his chin, put up his brolly, and started the long trudge through the avenue of beech trees, along the soggy grass path to the house.

For the next forty-five minutes, Kingston, with other visitors, including a docent-led group of seniors, made their way slowly around the grand echoing exhibit hall under the gimlet-eyed gaze of two uniformed guards. Graves's Asian art collection was, as the article had promised, extensive, museumworthy, and impressive. What with the Chinese bowls at Jenkins's place, his recent exchange with the Percival David Foundation, and now this magnificent display of old Asian artifacts, Kingston was quickly gaining a renewed interest and appreciation for Chinese antiques.

Kingston at last reached the end of the exhibit. He gazed at the jars, plates, tureens, and candlestick holders displayed in the last showcase: blue-and-white porcelain from the Qianlong period (1736–1795). He paused briefly, looking around the hall, thinking. There had been no Ming Dynasty Palace bowl resembling the one in Cornwall. He came up with only two reasons why not. The most obvious was that Graves didn't possess any. Considering their stratospheric value, that wasn't surprising. The second reason was that if Graves did have one or more in his collection, and was also implicated in the forgeries, he certainly wouldn't put one on display.

More visitors were entering and the room had become quite crowded. The guards' attention was focused mainly on the showcases and wall cabinets, making sure that the security systems were functioning and that some light-fingered person wasn't walking off with a Ming vase under his raincoat. Kingston saw several closed-circuit TV cameras mounted high on the walls and in adjacent hallways. Nobody noticed as he calmly slipped out the exhibit hall into one of the hallways farthest from the main entrance.

He was in an unfamiliar part of the house. On his earlier visit, Graves had mentioned that it contained forty-plus rooms. At that time Kingston had seen only a few. He had no idea what he was looking for, or what he expected to find, but it was too good an opportunity to pass up, nosey parker that he was. If he bumped into a staff member, he would surely be directed back to the hall or the exit. Turning a corner, passing several closed doors, he was soon out of sight and sound of the exhibit hall. If asked what he was looking for, he would simply say the bathroom. It worked every time.

He became a little bolder, quietly opening a door now and

then, each time peering into an empty room or storage area. He was starting to think that it had been a bad idea in the first place and that perhaps he should retrace his steps, when he heard voices. He slowed, approaching a door on his right that was slightly ajar. He stopped, straining to hear the conversation that sounded to be between two men. He stood still, no more than three feet from the open door.

"Can I help you, sir?"

The voice from behind startled Kingston. He turned, aware that he'd been caught eavesdropping. "I know it doesn't look like it, but I was looking for the gents," he said, with as much humility as he could summons.

For a moment the man didn't answer. He was wearing a black suit with a white shirt and tie, and looking at Kingston in an odd way. At last he spoke. "You're Dr. Kingston, aren't you?"

"I am, yes," Kingston replied. Then the penny dropped. It was Hobbs, Graves's butler, manservant, whatever. He wasn't wearing his glasses, which was what had thrown Kingston off.

"Would you looking be for Mr. Graves?" he asked politely.

Kingston smiled inwardly at the archaic phrasing. "I actually *was* looking for a bathroom. But yes, if it's not inconvenient. Just to say hello. I really came to see the exhibit and wouldn't want to disturb him unnecessarily."

"Wait here a moment." Hobbs stepped past Kingston, knocked lightly, opened the door and entered, leaving it ajar. Kingston wondered what kind of reception to expect from Spenser Graves. In seconds, Hobbs reappeared.

"He'll meet you in the library. He's just finishing his meeting. No more than ten minutes, he said. Come with me, Doctor."

Kingston nodded and followed Hobbs to the end of the hall, where he opened a large paneled door, holding it open for Kingston to enter.

The elegantly colonnaded room was magnificent. Row after

row of books covered three walls, from floor to vaulted ceiling. Each wall had its own library ladder connected to a brass track surround that projected from below the ceiling molding. Multipaned French doors occupied most of the other wall facing the garden. Too bad it was still pelting down outside, so the view didn't amount to much. In the center of the room a massive square table, low enough but far too big to be considered a coffee table, was surrounded by overstuffed chairs. A huge copper bucket containing fresh flowers—from the garden, no doubt—sat in the center of the table in the midst of stacks of books and magazines. Declining Hobbs's offer of tea, coffee, or "stronger beverage," Kingston settled into one of the chairs, picked up the top magazine, *The World of Interiors*, and started reading.

After several minutes, Spenser Graves entered. Kingston put down the magazine and stood. He was pleased to see that Graves's expression was agreeable.

"Good morning, Lawrence. Hobbs tells me you came up to see the exhibit."

"I did, yes."

"Why didn't you call me? I could have given you a private viewing."

"I thought about it but decided not to bother you. Having seen the displays, I can imagine how much effort went into staging the event. Superb, I might add."

Graves pulled up one of the chairs and sat. Kingston did likewise, crossing his legs.

A silence fell, while each waited for the other to say something.

"If I'd known you were that interested in Asian antiques, I could have shown you a good part of the collection when you were here last," said Graves.

"Other than certain Japanese pieces—Imari, tansus, netsuke, that sort of thing—I confess it's a subject I know little about.

That's why I thought it would be a good idea; that I could learn something. I saw the mention in *Country Life*."

Graves nodded, scouring Kingston's face, remaining silent.

Kingston cleared his throat. "I was coming up to Bedford anyway, to visit friends, so it wasn't as if I had to make a special trip." He realized now that he was babbling and sounding apologetic. By the look on Graves's face, he was thinking the same thing. In the brief silence that followed, Kingston wondered if he should apologize for the intrusion and make a graceful exit. As he was about to stand, Graves spoke. His eyes locked on Kingston's.

"Are you still working with the police on the Mayhew case?"

"I'm not, no." Kingston reasoned that it wasn't really a lie because, to all intents and purposes, his role in the case had run its course. "Why do you ask?"

Graves's eyes narrowed. Now he looked anything but friendly, a Graves that Kingston hadn't seen before. "I understand that David Jenkins is dead." His voice lacked any trace of emotion or sympathy. "The police say he was murdered."

Kingston saw the trap. If he admitted to knowing about Jenkins, he would have to explain how he came by the information. He had to think quickly.

A knock on the door gave him the time he needed. The door opened partway and Hobbs appeared. "Your guests are ready to leave, sir," he said.

Graves swiveled in his chair to face Hobbs. "Tell them I'll be with them in a few minutes. I'll be through with Dr. Kingston shortly." He turned back to face Kingston.

Kingston didn't like the implication in Graves's last remark one bit. Rather than try to change the subject, which would appear as if he were purposely avoiding Graves's last question, he waited for Graves to say something.

"Jenkins's death doesn't surprise you?" Graves asked at length.

"It doesn't," Kingston replied without hesitating. "Sally Mayhew told me. She'd called the police to find out if there had been any further developments in the case. It just so happened that she phoned them right after Jenkins was killed."

Graves searched Kingston's face momentarily, as if he were unsure whether Kingston was telling the truth. Seemingly satisfied with Kingston's explanation, he looked away and stood. "I have to say goodbye to my friends," he said.

Kingston got up and nodded. "I must get going, too. I'm due in Bedford in an hour." He followed Graves to the door. This was his last chance to ask Graves if the police had interviewed him again. He decided against it.

No words were exchanged as they walked along the hall to the room where Kingston had eavesdropped. With a curt "Goodbye, Doctor," Graves went in and closed the door behind him. Kingston stood by the door for a moment, then shook his head, turned on his heels, and headed for the exhibit hall and the exit. At the cloakroom, he was met by a queue of visitors waiting to retrieve their raincoats and umbrellas. A frail octogenarian lady, moving at the speed of treacle running uphill in winter, was taking forever to retrieve people's belongings. Ten minutes passed before his coat and brolly were handed over. He left her a nice tip, anyway.

It was still raining stair rods when Kingston drove out of the car park. He was reminded, once again, that his windscreen wipers needed replacing. Seeing a car coming toward him from the direction of the house, he slowed at the junction where the two roads met. That road was no longer roped off. He let the car, a black Jeep, go first. It was the same color and model as the one he'd parked alongside that day at Bell's farm. Kingston watched as the driver turned in front of him. Though visibility through the windscreen was blurry, Kingston got a good look at the car's three occupants.

The man in the passenger seat was Asian, as was the man in the backseat. The driver was Julian Bell.

TWENTY

On the drive back to London it was still bucketing down, with no apparent letup in sight. To the monotonous *click-clack* of the wipers and hiss of Michelins on the rain-slick road, Kingston hashed over his short and fractious visit with Spenser Graves, thinking how starkly different it was from his first. If Sheffield had questioned Graves, perhaps something had transpired at the interview that had caused Graves to be so tetchy. Maybe Sheffield had mentioned Kingston's name, hence Graves's question about his working with the police.

It was a dead cert that the Asian men Kingston had seen in the car and the "friends" that Graves had been meeting with were one and the same. Their presence would tend to bolster the idea that Graves, Bell, and possibly Jenkins were all involved in a scheme to replicate valuable Chinese relics and sell them to unsuspecting collectors. It was looking even more as if his original premise was correct. All roads kept leading back to the same place: Someone on the expedition—most likely Mayhew—had discovered what the three were up to, threatened to expose them, and paid the price. Seeing Julian Bell at the wheel had surprised Kingston at the time. Now, after more thought, it would be reasonable to expect—if his theory were right—Bell to be in on any meeting that concerned the Chinese ceramics.

Closer to London, the weather and crawling traffic were starting to get to Kingston. He couldn't wait to get home to a glass of Macallan and, afterward, an early dinner at the Antelope. Maybe he'd give Andrew a call and see if he was up for it. Tomorrow, first thing, he would call Inspector Sheffield and tell him about his visit to Audleigh and his meeting with Graves.

As he thought about his day trip, Kingston wondered just how much longer the detective inspector would put up with his telling him things after the fact. In retrospect, he really should have informed Sheffield that he was planning to go to Audleigh. On the plus side, Sheffield would find it hard to argue that Bell and Graves meeting with the two Asians was not germane to the case. When Sheffield had finished letting off steam, Kingston would inquire—delicately, of course—what had transpired at Graves's and Bell's sessions in the interview room. Then he would ask if the Percival David Foundation had responded with an evaluation of the bowl sent by Inspector Hannaford.

As it turned out, Andrew had just had a root canal, so Kingston's dinner companion that night was the *Times* crossword puzzle, which he almost completed. On the way back home, he rented a movie to take his mind off the day's developments and eventually turned in at the respectable hour of ten forty-five.

The next morning, Kingston waited until a reasonable hour before calling Inspector Sheffield. Over a breakfast of two softboiled eggs, toast, and marmalade, he had jotted down a few notes, which were now in front of him on the kitchen table. At five minutes after ten, he pressed the speed-dial number for Sheffield's direct line—he couldn't think why on earth he had added the policeman's number to the short list in the first place, but he certainly couldn't have known then that he would be calling the inspector with any frequency. In a few rings Sheffield was on the line.

"Good morning, Doctor," he said, in his soft brogue. "What have you been up to lately? Not sitting home watching the telly, I would imagine."

At least he was in good humor, thought Kingston. "When the test matches start, maybe," he replied. "No, I'm calling because I was up at Audleigh Hall yesterday. I managed to have a chance meeting with Spenser Graves."

"Chance meeting, eh?"

"Yes." Kingston resented the skepticism in Sheffield's voice.

"And how did you *manage* that?"

"I went up to see his exhibit of Asian art. It was written up in *Country Life*. It's a subject that I've become more interested in over recent years."

"I'd heard about it. Graves mentioned it when we interviewed him."

So the interview had taken place. Good. He would ask how it went, but not until after he'd further explained his reason for traveling all the way to Leicestershire. "I was going up to Bedford anyway, to visit a friend," he said. "I thought it might be worthwhile to go the extra few miles and see the collection. It turned out to be a good decision."

"And how is our friend Graves?"

"He wasn't overly friendly, I must say. Can't say as I blame him, though. I did drop by unannounced. He happened to be in an important meeting but was decent enough to give me a few minutes of his time."

After a brief pause Sheffield spoke again. "Where's all this going, Doctor?" There was a trace of impatience in his voice.

"Well, I believe the meeting was with Julian Bell and two Asian men. The three of them left the same time as I did. I saw them drive out together."

"So you think that it had something to do with the Chinese pots that were found in Jenkins's barn?"

"The bowls. Yes, I do." Kingston hoped his correction didn't sound too disrespectful.

"Well, if it helps any, I got an e-mail from Hannaford late yesterday. It included a copy of the response he'd received from the Chinese art foundation."

"The Percival David people. Excellent. May I ask what they said?"

"They said the bowl was a copy."

"That wasn't all, surely?"

"No. They explained how they came to that conclusion."

"If it's not too much to ask, could I get a copy of the e-mail?"

Sheffield's reply was a long time in coming, and Kingston thought he knew why. He just hoped the inspector wasn't going to pull rank. He'd heard it before: "This is a police matter and we don't give out evidence or information willy-nilly to anyone asking for it, chum." Kingston smiled. He shouldn't be so prejudgmental; for all he knew the inspector might have spilled his coffee in his lap.

At length, Sheffield deigned to answer. "I have it right here. It's not very long. Why don't I just read it to you?"

"That would be fine."

The inspector cleared his throat and started reading:

"Dear Inspector Hannaford,

"We are pleased to present our opinion as to the authenticity of the ceramic bowl that you submitted. The bowl is not an original work but rather a well-executed copy of a Ming Dynasty Palace bowl of Chenghua period (1465–87).

"The size and the shape of the piece accurately replicate that of a genuine bowl, as do the scroll design and brushwork. While the Imperial character marks at first appear genuine, closer inspection proves that they have not been executed by a Chinese artisan. Also, the glaze, wear, and patina are not consistent with an artwork purporting to be of such age.

"For your information, the bowl appears to be the same as, or similar to, the one depicted in photographs recently sent to us by Dr. Lawrence Kingston. We are presuming that you obtained the bowl from him.

"I hope this answers your questions. If not, please feel free to call me and I would be happy to discuss the piece with you further. We will return the item within the next few days.

"Yours truly, Warren Yee, Curator."

"It doesn't surprise me," said Kingston.

"Nor me. Unfortunately, it doesn't shed much light on who killed Jenkins."

"Or Jeremy Lester."

"Right. I hadn't forgotten him."

Kingston knew by Sheffield's tone and the brevity of his answers that the conversation was about to come to a close. He might just as well come right out and pop the question, no more subtlety or diplomacy. "How did the interviews with Graves and Bell go?"

"Not much help, I'm afraid."

"How did they respond to Jenkins's murder?"

"Well, both reacted the way you would expect—shocked, upset, denied any knowledge of it. I'll say one thing. If either *were* implicated in any way, they deserve bloody Oscars. Both had credible alibis that all checked out. That majordomo fellow of his,

Hobbs, said he had a touch of the flu that weekend and confirmed that Graves was home the entire week of Jenkins's murder, making last-minute touches to the exhibit. A woman who cooked for him and another staff member also confirmed that Graves was home all weekend."

"How about Bell?"

"He was attending a wedding at Midhurst, in Sussex—daughter of a close friend, apparently. It all checked out, too."

"Hmm. By the sound of it, we've run out of suspects."

"It looks that way, I'm afraid. If you come up with any ideas, Doctor, you might want to let us know. I'll do likewise."

Much as he tried over the following days, Kingston found it almost impossible to focus his thoughts on anything but the murders of Jeremy Lester and David Jenkins, and the mystery surrounding Peter Mayhew's accident. One side of his brain said, "Let it go and get on with your life." The other kept nagging, "There must be something you've overlooked. Perhaps you're presupposing too much, and the answer is right under your nose." If it was, then he was losing his touch. It gave him little satisfaction, too, that unless they were keeping it to themselves, the combined gray matter of the Thames Valley Police had been unable to find even a hairline crack in the case. He smiled, thinking about it. Where were Morse and Lewis when you needed them?

As each day passed, Kingston's enthusiasm for the case was diminishing slowly to a point where he was no longer losing sleep over it. He could remember no other time in his past when he had been so frustrated and felt so powerless.

All that changed when he got another phone call from DI Sheffield. Kingston was halfway out his front door, headed for Lea and Sandeman, his wine merchants in Fulham Road, when the phone started ringing. He went back and picked it up.

"It's Sheffield, Doctor. Glad I caught you at home. Thought you might have decided to dash off somewhere for a change of scenery, being summer and all that."

"I was planning to spend a few days in Wiltshire with friends, but that's been put off for a while. How are things going up there, Inspector?"

"Well, I promised to call if there were any developments in the Mayhew case, and though it's not exactly what you'd call a break, I thought you might like to know about it."

"I appreciate that, Inspector." Kingston tried to contain his eagerness.

"The Met got a call yesterday from the Chinese embassy in London. It seems that they received an inquiry from the Bureau of Criminal Investigation—I believe it was—in Beijing. It was regarding the remains of a body discovered recently in Yunnan, not far from the mountain pass where Mayhew lost his life."

"Interesting."

"It certainly is. In cross-checking their records, the Chinese authorities found that a group of British botanists, headed by an American, were exploring that area last October. Right away, the Met called us, knowing that we were investigating two murders involving a plant-hunting expedition that had taken place in China."

"Have they identified the person?"

"Yes. It's a male who was reported missing about the same time. He lived in a nearby village."

"The same time as the expedition? October?"

"Early November, actually. Because the body is so decomposed they haven't been able to establish a time of death, but the remains are consistent with a person having been dead and buried for that period of time. No cause of death, either."

"Buried, you said?"

"He was found in a shallow grave by a construction crew surveying the region."

There was a long moment of silence before Sheffield spoke again. "Unlike you to run out of questions, Doctor."

"Sorry, Inspector, I didn't mean to be so obtrusive. It's just that . . . well, obviously, it must have something to do with the expedition, don't you think?"

"It certainly looks that way."

"Do the Chinese authorities know what happened on the expedition? About the murders here?"

"They do. The Met didn't go into a lot of detail, only that we've been working on the case and haven't made much progress. With this new development, we're setting up a conference call with the Met and the Chinese police in the next twenty-four hours. Based on what we've told them so far, they may send investigators over here to interview Graves and Bell."

"Do you think one of them might have killed the man?"

"I don't think we can jump to that conclusion quite yet, but there is one thing that points to their being implicated. The chap I spoke with at the Met said the Chinese police told him that the crime rate for that area is exceedingly low, mostly family disputes, theft, and an occasional robbery. He said there hasn't been a murder in that region since they started keeping records over fifty years ago."

"Too much of a coincidence, if you ask me," said Kingston.

"What next, I wonder." Sheffield sighed. "Well, just give it some thought, Doctor." He paused, then said, "I know you will."

TWENTY-ONE

On the bus to the Fulham Road, Kingston was still thinking about his conversation with Sheffield and how the death of the man in China could be linked to the plant-hunting expedition. He could come up with only one idea: Like Mayhew, the man could have accidentally stumbled on something connected to the expedition that had cost him his life. Problem was, the only two people remaining—other than the American, Kavanagh— who might perhaps know what that "something" was were Graves and Bell. And if they did, they certainly weren't going to reveal it. So it looked dubious that the Chinese "connection" was going to help much, after all. Maybe, just maybe, he should contrive a reason to give Kavanagh a call. From everything Sheffield had said so far, it looked like the American was in the clear. But that didn't mean that he might not be able to shed some light on the case, to provide some information that might help put the pieces of the puzzle together. Questioning him would take some careful thought, and in order to do so, Kingston would have to get Sheffield's go-ahead. How could he manage to do that?

His stop was coming up, so he made his way to the back of the bus. As it slowed, he was still thinking about the American. Had he been a little hasty in writing him off as a suspect? Perhaps, before anything, he should first ask Sheffield where he now figured in their investigation.

Half an hour later, with the help of one of Lea and Sandeman's wine connoisseurs, Kingston had made his selections: a case each of mixed Bordeaux, Burgundy, and Rhônes, a case of Italian varietals, a mixed case of Australian and California wines, and two bottles of vintage port. They would be delivered in the next couple of days.

The delivery from Lea and Sandeman's arrived midafternoon Monday, as promised. Carefully comparing the labels to the packing slip, it took Kingston about fifteen minutes to restock and rearrange his wine cellar. The cellar was one of the first things he had had installed after moving in. It had been constructed by making a few simple modifications to a large clothes closet. With a thermal air-seal door, full insulation, and a professional wine-cellar cooling system that controlled the temperature and humidity, it housed approximately 250 bottles, with storage space for cases.

As he closed the cellar door, he heard the post fall through the slot in the front door. He flipped through the half dozen envelopes and junk mail on his way to the kitchen. The last envelope caused him to stop in his tracks. It bore the embossed logo of Audleigh Hall. Just about the last thing he was expecting was a letter from Spenser Graves. Kingston opened it, withdrew the handwritten letter on expensive stationery, and started reading.

Dear Lawrence,

A path has been reached in the police investigation into the death of Peter Mayhew that causes me serious concern. I have now been subjected to several police interviews. I have told them, to the best of my recollection, precisely what happened on the plant-hunting expedition and how Peter fell to his accidental death. They also questioned me concerning the deaths of Jeremy Lester and David Jenkins.

Yesterday, I received yet another phone call from Detective Inspector Sheffield, Thames Valley Police. He said that the Chinese police had found the remains of a man who had met his death about the same time as our expedition, and in the same locale. He informed me that the Chinese police might also want to talk to me.

You told me when you were here last that you were no longer helping the police on the case, not that it really makes that much difference to me. I have decided that rather than unburden myself to the police at this stage of the game, thereby risking irreparable damage to my reputation and future, I would like to talk with you and explain my predicament. There is, no doubt, little time left before the news media get hold of the story (I'm surprised they haven't already), and when that happens, the damage will have been done.

I am asking you to meet me at the cottage off the ridge path, Wednesday at 2 P.M. Come alone, and please do not visit the house before or after your visit. You can reach the cottage by parking at the end of Jackdaw Lane (off the main road to the house). It's just a short walk from there. Please phone me if you can't make it.

Cordially,
Spenser

Kingston sat down at the kitchen table and read the letter again. What was Spenser prepared to tell him but not the police, and why? His request that they meet at the cottage, and that Kingston not visit the house, could only mean that Graves didn't want Hobbs or any of the staff to see or talk with him. While he hadn't asked specifically that Kingston not tell the police about the meeting, it was implicit in the letter. Last, what was the "damage" Graves mentioned? Damage to his reputation, or something of far greater consequence?

Kingston put the letter aside and looked out the window, thinking about it for a minute or so. Was he finally going to learn exactly what happened on the slopes of that mountain in China? Or was he getting involved in something better left to the police? Graves insisting that Kingston go alone and not make his presence known to anyone at the house worried him. Somehow, though, he couldn't imagine Spenser wanting to do him harm. These apprehensions, however, were all outweighed by the possibility that Graves might open up and disclose what, if anything, he knew about the two murders and explain what the fake ceramics were doing in Jenkins's barn. It was an opportunity Kingston simply couldn't pass up. The man was asking for help, and Kingston would oblige.

Wednesday arrived, and with it somber skies and umbrella-warping winds. At eleven o'clock, dressed for nasty weather, Kingston started off for his garage. Three hours should be more than enough time to get to Audleigh Hall. With half the roads in England gummed up by road works on any given day, one never knew what kind of delays might be encountered.

Arriving in good time, he found Jackdaw Lane without trouble, parking the TR4, as Graves had suggested, at the dead end of the road by the path leading to the cottage. No sooner had he locked the car than it started spitting rain. With his folding umbrella in the pocket of his Barbour jacket, he set off down the path, buffeted by the gusting wind. He was hoping that the weather wasn't a portent of whatever was about to play out at the cottage.

On the drive, he hadn't given too much thought to the meeting;

he'd done enough of that already. But now that he was about to come face-to-face with Graves, he was starting to feel trepidation. Not necessarily bad vibes, but the sense that he was about to learn something he would rather not. Something unexpected. Too late to think about that now, he said to himself as the cottage came into view. In the shelter of the big trees, smoke was curling from the chimney, a sure sign that Graves was waiting for him.

Kingston rapped on the door with the lion's-head knocker. It opened almost immediately, and Graves, wearing corduroy slacks and baggy cardigan sweater over a checked shirt, ushered him inside. "Come through here and sit by the fire," he said, leading the way into a low-beamed living room with wood-plank floor and white plaster walls.

Graves took Kingston's wet jacket, and in a few moments was back. "Please sit down," he said. Kingston sat in one of the two identical wingback chairs located on either side of the fireplace. While Graves stoked the fire and put on another log, Kingston looked around, admiring the comfortable room with its country pine furniture, worn Oriental rugs, and watercolor hunting prints. After the grandeur of the big house, he could see why it would be a welcome "escape."

Graves sat, crossed his legs, then uncrossed them, and looked at Kingston, unsmiling. A Christie's auction catalog and a half-filled glass of what Kingston guessed to be whisky—his drink of choice at their last meeting—sat on the small table at Graves's elbow. His face was ashen and he appeared uneasy. He seemed thinner and more worn.

"Thanks for coming all the way up here to see me, Lawrence," he said. "To be honest, I thought you might decide against it—your having worked with the police."

Kingston wasn't about to tell him that he'd had some qualms about coming. He'd driven all this way to hear what Graves had to say, so the less he said the better. "If I can be of help, Spenser, it will have been worthwhile," Kingston replied. Before Graves could respond, he continued. "In your letter you said that you wanted to explain your... 'predicament' I believe was the word you used. I take it that this relates to Mayhew's death and the other incidents surrounding the expedition?"

"To some extent. Let me explain," he said, taking a long, solicitous look at Kingston. "To start with, I want you to know that most of what I told the police was accurate and true. Despite all the speculation, to the best of my knowledge, Mayhew's death was accidental. I saw it happen with my own eyes and so did all the others. Nevertheless, I have been guilty of withholding certain information about the case. I was forced to do so for the simple and painful reason that it would have incriminated me as an accessory in a crime." He blinked rapidly, a tendency that Kingston hadn't noticed when they last met. "Should that happen, I fear I would pay a very heavy price." He picked up his glass, taking not a sip but a gulp of whisky.

"Tell me about the—"

"Wait, Lawrence." Graves put down his glass and held up his hand. "This is difficult for me, but let me continue."

"All right."

As Graves lowered his hand, Kingston couldn't help noticing the slight tremor before it came to rest on the man's knee.

"Six generations of Graveses have lived at Audleigh Hall, Lawrence," he said, clenching his teeth. "And I represent the last. When I'm gone, all this will pass on to Alexandra, my daughter, whom you met. I deeply regret never having had a son and that the family name will no longer be associated with Audleigh. Not that it makes any difference, now." He took a deep breath and exhaled. "Don't mistake me. I love Alexandra more dearly than I can ever express, but she'll be married soon, and it's doubtful that she and her future husband will make their home here. He works in Paris, you see." Graves ran his tongue over his lips.

"Sorry," he said. "Rude of me. I didn't ask if you'd like something to drink."

"No, I'm fine," replied Kingston, not wanting to interrupt now that Graves was baring his soul with such unexpected candor.

Graves continued. "Have you any idea what it costs to keep a place like Audleigh afloat, Lawrence? The house, the gardens, the taxes?"

Kingston shook his head. "Only from what I've read—so many having been sold off to satisfy debts."

"Right. Dumfries House was the latest—or I should say, almost. One of the most spectacular historic houses in Britain, about to be broken up and sold off privately. That is, until Prince Charles intervened, forming the consortium that bought it. Dumped twenty million of his own money in it, too."

"I saw that."

"I tell you, the financial drain is intolerable. Over the last few years I've managed to keep Audleigh from going under, by one process or another, but the wolves will soon be at the door. It's a bitter pill, but there's no way to prevent it. Audleigh is finished. It will end up as a school, a corporate retreat, or a bloody sanatorium, just like all the other estates before it."

As moved as he was listening to Graves's outpourings about the looming demise of the Audleigh dynasty, Kingston was starting to wonder when Graves was going to move on to the matter of the expedition and the murders. In his letter he'd mentioned his worry about the media, and what would happen when the news got out. Surely he hadn't been referring to his personal hardships and losing Audleigh. Kingston was starting to realize that it was going to be up to him to steer the conversation to the expedition, the two murders, and the Chinese bowls. He watched Graves take another long sip of whisky, placing the glass on the table with a shaky hand. Rather than start questioning him about the murders, Kingston thought it would be easier on Graves if first he inquired about the bowls, to see where that led. Graves was about to speak when Kingston cut him off.

"May I ask where the forged Chinese ceramics fit into all of this, Spenser? The ones found at Jenkins's farm?" He tried to sound nonchalant.

The question didn't appear to faze Graves. It was almost as if he'd been expecting it. "Yes," he replied. "You'd know about those, of course, wouldn't you? Your working with the police." He shrugged. "There's not a chance in hell of our going back, so you might as well know."

Kingston wondered what he meant by "going back." He could only assume he meant back to China. He said nothing, waiting, while Graves had a brief coughing spell.

Graves drew a long breath, as if it was going to take a while to explain, then continued. "In order to answer your question, I must hark back to an expedition that took place a year *before* the last one." He leaned far into the wingback so that his face was partially concealed in shadow. The storm had now arrived in full force and windswept rain was spattering loudly on the leaded windows. The room had become quite dark, lit only by the dancing flames from the log fire. Somehow, China, snowcapped peaks, and plant-hunting expeditions seemed far removed, incongruous. Graves continued.

"Julian Bell was on that trip, too, as was David Jenkins. It also took place in the same region as last year's—not by accident, I might add. On that first expedition, we came across a small village temple in the mountains. You've been to those parts, Lawrence, you've probably seen them yourself."

Kingston nodded. "I have, yes. They're remarkable, very colorful."

"Well, late one afternoon, Julian and I took off from the rest of the party to visit the temple. As you know, I'm interested in Asian antiquities and Bell has a thing for Chinese architecture, or so he told me. The temple turned out to be little different from others in the region. Rustic would describe it, I suppose. The altar, not much more than a cloth-draped table, displayed the typical color statues, gold-painted figures, various plates, bowls, and other sacred offerings. You've seen the likes, I'm sure, Lawrence. I've never figured why they keep them so dark inside, though—all those curtains."

Kingston was wondering why Graves was taking so long to describe the scene, but he didn't interrupt; he sensed that Graves was leading up to something important. Graves continued.

"Behind the altar, off-bounds to worshippers and visitors, was another table. On it, the same clutter of statues and artifacts. From where we stood it was hard to determine exactly what they were. So, since we had the place to ourselves, I decided to risk going beyond the altar to get a closer look. I was about to leave when I spotted a small bowl, partially hidden by a small statue and a couple of those familiar yak-butter flower sculptures. I moved in closer. It was a blue-and-white palace bowl. At first I thought my eyes were playing tricks, but when I got close, lifting it down, carefully, so I could see the marks on the underside, I realized what I was holding. It was an extremely rare piece, more than five hundred years old. I'd read many articles and studied museum literature on Ming Dynasty bowls with this particular glaze and scrollwork, and knew that there were only a half dozen or so in the world. This one was in perfect condition. I remember my hands trembling as I held it. Conservatively, from what I'd read—if it was genuine, and everything told me that it was—I knew it was worth at least two million pounds. A priest arrived at that point and I hastily returned it to where it had been before he spotted us, moved away from the table, and we left."

A smoldering log fell onto the hearth. Graves got up slowly, using the blackened tongs to place it back on the fire, adding another log while he was at it. In moments he was back in his chair.

"Sure I can't get you something?" he asked.

Kingston shook his head. "I'll wait, thanks."

"So where were we?" Graves asked, pulling a handkerchief from his pocket and wiping his brow. "Right. Later, I told Julian Bell more about the bowl and what I thought it was worth. He was all for taking it, the next morning, before we left the area."

"Stealing it—from a temple?"

"I told him it was out of the question. I wanted no part of it. Not only that, but we'd been seen there and would be the first people the police would come looking for. On top of that, the bowl had no doubt rested in the temple for centuries without being recognized for what it was, or disturbed. If it were stolen at the same time that a group of foreign plant hunters was in the area, the jig would be up, as they say." Graves paused and rubbed his eyes. The room was getting smoky. He picked up where he'd left off. "It wasn't until after the expedition, when we were back in England, that Julian came up with what I thought was a brilliant idea—a way to get our hands on the bowl. I must say that the scheme was so damned ingenious that it would be doubtful the bowl's loss would ever be noticed. So much so that we would be able to sell it, most likely to a private collector, and nobody would be the wiser."

Listening to Graves, Kingston was thinking that he'd been right in assuming that plain and simple forgery wasn't the reason for the bowls in Jenkins's barn. But for the life of him, he couldn't guess where Graves was going with this. Whatever their scheme was, surely it had to amount to larceny—a serious crime. Kingston reflected on how often people managed somehow to rationalize actions that they knew to be illegal, unethical, or just plain wrong—as was clearly the case with the activities Graves was describing. His thoughts were interrupted by Graves, who seemed to be getting a certain amount of satisfaction in telling the story.

"You're wondering how we planned to pull this off, eh? It was simple, really, but I must admit it took an inordinate amount of planning and presented a lot of physical and logistical challenges. There was no need to rush, though. We had practically a year to work it all out. You see, the bowls you found at Jenkins's place— the damned fool swore he'd destroyed them—were all prototypes. They were part of a lengthy process to create as close a replica as possible to the bowl in the temple."

"Just one?"

"Right. Let me explain why: On this last expedition, Bell returned to the temple. Not to visit but to observe when it opened and closed, when the priests, the cleaners, and the villagers came and went. He was looking for a narrow window of time when we could slip in unnoticed and remain there undisturbed for no more than ten minutes. He established a time that would suit our purposes, and the next day he and I returned to the temple. We waited outside until we were certain it was empty, and then we entered. We discovered later that many of the temples remain unlocked late into evening." Graves broke off briefly to polish off the remainder of his drink.

"Once inside, we had to move quickly. We had a rucksack containing two jars of silicone compound to make the molds, and two small custom-made boxes to house them. The stuff reproduces the minutest detail, even a fingerprint. We had other equipment, of course. A digital camera, a battery powered lamp, scales, micrometer, color-matching kit, and other bits and pieces: everything needed to make a perfect mold and ultimately an exact replica of the bowl. Which is what we did. It took longer than we'd anticipated, though. In fact, Bell had to sneak in the next day to take the photos. When we got back to England, it was more than six months before we finally produced a copy that was so close to the original as to be almost indistinguishable. Switched with the one in the temple—which had probably sat there for

God knows how many years, maybe centuries—nobody would ever notice the difference, even if it were taken down and closely examined."

"Very ingenious. Where did Jenkins fit into all this?"

"He knew a lot about ceramics and found the man to make it. We couldn't use any old potter, for obvious reasons. First and foremost, we needed someone with exceptional skill, a person we could trust. As you know, Cornwall and Devon are crawling with artists of all kinds, plenty of them making high-quality ceramics. It didn't take David long to find just the right man, a chap in his late seventies who'd been working with China clay for the best part of his life. He was a widower who worked out of his house on the edge of Bodmin Moor. We offered him more money than he'd earned in his last five years working, and he swore to secrecy."

Kingston was impressed with the cleverness of it all, but his respect for Graves had plummeted. "So where's the bowl now?" he asked.

"In a safety-deposit box."

"Ready for your next trip when you switch them?"

"Which will never happen now, of course."

"Do you know who killed David Jenkins?"

"It wasn't me. I was here, at Audleigh. You can ask Inspector Sheffield."

"Why was he killed?"

"That I can't tell."

By "can't tell," did Graves mean that he didn't know or wouldn't say? Kingston wondered.

"And what about the other chap? Jeremy Lester?"

"Same thing."

"Did Lester find out what you and Bell were up to and threaten to expose you? Maybe blackmail you?"

Graves didn't answer. Instead, he stood, picked up his glass, and crossed the room to a butler's table where he poured a generous measure of Johnnie Walker Green Label into his glass, adding barely a splash of water. "How about a Schweppes? Something like that?" he asked, looking across at Kingston.

Kingston nodded. "That would be fine."

In half a minute Graves was back with the drinks and settled in his chair.

Kingston sipped his soda and looked at Graves. "Spenser, I hate to say this, but it looks like this has been a waste of my time. Frankly, I came here hoping, mostly, to learn about the murders of Lester and Jenkins. It's obvious you know a lot more than you're prepared to discuss. You know damned well that I'm more or less duty bound to tell the police what you've told me. That means they'll know that you've admitted to being implicated in a scheme involving grand theft."

"No crime has been committed."

"I'm not so sure about that."

"Is it a crime to replicate an antique bowl?"

"It damned well is, if you plan to palm it off as the original."

"But we haven't done that. Can they prove intent?"

Kingston shook his head in exasperation. "So why, for God's sake, ask me all the way up here, Spenser? There must be more than what you've been telling me for the last ten minutes."

Graves took a longer than usual draft of his whisky, drying his lips with the back of his hand, then leveling his now bloodshot eyes at Kingston. "I don't expect you to understand fully, Lawrence. Putting it as simply as I can, I suppose it's about vanity as much as anything else. Saving face, if you will. I fear it's only a matter of time now when all this will come to a head. Every newspaper in the country, TV, the Internet, you name it will have a feeding frenzy. The names Spenser Graves and Audleigh Hall will be on everyone's lips. The reporters and journalists will hound me, Alexandra, her friends, and our staff without mercy. It'll be sheer hell."

"How can you prevent it? If, as you've suggested, you're innocent of some of the charges, why not say so? You must tell the police everything you know—everything. Let them decide the degree of guilt. You have no other choice."

"It really doesn't matter anymore, Lawrence. However, I'm not the person who concerns me the most in all this mess. I'm finished. I don't give a sod now. It's Alexandra. The humiliation, the thought of disgracing her, making her suffer for the rest of her life, because of my actions and stupidity, is more than I can bear." He paused, his eyes never leaving Kingston's.

Kingston was starting to feel sorry for the man. "Why did you ask me here, Spenser?"

"You're right to ask the question. I thought long and hard about asking you in the first place. What purpose would it serve? Simply put, there is no one else. Sad to say, I no longer have any close friends—never did, really—only acquaintances. And, other than Alexandra, I have no family. You're no doubt aware of my reputation, Lawrence. The reclusive Spenser Graves. The eccentric—" He held up a hand. "Well, you know what I'm talking about. Not all of it's true, of course, but much of it has come about deservedly by my choosing to live a private life." He gave a wan smile. "The French have a saying: *'Pour vivre heureux, vivons cachés*—to live happily, live hidden.'" He looked away briefly, then sighed. "Anyway, I picked you to unload on."

Kingston waited before answering. "I don't know what to say. I should be flattered, I suppose."

"Flattered be damned. I had to get it off my chest. You know as much about this wretched affair as anyone. I believe you're a decent sort, you're good with words, and I trust you."

"Why don't you confess all of this to your daughter? She's the one who's going to be hurt the most."

Graves pursed his lips and shook his head. "I couldn't do it, Lawrence. You can call it cowardly or whatever you want, but I just couldn't look her in the eye and tell her how badly I've failed her. There would be too many questions that I wouldn't have the courage to answer with honesty."

"If you did, what exactly would you tell her?"

He gave the question a moment's thought. "Simply, that from the start, my only motive was to save Audleigh—pure and simple. With Bell's scheme to obtain the Chinese bowl, I'd found a way to get the money to do that. The scheme was so simple as to be almost foolproof, and the risk was negligible. It wouldn't settle the debt entirely but, with principal and interest, there would be enough to keep the estate going for quite a few years—probably for the rest of my life, anyway. I thought about it a long time. If you exclude nicking a box of pencils from a shop when I was about ten, I've never committed a crime of any sort in my life. Bell was persuasive, though. As long as the replica remained undiscovered in the temple—and the odds were overwhelming that it would— there was virtually no way the theft could be discovered. Maybe there's no such thing, but this was about as close as you could get to the perfect crime. We—that is, Bell and I—could have had no idea how wrong it could all turn out."

A lengthy pause followed, as Graves took another gulp of scotch. Kingston was amazed that the man wasn't plastered by now.

"Are you saying that you want me to tell the police all this?"

Graves put his hand over his mouth, pondering Kingston's question. He took it down and sighed despairingly. "You can tell them everything, Lawrence. It doesn't matter anymore."

Graves stood, and so did Kingston. They shook hands, Graves holding on to Kingston's longer than Kingston felt necessary. "As you wish," said Kingston, turning and heading to the door. "I'll call you in a day or so. Perhaps you should get some rest, old chap."

Graves looked unsteady, propping himself up on the back of the chair. "I will," he said. "Don't worry about me, Lawrence. Just be on your way."

The wind had died down, but it was still raining. Kingston stood in the shelter of the porch for a moment, taking his umbrella from his pocket and trying to open it. The button was stuck, and it took a half minute or so of jiggling before he managed to get it open.

He set off along the path back to his car, thinking about Graves and what would happen now. It hadn't been a complete waste of time. At least part of the mystery was solved. Then another thought struck him. How could he have been so blind?

That was when he heard it: the unmistakable *crack* of a gunshot. For a moment he thought it might be someone hunting rabbits. It wasn't and he knew it. From his army experience, he knew it was the report of a pistol. Then it dawned on him what it meant and how it confirmed his premonition of moments earlier. He turned and ran back to the cottage.

The door was unlocked. He walked in, his heart palpitating at the thought of what he would find. It didn't take long. Taking a few strides across the room, he rounded the wingback that Graves had been sitting in. Kingston stopped and stared. Graves was in the chair. He was slumped sideways, blood seeping into the fabric of the chair, forming a dark patch. The blackened entry wound in his temple was small. Kingston was glad he couldn't see where it had exited. The empty whisky glass was on the table, and a small handgun was on the carpet a few feet away. Now he knew why Graves had been drinking so heavily.

Kingston picked up the old-fashioned phone on a sideboard and dialed 999.

TWENTY-TWO

Kingston walked to the door for some fresh air. The room was dark and smoky, and the sight of Graves's dead body had unnerved him. He wished that he could leave right then. He stood on the porch staring absently at the perennial garden, the usually bright colors softened by the gentle rain. Minutes ago he had been talking with Graves and now he was dead. It was the strangest feeling, one that Kingston, in his many years, had never before experienced. While he and Graves hadn't been friends in any sense of the word, and Graves was an avowed criminal, almost certainly implicated in the deaths of Lester and Jenkins, and maybe the Chinese man—he'd forgotten to ask Graves about that incident—it did nothing to mollify the shock and despondency he was now experiencing.

Once again, the series of events surrounding the plant-hunting expedition had taken another unexpected and tragic turn. Despite his trying to dismiss the idea as frivolous, he couldn't help thinking of Agatha Christie's *Ten Little Indians*. Of the six people who were on the expedition, only two were still alive. And with one of those out of the country, virtually free of suspicion, that left only one suspect: Julian Bell.

He went back inside the house to the butler's table, being careful not to look at the body. He poured himself a whisky with a splash of water and carried it to a chair that was facing away from the fireplace. He sat down, took a long drink, and waited for the police and paramedics.

The anticipated call from Sheffield came early the next morning. It had been almost eight o'clock by the time Kingston had got back to his flat the night before, tired, hungry, and emotionally drained. He hadn't bothered to call Sheffield then, knowing that he would have to leave a message and that word of Graves's suicide would soon reach the inspector anyway.

"I got the report this morning from our blokes in Leicestershire," said Sheffield. "Rotten business. Might I ask what you were doing there, Doctor? Seems of late that every time someone is killed, you're Johnny-on-the-spot."

"It was at the invitation of Graves. He wrote, asking that I go up to see him. He wanted to explain his 'predicament,' as he called it. Wanted to get some things off his chest. He asked that I come alone."

"I see."

"I had no idea what he had in mind. There was nothing in the letter to even remotely suggest that he was going to take his life."

"So what did you two talk about?"

Kingston told Sheffield the substance of his conversation with Graves. How Graves had openly confessed to his financial problems and the impending demise of Audleigh Hall. That he had all but admitted to being implicated in, but not having committed, the murders of Lester and Jenkins. Following that, Kingston gave a much-abbreviated version of the scheme that Bell and Graves had hatched to steal the bowl from the temple. The conspiracy involving the ceramics seemed to intrigue Sheffield as much as, or more than, the more serious crimes.

After Kingston described Graves's last moments, Sheffield remained silent for a long moment.

"Looks like we're going to have to have another word with Mr. Bell," he said. "With his alibi, he's off the hook as far as Jenkins's murder is concerned, but from everything Graves told you, we can bring him in on a grand theft charge. We need to talk to him again about Jeremy Lester's death."

"Can he be charged with conspiracy, where the theft of the bowl is concerned?"

"He can. Even if the act is never carried out, it's still a crime. The Fraud Squad will probably be involved. Let's not forget the Chinese authorities. They'll want to press charges, too. There's also the unsolved death of the Chinese villager."

"I'm sure the temple will be pleased to know that their bowl is a priceless museum piece, too."

"They'll be told about it, don't worry. One thing's for sure, it won't remain in the temple for a minute longer."

"The sixty-four-thousand-dollar question is, if neither Graves nor Bell killed Lester or Jenkins, who did?"

"Someone they knew? Someone they paid? I don't know."

"The American chap? Is he crossed off your list?"

"According to the FBI, he's remained in the States all this time. Like I said before, there's no record of his having left the country since he returned from the expedition last year. At least, not under his own name."

Now was as good a time as any, thought Kingston. "Would you have any objection if I were to talk with him, Inspector? He may

202 • Anthony Eglin

be innocent, but maybe he could tell us something that we don't know. He organized the expedition."

A long pause followed. "I don't think that's a good idea, Doctor, at least, not for now. Let me think about it."

Kingston tried not to sound disgruntled. "I suppose there's always the outside chance that when Bell learns about Graves, and is told that Graves has implicated him in the theft, maybe he'll break down and tell his side of the story. That's about our last hope, I guess."

"We'll see, Doctor. By the way, we'll probably need you to make a full statement detailing your conversation with Graves. If we do, I'll let you know as soon as possible."

Next morning, all of Britain learned about Graves's suicide. The story was banner headlines on the front pages of the newspapers, given top billing on TV and radio newscasts, and on the Internet. Kingston was surprised at the amount and depth of the coverage. While Spenser Graves was not exactly a household name, he was sufficiently recognized, apparently, as one of the country's foremost horticulturists and antiques collectors and, of course, the somewhat idiosyncratic owner of Audleigh Hall, one of the leading jewels in the crown of England's stately homes. The reports were all positive, making him out to be one of a dying breed: a philanthropist of sorts, modern-day adventurer, horticulturist, and pillar of the Leicestershire community. Most of the stories cited overwhelming financial difficulties as the reason for his suicide, and many mentioned the tragedies that had befallen his last expedition.

The following afternoon, Kingston was surprised to get another call from Inspector Sheffield.

"Glad I caught you home, Doctor. We've got a new development."

"Really?"

"We went down to Dorset this morning with a warrant to pick up Bell for questioning. According to his housekeeper, he'd packed a couple of bags yesterday and left in rather a hurry. No explanation other than that he was just going away for a while. Not like him at all, she said. Looks like our Mr. Bell has done a runner. So you be careful how you tread from now on. He could be dangerous."

TWENTY-THREE

Graves's funeral was held one week to the day after his death. Kingston had decided to attend, more out of deference to Alexandra than to her father. The service was held in St. Anne's, a small church in the same parish as that of Audleigh Hall. Spenser would become the first of the fourth generation of Graveses to be interred in the churchyard. When Kingston arrived, he was guided into a field adjacent to the church used for overflow parking. The skies were sullen gray to the horizon. Mournfully appropriate, thought Kingston, but at least it wasn't drizzling.

Entering the church to the solemn cadence of an organ, Kingston took one of the remaining seats in the last pew. He was happy to be in the back of the nave, where he could see and not be seen. He sat next to a large lady wearing a floppy hat who had overdosed on Chanel. He prayed it would be a brief service. Watching the vicar approach the altar, he spotted a woman whom he assumed to be Alexandra, in the front pew. Driving up, he had wondered if there were others he would recognize at the service. He could come up only with Hobbs, the majordomo, and—most unlikely—Julian Bell.

The service was mercifully short. As the somber-faced mourners slowly inched along the aisle, exiting the church, Kingston had the opportunity to scan their faces. Alexandra and Hobbs were the only two people he recognized. Outside, as is often the case, the mood among the gathering was more convivial. Kingston spotted Alexandra in the midst of a group on the edge of the crowd and made his way over. She saw him and, to his surprise, recognized him immediately.

"Thank you for coming all the way from London, Doctor," she said with a trace of a smile.

He returned her smile, sympathy in his blue eyes. "Your father would be very upset were he to learn that I hadn't," he replied, hoping the light touch didn't come off as facetious.

"He would, I'm sure," she replied.

"I came for you, too, of course. I wish we'd had the opportunity to get to know each other sooner."

"You were with him when he died, I understand."

Kingston nodded. "I was, yes." He wondered if he should change the topic, for her sake more than his. "I didn't know your father that well, Alexandra," he said. "It was only recently that we renewed our acquaintance—through Asian art, actually. He might have told you that I came up for the exhibit."

"He did, yes. He said he wished he'd had more time to spend with you on that occasion." She went on to introduce the tall dark-haired man at her side as William, her fiancé, afterward introducing the rest of the small group. They chatted for another minute or so, and gradually the crowd started to disperse.

Kingston held Alexandra's hand briefly. "Well, goodbye, and do please keep in touch. You know where to find me."

"I will, Doctor. That's a promise." She paused, brushing a stray hair from her eyes. "There is one thing I'd like to ask."

"Yes?"

"Would you come up to Audleigh sometime in the next few days? I'd like to hear what you and my father spoke about that day at the cottage." Her voice faltered. "These last days have been difficult for all of us."

"I can understand," Kingston said softly.

"All I know, so far, is what the police have told me."

"Nothing would please me better. He would've wanted me to do that."

"Please call me and we'll set a date."

"I will," he replied with a nod and a quick smile.

Kingston, Andrew, and Desmond Scott were having an early dinner at the Antelope. It was more than two months since Kingston had last seen Desmond, who lived in St. Albans, about a forty-five-minute drive from Chelsea. Two years ago, Desmond had helped Kingston identify an Amazon lily hybrid that was central to a murder case—a water lily capable of desalinating salt water. Kingston had come close to losing his life because of it.

The three had just returned from Desmond's water-plant nursery in Finchley. The visit had inspired Andrew to install a water feature in his country garden. Desmond, who was meeting Andrew for the first time, had offered to donate the labor, charging only for materials, plants, and fish. Talk of koi, mosquito fish, flathead minnows, and water plants ended when the dinner plates arrived.

The waiter had whisked away the empty celebratory bottle of Veuve Clicquot, and they were now drinking an Italian red—in Desmond's case, a beer—with their steak and ale pie. Kingston knew that it was only a matter of time before the question of his involvement in the plant-hunting murder case, and Graves's suicide, was raised. He wouldn't mention it, of course, for several reasons. First, he knew that it would take the rest of the evening to fully explain; second, he was tired of thinking and talking about it; and last, because Desmond would have a right old time winding him up about his "Holmes" complex. It mattered little, because Kingston knew damned well that, sooner or later, Andrew would bring it up. Not a minute later he did.

"Lawrence, tell Desmond about the plant-hunting murders," he said blithely.

Kingston sighed. "Do I really have to? You've read all about it in the papers, for God's sake."

"Unless you want to pick up the tab, you do," said Desmond, grinning.

Kingston took a long sip of wine and started from the beginning, when he had received the first phone call from Clifford Attenborough at Kew.

Pretty soon, the first bottle of wine was empty, and Andrew had ordered another. Two glasses later, with few interruptions, Kingston was still at it. Finally, over coffee, he finished, telling them about his last call from Inspector Sheffield, warning him to be careful from now on.

Desmond looked at Kingston, shaking his head slowly. "Bloody hell! You're barmy, Lawrence. I can't for the life of me understand how or why you get involved in these bloody . . . misadventures. Last time, it almost cost you your life. Won't you ever learn?"

Kingston smiled. "Thanks for the compliment, Desmond. I thought I'd made it clear that this all came about as a result of my volunteering to help an old chum at Kew. This time I've tried to keep my nose out of it as much as possible. One can't change the natural course of events, dear boy."

After a brief silence, Desmond spoke again. "What about this Bell fellow? How well do you know him, Lawrence?"

"Hardly at all. Are you asking me if I think he's responsible for the murders?"

"Not necessarily. I was just wondering if, in your judgment, he seemed the type."

"The mild-mannered Dr. Crippen seemed hardly the type to chop up his wife," Kingston replied. "As far as Bell is concerned, we know for sure that he was up to his ears in the scheme to steal the Chinese bowl—in fact, he was the architect. As to the murders, the police say he had cast-iron alibis in the case of Lester and Jenkins. So no. To all appearances he didn't commit the crimes personally. That doesn't mean that he didn't have a hand in them."

"What about the poor sod in China?" Andrew asked. "Bell and Graves were involved in his death, wouldn't you say?"

"I would," Kingston replied. "The most plausible explanation is that he saw Graves and Bell handling the bowl in the temple and followed them, demanding to know what was going on. Maybe he thought they'd stolen it. Why it became necessary to kill him, I have no idea."

"So, let's get this straight," said Desmond. "Graves and Bell might've planned the murders but didn't commit them. The only other person on the expedition now alive is the American. But he wasn't in England when they happened, you said."

"That's right. I'm only going on what the police told me. Unfortunately, they don't like the idea of my talking to Kavanagh."

"Then that leaves who?" Andrew held up his hand, placing the index finger of his right hand on the tip of the little finger of his left, ready to count. "Let's see, the only other people you've mentioned, Lawrence, are Sally Mayhew, Graves's houseman, and—" He looked down momentarily at the table, then back to Kingston. "There is no one else. Just those two, right?"

Kingston nodded.

Desmond continued. "What about Sally Mayhew? What if she had information proving that Jeremy Lester was responsible for her brother's death? That would certainly be motive for wanting to kill him, wouldn't it?"

"She worked for a pharmaceutical company, too," Andrew interjected. "You know—drugs, right?"

Kingston found himself smiling. He looked at Andrew. "I know you're going to say that I'm a lousy judge of women, but I had lunch with her. In my mind, she's the very last person to be party to a crime, let alone commit murder. Besides, she's an accountant, not a bloody pharmacist. And what about Jenkins? You think she killed him, too?"

The waitress arrived with the bill on a tray. Kingston grabbed it before the others could reach it. "Maybe I can write this off as a business expense," he said, smiling.

"Shady business," Andrew quipped.

Kingston pushed aside the tray and downed the last of his wine.

"So, you had lunch with Sally Mayhew. You sly old dog you. Can we read something into that?"

Kingston smiled. "Anything you like, Andrew, except wedding bells. If she sticks around, I may even invite her out again. She's very nice, and not at all unattractive, I might add."

Andrew frowned. "Sticks around?"

Kingston grinned. "I forgot to mention. She may be leaving the country."

Andrew shook his head and sighed. "I knew it was too good to be true."

Desmond took over the conversation again. Evidently he was not ready to give up so easily on the murders. "All right, Lawrence," he said. "If we discount Sally Mayhew, that leaves, what's his name—?"

"Hobbs," said Kingston.

"Does he have a first name?" asked Desmond.

"They never use them though, do they, those types? Like Sherlock Holmes's Watson," said Andrew. "Never did know his first name."

"It was John," said Kingston. "Hobbs's is Arthur."

"This Hobbs," said Desmond. "You said he had an alibi, too?"

"That's correct. Inspector Sheffield assured me that on the day Jenkins was murdered, Hobbs was at Audleigh Hall—all weekend, in fact. Graves confirmed that, and so did two staff members."

"What about Lester's death? Did he have an alibi for that, too?"

"According to the police, he did, yes."

"So there are no suspects. Is that what you're saying?" asked Desmond.

Kingston pulled on his ear. "That would appear to be the case."

There was a lengthy silence, as the implausibility of Kingston's last remark sunk in. Then Desmond spoke again.

"There's only one other possible explanation for all this, then."

Kingston had a pretty good idea where Desmond was going— he hadn't overlooked it, either—but said nothing.

"Which is?" Andrew asked.

Desmond looked at Kingston. "You said that Peter Mayhew's body was never recovered, right?"

"Whoa!" Andrew exclaimed. "You're suggesting that he fell hundreds of feet into a ravine, with a river and rapids below, miraculously survived, climbed to safety, made his way back to England, unnoticed, then carried out the murders?" He paused. "And why? What's his motive?"

Desmond scratched his head. "I know it's bloody far-fetched, but do you have any other ideas?"

"I don't," said Kingston, smiling. "My exceptional powers of deductive reasoning seem to have failed me this time."

TWENTY-FOUR

L et me tell you, as close as I can recall, what your father and I spoke about that day at the cottage," said Kingston. It was a week after the funeral, and he was seated across from Alexandra Graves in the same gracious living room where he and Spenser Graves had met on his first visit to Audleigh Hall. Neither her expression nor her body language betrayed the anguish or nervousness she must have been holding back. He had declined her offer of tea or a drink, and had settled into his chair.

"First, your father wanted you to understand why he couldn't bring himself to tell you all this face-to-face. I'm by no means qualified to judge his state of mind but, on that day, it would've been clear to anyone that he was emotionally unstable, guilt ridden, and deathly afraid. The problems facing him had become insurmountable and, in his mind, were beyond solving." He paused, allowing her time, should she want to comment or ask a question. She nodded briefly, as if to say, "Go on," so he continued.

"He said he loved you, Alexandra. 'More dearly than I can ever express' were his actual words. He also begged your forgiveness for what he has done, for bringing such unpardonable disgrace to his family and friends. He knew it would be the end of him, and Audleigh. He was man enough to accept full responsibility, though."

Alexandra looked at him with a rueful smile. "I appreciate your doing this, Lawrence. I know it's not easy for you, either. Please continue. There's no point in holding anything back. I'm going to learn about it sooner or later. I'd like to know everything, please."

Kingston was encouraged by her candor and sangfroid. He was thinking that his earlier impressions had been right. Considering the grim circumstances—and the fact that he was hardly a family friend—she was showing remarkable composure and forbearance. It was going to make his task much easier.

"Go on, then," she said, jogging him from his momentary thought, looking at him with unwavering gray eyes.

It took almost twenty minutes for Kingston to recount the events of that day and the admissions and intimacies that Spenser Graves had unburdened on him. All that time, Alexandra had sat still, fixed on every word he said with hardly an interruption. Only once, when he was attempting to summarize her father's words without making them sound too taxing, had she turned away briefly to brush a tear from her eye. He wanted to get up and embrace her, to comfort her, but that was the last thing she would expect or want of him.

"Well, Alexandra, that's the best of my recollection," said Kingston, leaning back.

"Thank you, Lawrence," she said, softly. "Thank you for being so considerate and forthright." She paused, as if choosing her words. "You've been of great help in making me understand... try to understand why my father chose to do what he did. Though it may sound selfish, I still can't dispel from my mind the thought of walking down the aisle without him."

"I have a daughter about your age. She's still single, but I know that if and when the time comes for her to marry, that day will be one of the proudest moments of my life. So, in a small way, I can understand how heartbreaking it must be for you."

She tried to smile. "You're a very understanding man, and for that I'm thankful."

"Tell me about your wedding plans," said Kingston, sensing that she would welcome talking about it. She told him about William and the ceremony and reception, which was to take place in a villa outside Paris. She went on to tell Kingston that where Audleigh was concerned, she had already had one meeting with the family solicitor and their accountant, who were recommending cost-saving measures, which included staff cuts. "That's going to be awfully hard, both for the help and for me," she said. "Some of them have been on the payroll for years. Adam, one of the gardeners, has been here forever, it seems. When I was small he would take me for rides around the garden in his wheelbarrow." She smiled at the memory. "On the bright side, all of them were provided for in the will. And I must say, considering the sad state of things, Daddy was unusually generous."

"Better they have it than the banks," said Kingston. While they were on the subject of the staff, he figured now was as good a time as any to mention Hobbs. "Before I leave, I'd like to have a quick word with Hobbs, if I may?"

"Unfortunately, he's already left."

"He *has?*"

"Yes. He said that, with Father gone, he felt that his services were no longer needed, and that he wanted to move back to London, where he had friends and family."

"That's too bad. Perhaps best for you, though, considering."

There was no point in telling her that he was disappointed; that he had hoped to have a word with Hobbs about Graves's activities.

"Actually, there were things that your father wanted me to tell Hobbs," he fibbed. "Mostly along the lines of how much he appreciated his loyalty and good service over the many years, that sort of thing."

"Perhaps you could write to him. He left a temporary forwarding address. I'll be writing to him later, of course."

Kingston nodded. "Yes, I'll do that."

"Well," she said, standing, "why don't we go into the conservatory? Mrs. Coggins should have lunch ready by now."

"Mrs. Coggins? Your cook, I take it?"

She nodded.

He remembered now Sheffield's telling him that she had vouched for Graves—and Hobbs, too—attesting that both were at Audleigh the weekend Jenkins was murdered.

"Perhaps I could have a word with her before I leave?"

"I don't see why not," she replied, frowning. "May I ask why?"

Kingston had anticipated the question. The last thing he wanted was to give her the impression that he was still carrying out an investigation on the side. He smiled self-consciously, even though he knew his little fib would go unnoticed. "When I last had lunch with your father, Mrs. Coggins served salmon in pastry. It had a rather curious sweet ginger filling. I wanted to ask what the ingredients were. I was thinking of having a go at making it myself sometime."

Alexandra smiled. "A bachelor professor of botany, a plant hunter, and a cook, too. I'm impressed."

The lunch was as good as, or even better than the one he'd had with Graves—more reason to chat with Mrs. Coggins, to compliment her.

Afterward, Alexandra led Kingston to the kitchen, where she introduced a beaming Mrs. Coggins.

"A pleasure to meet you, Mrs. Coggins," said Kingston. "I can't tell you how much I enjoyed your lunch. I should be so lucky to have such a first-rate chef."

"Maud, please," she insisted, clearly embarrassed by the praise.

Alexandra departed, leaving Maud and Kingston seated at a ten-foot-long harvest table. Kingston went on to say that he cooked frequently himself—one of his hobbies, in fact—but he wasn't up to her standards by any means.

Maud, still smiling, thanked him.

"I won't keep you long," he promised. "It's about the visit that you had with the Leicestershire policeman when he was here making inquiries."

"Oh yes, I remember him well. A nice man—awfully young, though."

"If I'm correct, I believe you told him that Mr. Graves was at Audleigh the weekend in question, the one that the inspector was curious about."

"I did, that's right. It was the same weekend as our village fete. I always enter a few baked things. Mr. Graves came to the fete, too. He was one of its biggest supporters."

"I believe you said that was also true of Hobbs. That he was also here that weekend, I mean."

"Yes, Arthur was here."

"You're sure?"

She nodded without hesitating. "I am. He was under the weather that weekend. Spent most of it in bed. It was unusual for him. He was one of those people who are hardly ever sick. Touch of the flu, I figured."

"You saw him, then?"

She looked at him quizzically. "Well, yes, of course. I took some soup up to him. Saturday, I believe it was. He was in bed, fast asleep, or so I thought."

Kingston frowned. "So you thought?"

"Turned out he was just dozing and had heard me come in. He asked me to leave it on the nightstand, which is what I did."

"Did you see him again that weekend?"

"I might have done, though I couldn't swear to it. I know that one afternoon he came down to the kitchen to get some tea, but that could've been Sunday."

"Well, thanks, Maud. You've been most helpful," said Kingston, getting up from the table.

She stood also and smiled. "Hope I was of help."

"You were." Kingston snapped his fingers noiselessly. "Oh, there was one other thing."

"Yes?"

"Did Hobbs own a motorbike?"

Maud thought for a moment. "Not that I'm aware. At least, I've never seen him on one."

"Thanks, Maud." He then asked her about the salmon dish.

A few minutes later, they shook hands, and Kingston, with the scribbled recipe in his pocket, left the room to say goodbye to Alexandra.

Kingston looked in his rearview mirror as the redbrick confection of Audleigh Hall disappeared behind the tall trees on either side of the drive. What would become of it? he wondered. Though sad for Alexandra, he was feeling particularly pleased. In his pocket was also a London address for Arthur Hobbs. It wasn't letter writing he had in mind, however. It was a personal visit. Figuring that the address was likely to be temporary, he'd best go as soon as possible. He now had a strong suspicion that Hobbs was up to his neck in the whole business.

TWENTY-FIVE

Next morning, Kingston exited Stamford Brook tube station and set off up Goldhawk Road, heading for 25 Evelyn Close, the address Alexandra had given him. Hobbs hadn't left a phone number, which Kingston didn't think unusual. He was most likely renting, and before leaving Audleigh probably wouldn't have had one to give.

In less than ten minutes, Kingston had reached the quiet residential street and number 25. The house was typical of thousands that populated London's neighborhoods: a two-story terraced Victorian, redbrick with lace-curtained bay windows, and a low brick wall separating it from the pavement. Kingston opened the spindly wrought-iron gate, took four paces to the shiny red door, and pressed the brass doorbell.

After waiting for what must have been a minute or so, he rang the bell again. He heard it ringing inside. He was beginning to think that his trip might have been wasted, when the door was opened by a man holding a folded newspaper. He was medium height with disheveled graying hair and stubble on his chin. "Can I 'elp you?" he asked.

"I was told I could find Arthur Hobbs here."

"You were, were you?"

Kingston felt uneasy. The man wasn't hostile, but he certainly wasn't overly friendly. "Yes. I was told by his former employer's daughter, Alexandra Graves, that he might be here."

The man looked at him for a moment, sizing him up. "What's it about?" he said gruffly.

"Alexandra's father committed suicide recently. I was with him that day, and he told me things that he wanted me to pass on to Mr. Hobbs. Is he here?"

"He may be, I don't know. What's your name?"

"Kingston. Dr. Kingston."

The man pushed the door to, not quite closing it. "Wait here," he said.

A few seconds passed, then, through the crack in the door, he heard an exchange of voices inside. In short order, the man was back, opening the door again. With a nod over his shoulder, he said, "Come on in."

Inside, the lace curtains were drawn, and though it was sunny outside, the interior was gloomy. Kingston was starting to wonder what he was getting himself into. He was beginning to wish he'd asked Andrew to accompany him, something that he'd considered. He entered a small living room, Mr. Talkative following. The space was untidy and sparsely furnished. In a corner by the window, a small television was on but with no sound. An open beer can sat on the coffee table. The place was musty and stank of cigarettes.

The man said nothing. He stood by the window silently watching Kingston, presumably waiting for Hobbs. Kingston wondered if he should sit, but seeing the clutter of magazines and newspapers on the couch, and the clothes draped over the back of the only easy chair, he decided to stand and wait.

"Dr. Kingston."

The voice came from behind. Hobbs had entered from the stairway that led upstairs. Kingston turned to face him. At first he didn't recognize Hobbs. For one thing, he wasn't wearing glasses, and he was dressed in a leather jacket, gray silk shirt, and black slacks, a far cry from the ill-fitting houseman's jacket he'd worn at Audleigh. His hair was cropped, making him look younger than Kingston remembered. A carry-on bag hung from his shoulder. By the looks of it, he was about to leave.

"It wasn't a good idea, coming here, Doctor," he said, shaking his head slowly. "Not a good idea at all."

Kingston ignored the remark. "Since it looks like you're leaving," he said, "I'll make it brief. I was at Audleigh when your employer, Spenser Graves, killed himself. But then, you would know that, wouldn't you?"

Both men stood silent and expressionless, looking at him. Kingston was starting to feel uneasy. "He wanted me to tell you how much he appreciated all the things you'd done for him." As he was talking, Kingston realized how lame the words sounded, what a pitiful excuse it was for his arriving unannounced on Hobbs's doorstep. His mind was racing, trying to come up with something, anything, that would sound more convincing, to get Hobbs's attention.

"I pegged you as trouble right from the beginning," Hobbs sneered. "Wandering around the halls, eavesdropping, asking a lot of questions. Still working for the police?"

"I'm not, no."

"Then what did you hope to achieve by coming here?"

"Just as I said. To tell you that your boss wanted to thank you, and tell you that he was sorry for what he'd done."

"You expect me to believe that rubbish?" he said, eyes narrowing. "I should deal with you right here and now."

He looked across the room to the other man, then back to Kingston.

"But I'm not going to—not yet, anyway. We'll have to save that for later. In the meantime, you'll be in Ben's care."

What exactly did that mean? Kingston wondered, as Hobbs crossed the room to Ben. A few whispered words passed between them; then, with a light pat on Ben's shoulder, Hobbs left the room. The front door slammed loudly and Kingston caught a glimpse of him through the lace curtains, heading down the street.

Kingston looked at Ben, who had now moved closer. "Do you know what your friend has done?" he asked.

"Friend? You mean brother."

Only then did Kingston realize the resemblance. Same height, not many years separating them in age—two or three at most. If anything Ben was a little heavier. The beer, maybe, he thought.

Kingston was thinking quickly. It was all starting to make sense. The fragmented pieces that he'd been trying so hard to fit together all these weeks were suddenly falling into place. Coming to the house hadn't been a waste of time, after all. To the contrary. He now knew—or was almost certain—how one of the murders had taken place. He had to get out of the house and go after Hobbs. And he had to do it quickly or, like Julian Bell, Hobbs was going to do a disappearing act. He started toward the door.

In the narrow entry hall, Ben blocked his way. No more than two paces apart, they stood facing each other, one waiting for the other to make the first move. Kingston was taller by a good three or four inches, but Ben was a few years younger and looked like he could handle himself in a fight.

"Get out of my way," said Kingston calmly.

"Didn't you understand what Art said, you big git? You're going to stay here, with *me*," he snarled, stabbing a finger at Kingston.

Kingston stood still, not wanting to give Ben the slightest provocation or indication that he was prepared to put up a fight.

He needed to buy time, to figure a way of escape by some other means. "How much did they pay you?" he asked evenly.

"I dunno what you're talking about."

Keep asking questions, Kingston said to himself. "You're trying to tell me you don't know what your brother's done?"

Ben's expression had become less contentious but his stance hadn't changed. He was still tense, hands at the ready should Kingston decide to make a move. He said nothing, simply glared.

Kingston faked a sneeze, allowing him to lower and turn his head toward the wall on his left for a few seconds. Within arm's reach was a hall stand. He hadn't noticed it coming in. Not surprising. It was hardly noteworthy, and obviously the piece of furniture one would expect in such a location. Made of dark oak, it had a long vertical beveled mirror, below which was a closed storage area covered by a hinged bench seat. The arched top cleared the ceiling by a foot, and sundry articles of clothing hung from its several hooks.

Kingston straightened and brought his eyes back to Ben's. As he did so, he stumbled and grabbed the curved arm of the bench. In the same motion, using all the force he could summon, he pulled the hall stand crashing down.

He leaped back as the top of the stand struck the opposite wall. Its top panel snapped off and cartwheeled down the hall. Immediately, the beveled mirror shattered. Ben reacted quickly, but not quickly enough. Seconds earlier, Kingston had gauged the man's position, knowing there was a good chance that at least a part of the hall stand would strike him—disable him just long enough to give Kingston time to clamber over the back of it and escape.

When the dust settled, it was the clothes as much as anything that had bought Kingston the time he needed. Ben was buried under a pile of raincoats, jackets, parkas, and scarves, plus the contents of the storage space. Kingston climbed over the heap and opened the front door. Just before slamming it behind him, he glanced back. He was sweating, covered in cobwebs and muck from the back of the hall stand, but couldn't help breaking a smile. Ben was still trying to disentangle himself from the shambles.

Kingston ran out of the house and down the street in the direction that Hobbs had taken, the same route that Kingston had taken to get to the house. There was always the chance that Hobbs would have a car, but, in London, Kingston figured the odds were against it. Not only that, but if Hobbs was doing a runner, a car would be a liability, too easy for the police to track and identify. That meant that wherever he was going, unless he could find a convenient taxi—rare on these quiet streets—he must travel by bus or the underground. Hobbs had about a minute's lead, and it was going to take a stroke of luck to catch up with him.

Still running, he'd reached the end of Evelyn Close, at the T junction. Turning right would take him back to Goldhawk Road and eventually the station. It seemed the only likely choice. If Hobbs had managed to hop on a bus, he would be long gone by now. Kingston was getting short of breath and slowed to a fast walk. Waiting for a pedestrian signal, breathing loudly, his heart thumping, a morbid thought crossed his mind. He'd never hear the last of it from Desmond and Andrew, let alone Sheffield, if he had a heart attack and ended up in the hospital. He quickly dismissed the thought and crossed on the green light. The Stamford Brook station was now only two blocks away.

He entered the station and, using his return ticket, passed through the automatic ticket barrier. He was reasonably familiar with the layout because Stamford Brook was only eight stops from Sloane Square, his local station. Both were on the District Line, and the station had only two platforms. The first was for westbound trains, heading out of London. The second platform was for eastbound trains, heading into central London, the West End, and, eventually, the East London suburbs.

Without giving it a moment's thought, Kingston took the steps up to platform 2. His reasoning was simple: Hobbs was carrying a bag, meaning he wasn't going out for a stroll or to buy a pack of cigarettes; he was planning a more extended trip. If his purpose was to go into hiding or leave the country, he would head for one of the several big stations like Victoria, King's Cross, or Waterloo, all easy connections by tube. Trains from those stations would take him almost anywhere in the country. If Hobbs was planning to leave the country, then Waterloo would probably be the one; he could catch the high-speed Eurostar train, connecting the UK with Paris and Brussels via the Chunnel. If he were in Hobbs's shoes—given the ease, convenience, and relative anonymity of the train versus flying—he would take the train any day. Plus it terminated in the heart of Paris. In three hours, Hobbs could be dining at Chez Michel.

On the platform, Kingston glanced around. There were few waiting passengers, normal for that time of day. If Hobbs was among them, Kingston would have spotted him by now. He was becoming resigned to the fact that the chase had been in vain; Hobbs had got too good a start. Now that he was here, he decided he might as well wait for the train. There was always the long shot that Hobbs had gone to the gents, or had stopped at the station's newsagents. He cursed himself for not having looked in there.

Kingston could hear the train now. In seconds, it appeared around the shallow curve, a hundred yards from the platform. People were picking up bags and preparing to board, but there was still no sign of Hobbs. That was it, then, he thought.

The train doors opened and passengers started boarding. Kingston was about to turn and walk away when Hobbs suddenly appeared, as if from nowhere, at the other end of the platform. He must have been sitting out of sight all this time on one of the station benches, thought Kingston. He watched as Hobbs boarded. So engrossed was he watching Hobbs and congratulating himself for tracking him down, that he almost forgot to board himself. He lunged for the doors as they were closing. He almost lost his footing but managed to hold the doors back and squeeze through them onto the train. Nobody noticed. Londoners did it all the time.

Though there were plenty of seats, Kingston stood by the door, gripping the handrail. The distance between stations was short, and he had little time to think. As the train was approaching the next station, he knew what he had to do.

He guessed that the train had at least a half dozen separate carriages, and there was no way to go from carriage to carriage when the train was in motion. Hobbs was in the first carriage, and he was in the second to last. By now, he was betting all his chips that Hobbs was headed for Waterloo Station, twelve stops away. That meant Hobbs would have to change at Westminster, onto a Jubilee line train. Kingston had made the journey a number of times.

The train pulled into the next stop, Ravenscourt Park. Kingston stepped onto the platform and quickly moved up to the next carriage. He waited on the platform, staying as close to the door as possible while still able to see passengers alighting. Satisfied that Hobbs hadn't got off the train, he waited until he heard the "Mind the gap" and "Stand clear of the closing door" announcements. Only then did he step back onto the train. At the next two stations, Kingston repeated the procedure, each time moving up another carriage. Was Hobbs still on the train? Had he managed to slip off without Kingston's noticing? He would know soon.

At Westminster, Kingston was ready. As the train came to a stop and the doors opened, Kingston stepped onto the platform. The exit was close to the front of the train. This meant that if Hobbs got off, he would head away from Kingston but be close enough to be followed unseen. Kingston had to be extra careful not to lose him in the crowd. He also knew that more people would be disembarking, because of the Waterloo connection. It was the largest and busiest of all London's stations.

Sure enough, Hobbs stepped off the train and made for the exit amid the throng of other passengers, Kingston following at a safe distance. Leaving the tunnel from the platform, Hobbs took the escalator down to the interchange level. Then he took a second escalator leading to the Jubilee line, platform 3. There was no question now that he was heading for Waterloo. Once on the platform, Kingston stayed back, in cover of the entrance tunnel, until the train pulled in. Kingston watched as Hobbs boarded, then quickly walked to the next carriage and stepped onto the train. Waterloo was the next stop, so he remained standing.

Up until now, he hadn't given any thought to what he was going to do once they arrived at Waterloo. The twenty-one-platform station was humongous. Kingston remembered reading once that it covered twenty-four acres. The main concourse could be elbow-to-elbow with travelers, most in a hurry. Unless he stayed really close, he could easily lose Hobbs.

With Kingston several paces back, Hobbs entered Waterloo Station's main concourse. Kingston's intuition had been right. Hobbs was indeed headed toward the two-level International Concourse ahead. That's where the chase would end, Kingston knew.

At the concourse entrance, Kingston watched, powerless and dejected, as Hobbs passed through the automatic ticket barrier and disappeared into the Eurostar terminal. He'd obviously purchased a ticket in advance. Kingston thought briefly about hunting down one of the yellow flak-jacketed transport police who patrol the station but quickly realized how futile that would be. What would he tell them? Certainly nothing that would persuade them to apprehend Hobbs. If Kingston could provide tangible, credible proof that he was pursuing a man who had committed a murder, or could convince the police that Hobbs was armed and dangerous, that would be another matter. As it was, it looked as though Hobbs was going to get away, scot-free. Kingston stood at the International Concourse entrance for a few seconds more, checking the departure monitor to see that the next train departed in twenty minutes, at one forty-one, direct to Paris.

Quickly, he sized up his options. There was still plenty of time for him to buy a ticket and board the train, but he didn't have his passport. He couldn't get through the ticket and customs inspection without it. Even if he could, doing so would run the risk of Hobbs spotting him, either in the terminal or on the train. If he boarded, he would have to stay out of sight and wait until it arrived in Paris—and then what could he do? Nothing. Once on the train, the only practical thing would be to call Inspector Sheffield on his mobile and have him call the police in Paris, who hopefully would arrive in time to apprehend Hobbs. So why get on the train at all? He could call Sheffield right now.

He walked back to the main concourse to find somewhere to sit down—not easy at Waterloo—and make the call.

Kingston punched in 999 and, within seconds, was talking to an emergency operator. Quickly, he explained who he was, where he was, and why he was calling, asking that a call be placed immediately to Detective Inspector Sheffield of Thames Valley Police. Stressing the urgency of the situation, and speaking as calmly as he could—hoping that the operator took him seriously and didn't consider it a crank call—he asked that Sheffield be located as quickly as possible and told to call Kingston. He left his mobile number, closed the phone, and went in search of a cup of tea and a sandwich.

Having made the trip to Paris on several occasions, Kingston knew that Hobbs would arrive at Gare du Nord in approximately three hours. That should give Sheffield plenty of time to call back. When he did, Kingston would tell him what had transpired that morning and that he now knew—or thought he did—how the murders were committed, at least Jenkins's. He would also urge that Ben Hobbs be arrested as an accessory. If everything went according to plan, Hobbs would be having dinner that night in a Paris jail cell.

TWENTY-SIX

Kingston's mobile rang just as he got off the train at Sloane Square tube station. It was Sheffield returning his call. For a moment it was impossible to hear the inspector over the sound of the departing train. He stood, staring at a Guinness poster on the wall opposite, until the train disappeared through the tunnel. Without wasting words, he told the inspector how he'd obtained Hobbs's address and what had happened at the house that morning and on the underground chase.

"I've got no proof, but I'm positive that Hobbs is mixed up in all this," he said.

"Give me a brief description."

"About five ten, slim, short-cut graying hair. He's wearing a black leather bomber jacket, gray shirt, black pants, and carrying a black shoulder bag."

"Good. We'll let the Paris police know immediately. We've still got plenty of time. They should have a welcoming committee waiting for him when he arrives."

"I hope so."

"I've got to go, Kingston. I'll let you know what happens. I'll have a lot of questions to ask you then," he added, before hanging up.

The veiled reprimand in the inspector's last comment didn't sit too well with Kingston. I go to all this trouble to help Sheffield solve the case, and a lot of thanks I'm likely to get, he thought. His conscience was clear, though, and he was pleased with his day's work. He also took comfort in knowing that policemen generally—admittedly for good reason—do not look too kindly on citizens who take matters into their own hands where police matters are concerned. Thinking on it, perhaps he had crossed the line yet again. Not by much, though.

On the way back to his apartment, Kingston stopped at Partridge's deli and picked up a generous slice of veal, ham, and egg pie and a jar of pickled onions. He was reminded that six hours had passed since he'd last eaten. The Eurostar was scheduled to arrive in Paris at roughly four thirty London time, so it would be a while before Kingston could expect a call back from Inspector Sheffield, if at all today. He would go home, have a leisurely lunch with a half-pint of London Pride, and try to finish the crossword. After that, he should be in a more receptive mood to worry about the rest of the day—or not worry about it.

The phone rang shortly after five. Kingston picked it up, putting down the book he was reading.

"It's Sheffield," the inspector said curtly.

"Good news, I trust?" Kingston replied.

"'Fraid not. Looks like he gave us the slip."

"Really?"

"The French police think it was doubtful that he ever got on the train at Waterloo. They had police swarming all over the platform when it arrived, and went through it, stem to stern, after everyone disembarked. He must have got wind somehow that he was being followed."

There was a moment's silence.

"Damn!" said Kingston. "Why on earth didn't I think of it before?"

"What?"

"It's the only answer. I'm positive he wouldn't have spotted me. It had to be his brother. The minute I escaped from the house, he must have called Hobbs's mobile. Told him that I was chasing him."

"Of course. He only had to watch you leave the terminal, wait until boarding time to make sure you didn't come back with a ticket, then leave. Everyone has a bloody mobile these days, even my seven-year-old nephew."

"Convenience and a curse."

"Right. Well, I think we'd better have a word with this brother of his. He tried to hold you in the house against your will. Is that right?"

"It is."

"That's unlawful imprisonment."

"You might also want to ask him if he owns a motorcycle and, if he does, impound it."

"Motorcycle? You know something that we don't, Doctor?"

"Just a wild theory," Kingston replied. Now wasn't the right time to tell the inspector that, at last, he had come up with a plausible, all-inclusive hypothesis as to how the murders were committed and why. That was going to require more than just a phone conversation.

"All right, we will. I won't ask you why now, but if it's not too much trouble, it would be most appreciated if you could fill me in when we next talk—Doctor."

There was no doubting the insinuation in the inspector's tone.

The next day's post brought the usual junk mail and bills, as well as a small pale blue envelope with Kingston's address in neat cursive handwriting. The letter inside, on matching paper, was from Sally Mayhew.

Dear Lawrence,

You will remember, I'm sure, my saying that, given the right opportunity, I might consider moving abroad. Well, out of the blue, that opportunity has presented itself. A friend, whose husband passed away recently, has offered me the use of their farmhouse in a village close to Émilion. She doubts she will use it much now and plans to sell it eventually. In the meantime, she said that if I agree to maintain it, I can live there as long as I like. My French is awfully rusty but I'm sure it will come back after a while.

I'd hoped that we could meet again so that I could tell you my good news over a glass of wine, but this has all happened so quickly, and I must leave in the next few days, or she'll have to rent it. Once settled in, I may try to find a temporary job in St. Émilion before looking for something better-paying in Bordeaux, which, as you may know, is only about a half hour away.

When I've found my feet, I'll give you a call and let you know how things are working out. At that time, perhaps you will have more news on Peter's death and the other wretched business, though I doubt it. Thanks again for the wonderful lunch, and for being so kind. I wish you well.

Fondest regards,
Sally

Kingston was pleased at Sally's good fortune, even a trace envious. For a moment he was lost in a distant memory of a sublime weekend once spent at a small villa in the vineyards of St. Émilion, during the vendange. Glancing at her letter again, an unexpected sense of disappointment dislodged his first thoughts. But as quickly as it came, the flicker of self-pity evaporated. If she were agreeable, perhaps he could go over for a visit once she'd got herself established. He could picture Andrew's reaction already.

What was going on? he wondered. Suddenly everybody was skipping out of the country, or trying to. First Bell, then Hobbs, now Sally. In Bell's case, maybe not the country, but there was no doubt now that he'd gone underground. The way Kingston now had it figured, Arthur Hobbs had murdered David Jenkins. Whether or not this was done at Spenser Graves's bidding was a big question mark. The idea of Graves being involved in such a heinous act seemed out of character. He might have been able to irrationally justify stealing the bowl, but murder was another thing entirely. That is, unless Kingston had completely misjudged the man.

With his alibis, Julian Bell's role in the murders was equally perplexing. Disappearing the way he had strongly suggested that he wasn't prepared to face any more questions from the police, either about the hijacking of the bowl or as a possible murder suspect. Then again, giving him the benefit of the doubt, there was always the long shot that he had been called away for good reason. Kingston pulled on his earlobe. He didn't believe that for one moment, though. Once again, he appeared to be up against the proverbial brick wall. Perhaps he should go over the alibis again.

Kingston wasn't expecting a call from Inspector Sheffield quite so soon. Only two days had passed since their last conversation. When the inspector announced himself, Kingston's immediate thought was that he might be calling about Ben—if he'd been arrested—and about the motorbike. He couldn't have been more wrong.

"Well, Doctor," said Sheffield. "I've got bad news. Bad, depending on how you look at it, I suppose." He paused. "Arthur Hobbs is dead."

"Good grief! When did that happen—how?"

"His body was pulled out of the Thames last night, at Wapping."

"Drowned?"

"No, blunt-force trauma, according to the SOCO. What you might call fatal whacks to the head. No water in the lungs."

"A homicide, then?"

"Could be. Or a botched robbery."

"Any witnesses?"

Sheffield's sigh was unmistakable. "In answer to your question—which I do hope will be your last—no. Not yet, anyway. The only eyewitness accounts, according to the Met, are a barmaid and the inebriated patron of a nearby pub. Both confirm that a man answering Hobbs's description was drinking with another man that night, a bigger man. They left the pub together, apparently."

"Not much to go on," said Kingston, the inspector's stern admonition still in mind. He risked a rhetorical question. "I wonder if Hobbs was involved in the theft of the bowl? If he knew what Graves and Bell were up to?"

"I know where you're going, Kingston, but until we catch up with Mr. Bell, I doubt those implicit questions of yours will be answered."

Until now, Kingston had been ready to tell Sheffield about his theory: who had murdered Jenkins and how it was accomplished. Now, with Hobbs dead, he needed more time to figure how this might alter things. Now that Sheffield had ruled out further questions, nothing remained to be said. He would just have to save all his questions and thoughts for the next time they talked—or the next time they met face-to-face, which was much more likely.

The inspector must have been reading his mind. "I think you'd better come to Oxford again." He was using the policemanlike tone that Kingston had come to recognize so well over the past few years. "We need a formal statement on this Hobbs business, and perhaps you and I should compare notes."

"I'd be happy to come up," Kingston replied. "There's a lot I want to discuss with you."

"You'll be hearing from me, then. You might want to keep the next couple of days open."

"I will." He hesitated, recalling his earlier thought. It was on his mind anyway, so he might as well say it. "This is becoming like *Ten Little Indians*," he remarked.

"The similarity hadn't escaped me."

"The fifth got dumped in the river, and then there was one." Knowing how touchy Sheffield could be, Kingston hoped the mild humor would be appreciated.

"One being Julian Bell."

"Exactly," said Kingston, relieved.

After they'd hung up, Kingston realized that he'd forgotten to ask about the motorcycle. He presumed that Sheffield had been preoccupied with the grim news about Arthur Hobbs, and it had slipped his mind to say whether the police had arrested Ben yet. Unlawful imprisonment sounded like a serious charge. Ben was surely under lock and key by now, he assumed.

TWENTY-SEVEN

T
o start, Doctor, why don't you give us an account of your meeting with Arthur Hobbs and his brother, at the house in Shepherd's Bush, and what followed as a result."

The two were seated across from each other in an interview room. The inspector had taken Kingston aside earlier, explaining that unlike their first meeting, this one would be formal. Sheffield had stressed that it was as much for convenience and comfort as anything else.

A plainclothes policewoman, introduced as DC Underwood, sat next to the inspector, a cassette recorder in front of her. The room, though sparsely furnished, had the intended calming effect: comfortable, upholstered chairs, designer-color walls, and Berber carpeting.

Kingston knew the drill, having been through it years earlier, when he'd been helping the police solve a crime in Somerset. Paradoxically, he enjoyed these exchanges. There was something about them that was perversely appealing to him, a sense of noble purpose about being on the side of justice and the law, observing the thought processes and dynamics of police investigation and procedures. That aside, he knew that he had to be careful not to come off as being overconfident or give the impression that he was matching wits with them. Above all, he must forget that he was once a professor and not assume the authority or language that he'd used in the classroom.

This interview would be different. Unlike his first face-to-face with Sheffield, this time he was close to having figured out how the murders were committed—at least Jenkins's—and by whom. His hypothesis wasn't entirely unassailable but it was sufficiently cogent and persuasive to be credible. It would be interesting to see whether Inspector Sheffield and his team of investigators agreed.

"I will," said Kingston, in answer to Sheffield's question. He allowed Underwood a modest smile, glanced at the red Record light on the recorder, and started. For the next ten minutes he related, in detail, how he had obtained Hobbs's Shepherd's Bush address from Alexandra Graves, described his confrontation with the Hobbs brothers at the house on Evelyn Close, how he had managed to escape, and the ensuing chase through the underground, "where," Kingston said with an apologetic smile, "I met my Waterloo."

Sheffield either didn't get the humor, or chose to ignore it. He leaned back and folded his arms, eyes leveled at Kingston.

"Well, Doctor," he said at last. "This case is going from bad to worse. We've now got four deaths and one suicide, all linked to this damned plant-hunting expedition. Two—possibly three—of those deaths are homicides."

"Not including the Chinese villager," Kingston added.

"Right. Because we're a nation of gardeners, and this case involves well-known people in that world, every Tom, Dick, and Mary in the country is glued to the telly and the newspapers. My people upstairs are wondering why the hell we don't have someone in custody by now. Or at least have viable suspects." He paused, eyes leveled at Kingston.

Kingston knew that from now on he'd better adopt a play-by-the-rules attitude. "Let me speculate on Jenkins's murder," he said. "Doing so may provide clues or motives for Lester's murder, too—even Hobbs's death, perhaps. One thing I'm sure we can agree on is that they're all connected."

"Very well, why don't you proceed, Doctor?"

Kingston took his notes from his inside jacket pocket, unfolded them, and laid them on the desk, smoothing them with his hand.

"To begin, let's focus on Arthur Hobbs. How, in my opinion, he conspired to murder David Jenkins at Jenkins's house in Cornwall. Because of his alibi—which we judged good enough to go unchallenged—I had ruled him out as a suspect. Graves testified that Hobbs was at Audleigh the weekend of the murder. If you recall, he remembered well, because Hobbs was sick at the time. The same goes for the housekeeper. She actually saw him in bed. He even talked to her. Plus, if my memory serves me correctly, one other staff member said that Hobbs was present at that time."

Kingston referred briefly to his notes, encouraged that he now had Sheffield's undivided attention. Then he continued.

"I don't think Hobbs was at Audleigh that weekend."

"Then who was?"

"His brother, Ben. When you meet him, you'll see that he looks remarkably like his brother. Not to the point where they could pass as twins, but close. Their voices are similar, too."

"Are you suggesting that Graves was in on the conspiracy?"

"Not necessarily. But even if he were, that wouldn't change things. Under normal circumstances, it would've been impossible for Ben to masquerade as his brother at Audleigh—not even for a few minutes, let alone the several hours that, in fact, he did. Feigning sickness was ingenious. It kept Ben out of sight, and even if someone entered the bedroom, he could easily pass as his brother under the bedcovers with a faked head cold." Kingston pinched his nose. "Speaking like this," he sniveled.

"We get the idea, Doctor."

"Which, in fact, is what he did with Maud, when she took soup up to his room. To set it up, Arthur likely complained to Graves and others of feeling under the weather. He then retired to his room, instructing that he not be disturbed."

"Is this why you asked me about Ben having a motorcycle?"

"Yes. Speed was crucial. Also, for obvious reasons, Arthur Hobbs's car had to remain at Audleigh, so he borrowed Ben's bike. Ben most likely rode it up to Leicestershire, parked it out of sight near Audleigh, then took his brother's place in bed— sometime on Friday evening. Arthur then took off on the bike for Cornwall, killed Jenkins, and hightailed it back, changing places with his brother early Saturday morning."

"So you're saying that Ben needed to be at Audleigh only during the time that it took Arthur to drive to Cornwall, kill Jenkins, and return?"

"Correct. Allowing Hobbs time to locate Jenkins's place at night and carry out the murder, I calculated that he could be back at Audleigh within about nine and a half hours, with time to spare. It's about a five-hundred-mile round-trip but mostly Motorway. The M5 goes all the way from Birmingham to Exeter in Devon."

"That could account for the farmer's wife hearing a motorbike after midnight, early Saturday morning."

"It would," Kingston replied, glancing at his notes.

"Well, your theory sounds plausible. We'll have to go over our notes and transcripts to see how it all checks out."

"Before getting to Lester, can we talk briefly about the way Jenkins was killed?"

"Is that relevant?"

"It could be."

"Go ahead, then."

"Chloroform and blunt-force trauma, you said?"

"Correct."

"I'm sure you know, Inspector, that chloroform is a dangerous chemical compound, employed mostly for pharmaceutical and industrial purposes. It was once used as an anesthetic, but too many patients were dying of cardiac arrest, and it was abandoned in favor of ether. Because my scant knowledge was based solely on what I'd read in whodunits and seen in the movies, I did a little research. How did Hobbs obtain the chloroform? I asked myself. I discovered that, because of its solvent properties, one of its principal uses is to prepare organic tissues for testing. Research laboratories store gallons of the stuff. In most cases, the lab would be a biochemistry outfit. However, these places are well guarded, requiring passes and other identification before entry is permitted. So whoever acquired the chloroform had to know someone who worked in such a lab, or worked there himself—or herself. Or got it elsewhere, of course."

"So how do you propose he obtained the chloroform? Broke into a research lab?"

"Doubtful. It's much more plausible that he got it from someone on the inside, or someone who knew a lab employee. You could check all labs for break-ins, though."

Sheffield didn't look too convinced, but he said nothing.

"So, once having got his hands on the chloroform—most likely through a second party—would he have sought instruction on how to handle and apply it? I asked myself this, because I also discovered that contrary to common belief, disabling an able-bodied person with chloroform is no easy task. It can take a minute or so to render even a passive victim unconscious."

Sheffield's expression had changed. He looked fidgety, less interested in what Kingston was saying. "Look, Doctor," he said at

240 • *Anthony Eglin*

last, "I appreciate the encyclopedic knowledge you've dug up on this stuff, but unless it's relevant, could we please get on with it?"

Kingston nodded. "I'll hurry it up." With a tug of his shirt cuffs, he continued. "I've concluded the following: Hobbs likely surprised Jenkins and tried to kill him with a lethal dose of chloroform. When Jenkins, who we know was a fit man, put up an unexpected struggle, Hobbs was left with no choice but to beat him to death. That would explain the burns on Jenkins's mouth. Chloroform applied to the skin for a few seconds will leave no trace. To burn and blister, it must be left on longer."

"This was all discussed with our forensic chaps. We'd requested that the Metropolitan police pathologist check Hobbs's hands and arms for burns. I was told there weren't any."

"No fingerprints at the crime scene?"

"None."

"Not surprising."

Sheffield looked dubious. "I must confess it's the first time I've run across chloroform used in a crime." His expression changed to puzzlement. "You said you thought that Hobbs might have obtained the chloroform from a second party. You had Bell in mind? Right? He's a doctor. He could probably lay his hands on it easily."

"I did, and he could have, but until we find him, and he confesses, we'll never know."

"All right, Doctor, if we're to accept this... shall we say, resourceful hypothesis, of how Jenkins was murdered, what about motive? Why had it become necessary to kill Jenkins?"

"Before I try to answer that, Inspector, may I just say one more thing about Hobbs?"

"Go on."

"Well, if Hobbs had indeed committed the murder, it raised a number of questions. Even considering the fact that we know virtually nothing about him, or his past, I still find it doubtful that he personally had it in for Jenkins. There's no evidence what-soever to suggest that."

"We're hoping that Ben can shed some light on all this. The Met have him into custody on the unlawful imprisonment charge. I'm going down there the day after tomorrow to interview him."

"He knows his brother's dead, I take it."

"He does, yes. If your theory turns out to be correct, he'll also be charged as an accessory in Jenkins's murder."

"Getting back to Hobbs, he had no direct connection with Jenkins that we know of. So, if someone had ordered him or paid him to do it, that would logically be Spenser Graves, or Julian Bell, or both."

"We've rather deduced that by now, haven't we? You haven't an-swered my question: Why do you think it became necessary to kill Jenkins?"

"I was coming to that."

"Go on, then." Sheffield's impatience was palpable.

"To best answer that question, we must reconstruct the case from the very beginning, starting with what happened last year, on that mountain in China, with Peter Mayhew's death."

Sheffield was shaking his head. "For God's sake, man. How many times have we done that?"

"Surely one more time won't hurt, Inspector? Besides, with Hobbs implicated—and it certainly looks that way—it's reason-able to expect that his complicity may help explain certain of the other incidents."

"Go on then, if you must."

Kingston adopted his barrister summing-up mode. He would have preferred to stand so that he could pace and use hand ges-tures, but Sheffield would never go for that. Instead, he would em-ploy a little verbal theatricality. He knew that doing so could easily invite Sheffield's scorn, but the quotation was germane, and he de-cided to risk it. He cleared his throat and began.

"Sherlock Holmes stated, 'When you have excluded the impossible, whatever remains, however improbable, must be the truth.' However, it was a gentleman from the *Times* who pointed out that, while it was a fine notion, it was too elementary and imprecise. If we are to rule out the impossible, he maintained, all that remains is what is possible; indeed, an infinite number of possibilities, but only one of which is the truth."

Sheffield's sigh was louder than necessary for Kingston's liking. Its meaning was clear, though.

Undeterred, Kingston continued. "I'm theorizing—for now, anyway—that Peter Mayhew's death was indeed an accident. If it turns out to have been murder, it doesn't change things. So from the beginning, trying to establish who would have wanted to kill Mayhew, and why, was a specious line of reasoning. It led us—me, I should say—in the wrong direction." He looked down for a moment, not at his notes but only to give himself sufficient time to couch his next words.

"The crux of this case is the planned theft of the Chinese bowl—specifically, what happened on the day Graves and Bell were in the temple, and no less important, what took place in the hours that followed. The discovery of the remains of the Chinese man near where the fieldwork was being conducted could be chalked up to coincidence. But the fact that forensics has determined that his death occurred at approximately the same time the plant hunters were in exactly the same area brings us closer to the truth."

"Closer to the truth meaning what?"

"What actually happened."

Sheffield sighed. "All right, go on."

"The Chinese man in question observed Bell and Graves in the temple, seeing them where they shouldn't be, handling the highly visible blue-and-white bowl, and assumed that they were up to no good. What were they to do? Their carefully laid plan was about to be torpedoed. If they were exposed, it would be a disaster. Certainly, criminal charges would be filed against them. Exactly what happened next we may never know, but it would be logical to conclude that an argument followed, threats were made, and a struggle ensued, during which the man was killed before he could sound the alarm. Most likely it was Bell who did him in. They couldn't leave the body in the temple; they had to take it with them. With their vehicle right outside, that posed little risk. On the way back to the camp, they hid the body until they could return later, to bury it."

"All right, Doctor. I'll buy what you're saying but how do Jenkins and Lester fit into all this? Their murders?"

"It's my theory that Lester, curious to know where Bell and Graves were going that day, followed them to the temple and witnessed that murder, unseen."

Sheffield frowned. "Wouldn't Lester have followed them afterward? He must have been curious as to how they planned to dispose of the body."

"It's possible, but it would have been difficult to do so without being spotted. But there is the possibility that Lester trailed Bell when he left, later that day, to bury the corpse. Remember, Lester was a photographer. One of the reasons he was on board was to document the expedition."

"So he could also have taken photos of Bell burying the body."

"He could have."

"That would have been incontrovertible evidence."

Kingston nodded.

"That's your theory, eh?"

"More than a theory now. It's supported by hard evidence."

Sheffield looked perplexed. "Evidence? You've been withholding evidence?"

"If you call forty-eight hours withholding."

"Christ! Explain yourself, Doctor."

"Two days ago, I received a letter from Alexandra Graves. She said that in combing through the estate's financial affairs, the auditors had discovered an offshore account belonging to Graves. Further investigation showed that over a period of time, large sums had been withdrawn in cash. Curiously, the span of time corresponds with the period immediately following the expedition up until the time Lester was killed. No withdrawals thereafter."

"You'd better let me have that letter."

"I brought it with me." Kingston reached in his pocket, pulled out an envelope, and handed it to the inspector. "She also included the two photographs," he said.

Kingston waited while the inspector read the letter and studied the photographs.

At last, Sheffield looked up at Kingston. "What do the photos prove?" he said. "It's just Bell and Graves exiting a building, and the two of them looking up the street. China by the looks of it."

"I'm certain that it's the door to the temple. We can easily find out."

"Even so, they're hardly what one would call proof."

"Not on their own. I'd be willing to bet that Graves and Bell received other photos along with these."

"From Lester?"

"That's what I'm suggesting. He'd followed them and captured much of it on film. Maybe not the killing inside the temple, but certainly their removing the body from the temple and loading it in the car."

"Why would Graves have kept these two?"

"Hard to say. They weren't incriminating. Maybe he simply put them aside as a reminder of his guilt. Atonement, maybe, mea culpa ... who knows? He was a complex man."

"So how do you think Lester found out about the planned theft of the Chinese bowl? How he came to be at the temple in the first place?"

"We'll never know for sure. The most likely answer is that it was by chance. He might have become suspicious, figuring that Bell and Graves were up to something other than collecting seeds. Like I said, he might well have become curious when Graves and Bell took off for the temple. We'll never know."

Sheffield looked into space for a moment, then back to Kingston. "If you're right about all this, it confirms that Lester was blackmailing Graves and Bell."

"Which explains why they would want him dead."

"Why did you say that it was most likely Bell who did the killing?"

"I did say Bell, didn't I?" Kingston paused, thinking to himself, then continued. "Let me explain. You see, over time I met Graves on several occasions, and while I don't claim to be a good judge of character, I came away each time convinced, almost beyond doubt, that Graves was not the kind of man to take another's life. Discounting his station in life, his lineage, his reputation as a pillar of the community—and taking into account our brief relationship—I still perceived him as a man of character with a strong sense of family and moral values. Knowing what we know now, that may sound contradictory."

Sheffield didn't venture an opinion.

"What I'm getting at is that even with everything at stake—Alexandra, his reputation, his estate—he could still rationalize the theft of the bowl, as he tried to, on that awful day at the cottage. His misguided logic was that if the scheme were scrupulously planned and executed properly, the chance of discovery was negligible. The temple would be none the worse off. Nobody would suffer. The fake bowl would likely remain there for another century. But being complicit to murder was another thing entirely. I still refuse to believe that Graves would willingly accept it."

Sheffield frowned deeply. "You're trying to tell me that

Graves didn't know what Bell was up to? Didn't know that it was Bell who might have killed Jeremy Lester? Wasn't aware that Bell and Hobbs had conspired to kill Jenkins? That he wasn't in on *any* of it?"

Kingston shook his head. "I just don't know. I prefer to think that either he wasn't aware of some of the things that Bell was up to or, as long as he wasn't involved personally, he could turn a blind eye to what Bell was doing. It wasn't until Bell killed the Chinese villager, in front of Graves, that everything changed. From that sickening point on, Bell took complete charge, and Graves was left to sit by, repelled and impotent, while Bell ruthlessly pursued their original goal—to steal the bowl. It wouldn't surprise me if we eventually discovered that Bell needed the money more desperately than Graves."

"That's possible, I suppose."

Kingston frowned. "I forgot to ask. Did you find the safety-deposit box containing the forged bowl, the one that Graves told me about?"

"We haven't. Graves dealt with three banks. None had record of any safety-deposit box rentals. We're assuming that Bell must have taken care of it."

"A more likely answer, when you think about it."

"So Bell murdered Jeremy Lester?"

"Yes."

"You seem pretty sure of yourself."

"There're not too many other suspects. For reasons I've already explained, I've ruled out Graves as a murderer."

"Graves was an accomplice, though."

"In the eyes of the law, yes." Kingston leaned back, lost in thought for a moment, then continued. "I tried to put myself in Graves's and Bell's place when they opened their newspapers a couple of days after the abortive motorcycle accident. What must they have thought when it was reported that the man in hospital was Peter Mayhew? Had he come back from the dead? Between the two, their phones must have been ringing off the hook that day. When it was confirmed that it was indeed Lester, they were in a real bind. If Lester survived, it was all over for Bell—Graves, too."

Sheffield was looking antsy again. "Yes, we've already assumed all that, Doctor. No doubt you have some ideas as to how Bell managed to murder Lester in broad daylight, in a hospital."

"I've given it a lot of thought, yes."

"Go on, then."

"As a doctor, he knew his way around hospitals, understood drugs, had access to them, and knew how to administer them. He probably had a white coat lying around, even an old identity badge and a stethoscope. Even if he were seen entering Lester's room, who would ever question him? No one looks at identity badges, anyway. They would simply assume he's a doctor."

"You might like to know, Doctor, that we reviewed the hospital's CCTV tapes—roughly forty hours of tape covering the period after Lester was moved out of the ICU until discovery of his death. The tapes revealed no suspicious activity by persons who might have been posing as hospital staff or service or delivery personnel."

"Really? Maybe Bell got lucky, or knowing that the hospital had cameras—which he would, I'm sure—found a way to bypass them. It might be a good idea if I were allowed to review the tapes. I'm the only one who knows what he really looks like now."

Sheffield looked puzzled. "What do you mean *now*?"

"Well, if I'm right, Bell made one mistake."

"He did? Enlighten me."

"Yes. It couldn't be avoided."

"Which was?"

"It was something he had to do before committing the crime."

"What was that, may I ask?"

"He had to shave off his beard. A doctor resembling Rasputin roaming the corridors of St. George's would hardly go unnoticed by the staff. In pictures of him in the magazine I'd read, he had a full beard. Sally Mayhew described him as having a 'bushy beard.' But when he and I met at his farm in Dorset, his beard was trim. I figured enough time had passed since the crime for it to have grown back, somewhat."

Sheffield no longer looked relaxed. He held up a hand, fixing Kingston with a jaundiced eye. "Look, Kingston. I'll accept most of what you're suggesting—despite what the tapes showed, and I'll let you review them—but aren't you forgetting one important thing? Bell's alibi?"

"It's damned convincing, I'll be the first to admit. Even to the point where—according to what you said—he was in no rush to volunteer producing the petrol receipt until you inquired about it. That was brilliant. Then I reminded myself that we were dealing with a clever and ruthless man. Don't forget, he was the one who came up with the ingenious scheme to steal the bowl."

"So how do you explain his alibi?"

"I'll try to make this brief."

"That would be appreciated."

"The first part of his alibi—his being in Cornwall, staying with Jenkins and dining out that evening, was factual. Although the restaurant waitress couldn't describe the man with Jenkins, the meal was paid for with a credit card, with Bell's signature. But this was the evening before Lester was murdered. That was a setup."

Sheffield nodded. "That would jibe with your beard theory. She would more likely have remembered him if he still had his beard."

"Exactly. Next, they had to account for the following day, when Lester was killed in Oxford." Kingston paused. "By the way, what time of day did that happen?"

"About one o'clock in the afternoon, as I recall."

"That would agree with my time line."

"Then what?"

"The next morning, Bell left Cornwall driving a car lent to him by Jenkins. Using the M5, he drove to Oxford, arriving with plenty of time to do Lester in. Later, probably sometime after two, Jenkins leaves Fowey, drives Bell's Jeep to the petrol station at Buckfastleigh and fills the tank, paying with Bell's credit card. Yes, Bell's Jeep was at the station all right, but Bell wasn't in it."

"The time on the credit card receipt puts the car there a little after three, as I recall."

"That would be about right. I timed it out on a map."

"So later—after Bell had killed Lester—the two met and switched cars. Right?"

"Yes. At a prearranged midway location that suited both of them, probably somewhere near Yeovil in Somerset, I figured. There, Jenkins gave Bell the receipts for the petrol and returned his credit card. They then exchanged cars and Bell returned to Dorset in his Jeep while Jenkins drove back to Cornwall." Kingston leaned back and folded his arms. "What do you think, Inspector?"

"It all sounds plausible. We'll have to go back and read the transcript of Bell's and Jenkins's testimonies, of course."

"That would be necessary, yes."

"Well, you *have* been doing a lot of thinking, I must say," said Sheffield. "So when they came back to England, that's when Lester started blackmailing Bell?"

"That's what Graves's withdrawals tend to confirm."

"Are you saying that it was Bell who attempted to kill Lester on the motorbike?"

Kingston shook his head. "It's possible but doubtful. It's more likely that Hobbs was driving the car."

"Why do you think that?"

"Something that you'd said earlier, Inspector, plus . . . let's call it intuitive reasoning."

Sheffield looked perplexed.

"You said that attempted vehicular homicide cases were quite rare because there's usually no guarantee that the victim will be killed. That suggested the risk of its backfiring, for something to go wrong—even the possibility that the driver of the car could also be injured in the accident or his car disabled. If it were revealed that Bell was behind the wheel of the car that killed Lester, it would raise a lot of awkward questions. What were they both doing on the same road at the same time? Why didn't Bell stop after he hit the motorcyclist? Did he know it was Lester on the bike? Added to which, Bell wouldn't have known that it was Mayhew's bike; that could have created a real problem, given the manslaughter charge in the death of Bell's daughter. Then there's the car, which could have been traced by forensics. On top of that, it was well established that the two knew each other. It would be far too risky for Bell. I think that Bell and Graves paid Hobbs or someone else to do the deed."

"If you're right, it would suggest that Hobbs has a criminal record."

"Very probable, I would say."

"With no paint samples, I doubt if we'll find the car anyway."

"On that subject, did any DVLA transfer papers show up for Mayhew's bike?"

"No. The only explanation we came up with is that Mayhew had sold the bike to Lester and the completed transfer of ownership papers were in the tank-top bag or one of the saddlebags, ready to mail, and were destroyed in the fire."

Kingston nodded, not convinced. "You might want to check Mayhew's bank statements, to see if he made a sizable deposit around that time."

"We did, and he didn't," Sheffield replied.

"Going back to Hobbs, I doubt he'd be stupid enough to use his own car, or one from Audleigh. That car, wherever it came from, has probably been ditched or destroyed. It wouldn't surprise me if Jenkins had supplied it and, after the accident, it was driven straight back to Cornwall, where it conveniently vanished or was taken apart."

Sheffield sighed, glancing at the clock as though he'd already heard enough for one day. "That brings us to Jenkins," he said.

"Yes. David Jenkins. If one must feel sorry for anyone in this damned mess—save for Mayhew, perhaps—it might be Jenkins. I'm now convinced that he became involved at the start in a lesser role and was never really a third partner in the scheme to steal the bowl. We know, from what Graves told me, that Jenkins's job was to find someone who could make the replica. Remember, the scheme was hatched long before this last expedition—it started almost two years ago. I asked myself if Jenkins had become aware of the plot to steal the bowl, or whether Bell and Graves had come up with some cock-and-bull story as to why they wanted the bowl replicated. Given everything that followed, it is more likely the former. It's possible, too, that Jenkins was promised payment for his services."

Sheffield was showing signs of impatience again. From his fixed stoical expression, he was clearly tiring and probably no longer considered it an interview but rather an amusing demonstration of Kingston's amateur detective work. How much of what he had hypothesized thus far had already been concluded by Sheffield and his team? Kingston wondered. With all the resources available to them, they certainly hadn't been wasting their time all these weeks, and had doubtless built a case of their own. Sheffield interrupted his thoughts.

"Explain the letters that Jenkins wrote to you, and the one he sent to Mayhew."

Kingston was pleased the inspector had posed those questions, pleased that he'd been given a reprieve, even if only temporary. From now on he would keep his answers and explanations concise, or Sheffield would simply have the tape turned off.

"Why he wrote them was perplexing, I must admit. Both letters—the one asking me to meet him at Lydiard Park, and the second, delivered by the schoolboy at the churchyard—indicate that he wanted to tell us everything he knew, but it had become too dangerous for him to risk doing so. The letters and the clipping suggest that his original arrangement with Graves and Bell—to find someone who could replicate the bowl—had escalated far beyond what he'd originally reckoned on. Helping with the bowl was one thing, but by agreeing—more likely being coerced—to set up an alibi for Bell, he had placed himself in jeopardy. Indeed, if he had prior knowledge of specifically why Bell needed the alibi, that would make him an accessory to Lester's murder. Am I correct?"

Sheffield nodded. "It would. Yes."

"He had to do something—anything—to distance himself from Bell and Graves, to somehow pin the crimes on them. He dare not go to you—the police—squealing on them, because, knowing what had happened to Lester, he feared for his life. So learning from the newspapers that I was helping in an advisory capacity, he chose me as the next best thing. By telling me, he could pretty much count on it getting back to you. The clipping about Mayhew's accident and Samantha Bell's death were also an attempt to place suspicion on Bell by providing a motive for his wanting Mayhew dead. It's conjecture, but perhaps Jenkins thought that if Bell and Graves were arrested and charged with conspiracy to commit grand theft, he might be exonerated, or at least let off more lightly."

"So you think that the letter he delivered to Mayhew, urging that he reconsider going on the trip, was simply to call attention to Jenkins's concern about Bell and Mayhew being on the expedition together?"

"A little more than that, perhaps. To Jenkins, going on the record *before* the expedition meant that afterward—if things took a turn for the worse—he could legitimately point out that he had sensed, ahead of time, potential for serious trouble between Bell and Mayhew. It could be damning enough to make Bell a prime suspect in Mayhew's death. Not only that, but Jenkins could prove that he'd tried to do something about it. At what point Jenkins knew that Bell had killed Lester, or whether he knew all along, is moot, I believe. With Lester's murder, Jenkins rightfully feared a similar fate, if Bell got wind that he was going to squeal. The newspaper clipping about Mayhew's acquittal in Samantha Bell's death served the same purpose: Both would incriminate Bell, make it appear that he was responsible for Peter Mayhew's death."

"Which you don't believe to be the case."

"Correct." Kingston glanced at his notes again, then leaned back, motioning with both hands that he was finished. "That's about it," he said. "Quite a few gaps, but until Bell surrenders or is captured, we may never know the full story."

Inspector Sheffield told DC Underwood that he was going to conclude the session and proceeded to sign off. Soon thereafter, Underwood departed with the recorder, leaving Sheffield and Kingston alone in the room.

"Well, I must compliment you, Doctor," said Sheffield. "I confess I hadn't expected quite such a thorough and compelling presentation." He granted a rare, thin smile. "At the same time, I think I'll give myself a pat on the back for deciding to tape the session. I never would have been able to commit the details of your . . . rationalization to memory."

Kingston wasn't quite sure if this was another one of the inspector's sly digs at his prolixity. Sometimes it was hard to figure the man out. He was about to respond, when Sheffield continued.

"Well, thanks, Doctor. I assure you that your insights, particularly where Hobbs is concerned, will be given serious consideration."

They talked for another five minutes before shaking hands, and then Kingston went on his way.

TWENTY-EIGHT

Back at his Chelsea flat, Kingston felt like a man who had just returned from a long and exotic vacation. Life over the next days seemed dull and sluggish. Even London, his happily adopted city, seemed grayer and more threadbare than usual. Andrew, whom he relied on more than he would like to admit to liven things up, was in France with a friend on a Champagne Rally or some such indulgence. His phone message had been customarily vague. Kingston did remember "tooling around, half plastered every day, in an XK150." He hoped Andrew had meant as a passenger.

Even the modest pleasures in which Kingston indulged occasionally lacked their usual rewards: visits to galleries, trawling for art and antiques at Camden Passage, Antiquarius in the Kings Road, Saturday mornings at Portobello Road, predawn Bermondsey— where a torch was advisable, taking in a new West End play, afternoons at Kempton Park racecourse, uninterrupted hours of reading, even something as simple as trying his hand at a new recipe. Rather than buck him up, they only succeeded in making him more apathetic. He knew what it was, of course. There was nothing to challenge him anymore. The Mayhew case was in the past, at least for now. He doubted that he would hear again from anyone at the Thames Valley Police—unless Bell was tracked down. Even then, it was more than likely that he would read about it in the papers. Sheffield's farewell words, when they had parted in Oxford after the interview, had had a marked ring of finality to them. Perhaps what irked him most was that the case was unsolved. Thinking back on everything, as he did almost daily, not one of the deaths could be laid at the feet of any one person. No proof, beyond doubt, existed for any of them. It was all speculation and hypotheses—for him, exasperation. Perhaps he should take a holiday? It had been a long time since he'd done so. He hadn't heard from Sally Mayhew, not that he'd expected to so soon. He had to admit, a week in and around St. Émilion would be a pleasant change. As quickly as the thought came to mind, he dismissed it. He would think about it again tomorrow, he told himself. Find a way to contact her somehow.

Friday morning, Kingston was driving home from Princes Risborough, Buckinghamshire, after dinner with the Conquests the night before. He smiled. Up until yesterday he'd reached the point where he'd almost put the Mayhew case behind him, getting on with day-to-day living; last night he'd had to resurrect it all. He couldn't blame Penny and Bertie for wanting to know. Like the rest of the public, they'd been following it in the papers, and for him to not have given them the inside scoop on everything that had taken place would have brought howls of protest and a few choice words thrown in. This time at least he'd been spared a tour of the stables.

On the outskirts of High Wycombe, he stopped at a traffic signal. Glancing at the car next to him, he saw two Asian men in the backseat. Immediately he thought of the Jeep he'd seen leaving Audleigh, with Bell at the wheel and the two Asian passengers. The light turned green, and Kingston headed for the Motorway. He was still thinking about that incident. Had he mentioned it to Sheffield? He couldn't remember. At the time, he had assumed what he thought the most plausible explanation: The men had met with Graves and Bell to discuss the sale of the Chinese bowl. The more he thought about it afterward, however, the more he realized that there could have been any number of other reasons. Graves was, after all, a collector of Asian art. They could be collectors, too. They could be representatives of a museum, specialists of some kind—even nothing whatsoever to do with Asian art, perhaps botanists or horticulturists visiting the arboretum.

On the M40, he stayed in the slow lane so as not to have to concentrate as much on the traffic. He was thinking, thinking about the real bowl. By now, it was no doubt in safekeeping. The blast of a horn jolted him into the here and now. Glancing in his mirror, he saw a truck's gargantuan radiator only a few yards behind. He accelerated, realizing that while he'd been engrossed with the bowl and the temple, his speed had dropped below 40 mph.

He moved over two lanes and was soon doing a shade over the speed limit. At that speed the TR4's exhaust note was music to his ears. He was now intent on getting home as soon as possible. He had an idea, the kernel of a plan. The more he thought about it, the more he realized that it might work. It was eminently simple, and he wondered why on earth it hadn't occurred to him before. He debated pulling off at the next rest stop and calling Sheffield on his mobile but decided to press on. Now, at last, he was excited. With luck on their side, his plan, executed quickly, just might bring Bell to justice.

Kingston and Sheffield connected that afternoon at four

o'clock. The Inspector explained that he was in London for three days of ACPO South East Region meetings with other police forces. They were in a break, he said, and he couldn't talk long. They arranged to meet the next morning, during a tea break, at ten forty-five. Kingston would have fifteen minutes to lay out his plan. Kingston was enthused that the inspector had obviously placed sufficient importance on his call to warrant the ad hoc meeting.

Inspector Sheffield and Kingston sat at a small table in the far reaches of the Park West hotel's coffee shop. The hotel was a five-minute walk from the Metropolitan Police Headquarters, which was located behind the St. James's Park tube station. The inspector glanced at his watch, as if to signal go. "So what's all this about?" he asked. Clearly, there was no time for niceties.

"First, a couple of questions, if I may?" Kingston replied.

"Go ahead."

"Your people still have the fake bowl, returned by the Percival David Foundation?"

"Certainly. It's tagged and bagged as evidence."

"What about the bowl in the temple? I take it that it's in safe-keeping by now?"

"It is. The Chinese authorities were informed of the aborted scheme, and they contacted the temple, and the bowl was removed immediately. At least, that's my understanding. I'd have to double-check with the Met. They dealt with all that."

"Good—"

Kingston paused because the waitress had arrived with coffee for Sheffield and Earl Grey tea with lemon for Kingston.

"Next," said Kingston, "the success of what I'm about to propose rests entirely on how much Bell knows about was has happened since he did a bunk. By that, I mean, if he's aware that we know all about their scheme to steal the bowl. Put another way, would he know that the bowl is no longer in the temple?"

"I don't see how he could."

"If he doesn't, then the plan—which is more of a trap—might work. It will also depend on the cooperation of the Chinese police, which, one would assume, we can count on."

Sheffield frowned. "Are you saying that the possibility could still exist? That Bell might try to steal the bowl?"

"Not himself."

"Kingston, give me credit, for Christ's sake. To get there, he'd have to pass through all kinds of passport, immigration, and security checks. He'd be nabbed the minute he stepped into the Heathrow terminal."

"I understand that. It'll obviously be someone whom Bell recruits. To answer your question; do I think he might try it? Yes, I do. Two or three million pounds is mighty tempting." Kingston picked up his cup and gave the inspector a long look over its rim. "That's where your bowl comes in," he said, taking a sip of tea.

"I think I'm starting to get your drift."

"Good. We place your bowl in the temple, in exactly the same spot where the original was. Even discounting the dim light, anyone switching the bowls won't know that the one he's stealing isn't the real thing. And here's where we need the help of the Chinese. The bowl has to be rigged with a silent alarm, and the temple must be installed with twenty-four/seven electronic surveillance. I'm the last person to know how all this MI6 stuff works, but setting up a concealed CCTV camera, with a monitor in a nearby building, plus a silent alarm, should be sufficient to nab anyone who attempts to pick up the bowl."

Sheffield nodded. "Not a problem. All that stuff is standard procedure these days. Wouldn't surprise me if there was a camera trained on us right now."

Kingston found his comment vaguely disturbing but knew that the inspector was right. Kingston had read somewhere that—because of soaring incidents of crime and increasing acts

260 • Anthony Eglin

of terrorism—four and a half million cameras were watching people and places in Britain. Dismissing the Orwellian thought, he bided his time, sipping his tea, waiting for a sign of acquiescence, an indication that Sheffield approved of his idea. The inspector put down his cup, then looked at Kingston—more of a stare, actually.

"I can't think of any reason why we shouldn't try it," he said at last. "Let's just hope it's not too late and someone's been there already."

"That's a real possibility, and that's why we have to move quickly."

"Right. Let me discuss it with my people and I'll let you know if and when it will be instigated."

They shook hands and went their respective ways.

Late in the next afternoon, Sheffield called. He'd been given the green light, and the Chinese police had informed the priests what was taking place. A team of police surveillance specialists was now in the village, setting up their equipment in the temple and in a nearby house, and had advised the local police and temple workers what the plan was and what was expected of them. "From now on, all we can do is wait," said Sheffield. *Where have I heard that before?* Kingston said to himself.

TWENTY-NINE

Kingston set aside the newspaper, took a sip of Macallan, leaned back into the sofa, and thought back on Sheffield's parting words. "All we can do is wait" was clearly a platitude, a way to close the conversation. Their search for Bell certainly wouldn't have been abandoned. One thing was clear, though the inspector hadn't mentioned it in so many words: They'd had no success tracking him down. In retrospect, Kingston had to admit that it would be doubly difficult to find Bell if he'd left the country. How would they go about it? he wondered. How would he go about it? He got up and poured himself another whisky.

He mulled over the problem. He doubted that Clifford Attenborough at Kew would be of help. Perhaps Bell had relatives or friends who might provide a clue, something that the police had overlooked. Obviously those people would have been first in line for questioning. After considerable thought, he could come up with only one idea. Hardly a brilliant one, but at least it was better than sitting on his duff waiting. He would go back to Bell's farm and talk to the housekeeper. If she was no longer there—which was likely—it shouldn't be hard to find her. Failing that, perhaps there might be a worker or neighbor who knew something about Bell's habits and travels. He had nothing planned for the next few days, and the weather forecast was good. A spin down to Dorset with a pub lunch thrown in was as good a way of spending the day as any other that came to mind. At least he was *doing* something.

Driving slowly along the now familiar gravel road to Magpie Farm, Kingston saw the thatched roof of the house come into view over the trees. Seconds later, as the front of the house was revealed, he slammed his foot on the brake. Parked by the front door was a blue and yellow BMW police car. "Damn," he said under his breath. Should he proceed, having to explain to the police what he was doing there? Or try to sneak behind one of the outbuildings and park until the police left? He decided on the latter. Explaining what he was doing at the farm could be a problem. Word could easily get back to Inspector Sheffield. He preferred to avoid that possibility.

Kingston parked the TR4 behind a corrugated building, about one hundred feet from the house. He walked to the corner of the building where, hidden from view, he could see the front of the house. So far no one had come out. Ten minutes passed before the door opened and two policemen emerged. Getting into their car, one of them waved goodbye to Mrs. Hudson, who had appeared on the threshold. Not until the police car had disappeared from sight did Kingston get back in his car and head for the house.

He rapped twice on the iron knocker. Within seconds, the door creaked open to reveal Mrs. Hudson. No apron this time, no smile, and no baking aroma drifting from the kitchen. It took a moment for her to recognize Kingston. Only then did she break into a smile. "Well, I never! Dr. Kingston. What a surprise. Come on in. Can I make you a cup of tea?"

"That's kind of you, but no thanks, I won't be staying long. If it's all right with you, I just want to ask you a few questions about Julian." He used Bell's first name because it implied that they were closer than they really were. She wasn't to know that his last meeting with Bell had been less than cordial.

Kingston lowered himself into the same overstuffed chair as on his last visit. Mrs. Hudson sat opposite, perched on the edge of the leather sofa, hands in her lap.

"You're lucky to have caught me here. I only come by twice a week now—just to check up on things, make sure there are no problems. Sad to say, we've had a few burglaries in the area lately."

"Seems to be widespread these days. Any word from Mr. Bell?" he asked offhandedly.

"No. Nothing. The police were here a few minutes ago. You just missed them. You must have passed them on the way in." She paused and smiled demurely. "Please, call me Maureen."

"All right." Kingston nodded. "I saw them as they were leaving, yes," he fibbed. "Did they have any news?"

"No. It was one of their routine stops. They come by every once in a while to check on the place—me, too, I suppose. Half the time, I think all they come for is a cup of tea."

Kingston smiled. "It wouldn't surprise me."

"They still don't have the foggiest idea where he is. They think he might have left the country. It's awful, isn't it? Mr. Bell, of all people."

"Have they told you why they're looking for him?"

"They have, yes. They came to interview me soon after Mr. Bell ran off. Said that he was involved in a swindle, trying to steal a valuable work of art in China. It gave me the collywobbles when they told me. I didn't believe 'em at first."

The housekeeper apparently didn't know that Bell was also wanted for questioning on murder charges. For whatever reasons, the police had chosen not to tell her. He thought it odd, but perhaps they'd felt it was shocking enough for her to know that her boss was wanted for grand theft. He decided that he shouldn't tell her the worst, either.

"I can just imagine how distressing it must have been for you, Maureen," said Kingston softly.

Mrs. Hudson looked down at her lap for a moment. "Sorry," she said, looking up. "I'm convinced he didn't mean to do anything wrong. There must be some other explanation—like maybe he's been in an accident."

"Who knows," said Kingston. "It could all turn out to be a huge mistake."

She nodded. "I only hope so." After a brief pause she added, "You were friends, weren't you?"

"Colleagues might be a better word. We were planning to work together on a botanical project. If we can find Julian, it would help me, too. To be truthful, that's the reason I'm here. Is there anyone you can think of whom Julian might have contacted? A relative, a friend, a priest, his accountant, or maybe a lawyer?"

Mrs. Hudson was shaking her head slowly. "The police asked me pretty much the same," she replied, looking momentarily into the distance.

"Did he have any relatives?"

She nodded. "A brother, but he died about three years ago, in a climbing accident."

"What about friends?"

To the best of my knowledge, he didn't have many; kept to himself most of the time. I gave the police the names of the two or three that I knew of."

"Do you recall who they were?"

She rattled off the names of two men and one woman, and Kingston jotted them down in a notepad taken from his pocket.

"I don't think they'll be of much help, though. The police said that they'd interviewed each of them and none had been contacted by Mr. Bell or knew of his whereabouts."

After another ten minutes of solicitous probing by Kingston, it was clear that Mrs. Hudson was not going to be of any further help. He stood and smoothed his trousers, about to leave. Looking past Mrs. Hudson, who had also got up, his eye was drawn to a landscape painting on the opposite wall. He hadn't noticed it on his last visit. From where he stood, it looked remarkably fine— good enough to have been painted by one of the nineteenth-century Barbizon School artists. He squinted at it. Not a Corot, surely? "What an excellent painting," he said, crossing the room to get a better look.

"Hmm. Not what I thought," he said after a few moments. "Damned good, nevertheless." He turned as Mrs. Hudson spoke.

"It was painted by Mr. Bell's brother, Timothy."

"Really? Was he a professional artist?"

"I don't think so, but he'd won several awards."

"I can see why. Looks like the Lake District—Scotland perhaps."

"Wales, I think."

"It's beautiful."

"I believe most of his landscape paintings were of Wales."

"You said he died in a climbing accident. Was that also in Wales?"

"It was."

Kingston took his eyes off the painting. "Did he live there?"

Mrs. Hudson nodded. "The last years of his life, yes."

Kingston smiled. "Well, Maureen, I'd better be on my way," he said, taking out his wallet, withdrawing his card, and handing it to her. "Thanks for being so understanding and cooperative. You will let me know if you hear anything, won't you?"

"I will," she replied.

No more was said as they left the room. At the door, Kingston stopped and looked at her. "Would you by chance have the address where Timothy used to live?"

"Unfortunately I don't, no. The police took all Mr. Bell's records. They left virtually nothing. All I can tell you is that the house was near Brecon, that I do know, because that's where the funeral was held."

"Never mind. You've been very helpful," said Kingston, thanking her one more time at the front door before driving off.

No more than ten minutes into the drive back to London, Kingston pulled off the road into a lay-by. He studied his AA road map for a couple of minutes. Satisfied, he backed up, made a U-turn, and returned to the road, heading in the opposite direction of London. He had a plan. Tonight, he was going to stay in Bath.

THIRTY

Next morning at eleven o'clock, after a restful night and a continental breakfast at the Priory Hotel, Kingston crossed the Severn Bridge into Wales, headed for the town of Brecon. There, he would go to the Town Council's offices and obtain a list of the funeral homes. Assuming that the list wouldn't be as long as his arm, he planned to call each one, inquiring about Timothy Bell's funeral, with the idea of finding out where he had lived. This could be his last-ditch effort, and he knew it.

Four hours later, he was sitting at an outside café table in a back street of the old market town on his third cup of coffee. In front of him was a list of the names, addresses, and phone numbers of the Brecon area's ten funeral homes. Eight were already crossed off. The penultimate call was to Barry and Sons. He took a last sip of tepid coffee and thumbed in the number on his mobile.

"Barry and Sons, Trevor Barry speaking," a benevolent voice answered.

"Good afternoon, my name's Kingston," he replied. By now, his questioning was well rehearsed and concise. "I'm trying to obtain information on the death, about three years ago, of a Timothy Bell. I'm given to understand that he lived in the area, and that the funeral service was held in Brecon."

"Three years ago? I'd have to go back through the records. It could take fifteen minutes or so. Is there a number where I can reach you?"

Kingston provided his mobile number.

"Specifically, what information are you seeking, may I ask?"

"I'd like to know the date of the service, where it was held, and—this is important—the address of the deceased at the time of his passing."

"That shouldn't be difficult. Mr.—"

"Kingston."

"Are you a family member?"

"No. I'm a friend of Timothy's brother, Julian, who's gone missing. I'm trying to help the family locate him."

"Very well. I'll see what I can do."

Ten minutes later, Trevor Barry called back. He remembered the house, he said, reading off the address. "It's a bit remote, about five miles from the village of Llangedwyn on the B3654. Don't sneeze, or you'll miss it," he added with a chuckle.

Kingston thanked him, ending the conversation. He left a tip, picked up his notes, and left. Back at the parking lot, he studied his AA map. He found Llangedwyn quickly and, within a few minutes, the outskirts of Brecon were in his rearview mirror. What, or whom, would he find at Timothy Bell's house? he wondered.

About a half mile in, on a narrow lane, Kingston found the house: a simple gray stone building with a dark slate roof, partly concealed by a circle of conifers. He studied the house for a moment before approaching the front door. The curtains were drawn and no vehicles were in sight. It appeared that nobody was home;

either that, or the house was at present unoccupied. He rang the brass bell that hung alongside the door. The clang was surprisingly loud, echoing through the surrounding woods. After a minute's wait, he knocked hard on the door; still no response. The ripple of disappointment he'd felt when no one had answered the bell had passed. Now he was faced with accepting the harsh reality that the journey might have been a waste of time; that his inchoate plan was already doomed. He wouldn't leave until he'd checked the back of the house, though.

As he suspected, the back door was locked. Like in the front, the curtains were also drawn. This was it, then, he said to himself. His search for Bell ended. He studied the surroundings: no garden to speak of, simply a few shrubs and parched annuals dotted here and there, a threadbare lawn that ended at a small orchard of gnarled apple trees, and beyond that, woodland. Timothy certainly lacked inclination or appreciation for gardening. Unusual for an artist, thought Kingston. He looked at the back door one more time. The lock was both old and simple. He studied it closely, pulling on his earlobe. It should be relatively easy to pick, particularly since there was no hurry. He'd done it several times in the past, using skills that he'd learned on a Special Services army course. He just hoped the door wasn't bolted inside. He went back to the car and took his Swiss Army knife out of the glove compartment. Returning to the back door, he went to work, probing and jiggling with the miniature screwdriver tool. After little more than a minute, he heard the pin click, and the door handle turned freely.

It took a moment for his eyes to adjust to the dimness. He pulled back the curtain nearest to him, filling the room with light. He was in a mudroom–cum–laundry room adjoining the kitchen. He passed through the kitchen into a hallway, where he switched on the light. A door on his left was ajar. He pushed it open to reveal a neat bedroom: single bed, sparsely furnished, a large pine wardrobe with the door partially open. It appeared to be empty. A few paces on, another bedroom on the right, this one larger. He went in and opened the armoire. Inside hung men's clothes. Leaving the bedroom, he entered a spacious room with wood-plank flooring, throw rugs, and very little furniture. There was no need to flick on the light switch; a large skylight flooded the room. It had probably been Timothy's studio. He hadn't noticed it on entering, but he could now detect the faintest whiff of turpentine. Even after three years, the pong lingers, he thought. Finally, Kingston entered what he figured was the last room in the house. It must be the living room. Flicking on the wall light switch, he could see that it was. He detected a different odor. Right off, he noticed that the room-size Oriental carpet was folded back at one end, covering a bulky object. Suspicious, he walked over and nudged it with his foot. He knew immediately what was inside. He pulled back the carpet. "Bloody hell," he murmured.

THIRTY-ONE

The body of a large man sprawled, facedown, in front of him. Blood had soaked into the carpet, leaving a dark, irregular patch. Kingston knelt by the body, took the man's wrist, and checked for a pulse. There was none. He stood and stepped back, staring down at the corpse. He took a deep breath, bent over, and with considerable effort managed to roll the body over. He recoiled, the fine hairs on his neck crawling. He was staring down at the bearded, alabaster face of Julian Bell. His blue shirt was stained black where it appeared that more than one bullet had entered.

Kingston backed off, holding a hand to his mouth and nose. The sickly odor was getting to him. How long had Bell been lying there? he wondered. From the color of the blood, some time, it would seem. In the relatively cold house, he could have remained like this for several days, Kingston figured. He walked outside into the welcome fresh air and called 999.

Knowing that it would be some time before the police arrived, he decided to go back into the house and take another look around. Passing quickly through to the kitchen, he took a clean dishcloth from the rack, held it over his nose, and proceeded to examine the house. He had no idea exactly what he was looking for—anything that might offer clues to Bell's murder, or evidence that others might have been living in the house, too. After fifteen minutes of searching, he was down to the small bedroom. By this time, he was convinced that the place had been "sanitized." Someone had gone to the trouble of removing all personal belongings: computers, photos, files, papers, even toiletry items, like aftershaves and perfumes. The place had the orderly, scrubbed appearance of a summer rental.

In the last bedroom, there were few places to look. The bed was made with clean sheets, the nightstand filled with paperbacks, nothing out of place. He knelt, lifted the lace bed skirt, and peered under the bed—nothing but a layer of dust. He opened the empty closet, in case it might contain an interior drawer. No drawers, just a dozen or so wire hangers bunched together. Without knowing why, he ran his hands through them. Two or three still had protective sleeves on them. As the last one slipped through his fingers, he stopped abruptly. It still had the dry cleaner's receipt stapled to the back. He tore it off and read the handwritten slip. Date: August 6. Name: Mrs. Leslie. Phone number: 0207-938-1624. Items: 1 blouse, 1 wool twin set, 1 pair tan pants. Odd, he thought, 0207 was a London area code. Perhaps she, or her family, had rented the house for their holiday. On second thought, he couldn't think why anyone, other than die-hard hikers or ornithologists, would want to vacation in such a remote area. As he put the slip in his pocket, he heard car doors slamming. He went outside, where two plainclothes stood talking, and two uniformed policemen were taking equipment out of their cars. An ambulance was coming up the lane to the house.

Kingston introduced himself, handing his card to the detective inspector, a burly, tweed-jacketed man named Broadhurst.

He explained that he'd discovered the body after finding the back door unlocked and entering, verifying that the deceased was Julian Bell, a fugitive wanted for grand theft and possibly murder. He went on to describe his role as a consultant of sorts to the Thames Valley Police, in the search for Bell. The DI was well aware of the case and assured Kingston that Detective Inspector Sheffield would be informed of the discovery right away. Approximately twenty minutes later, satisfied that Kingston had nothing to do with the crime, Broadhurst gave him permission to leave.

Kingston got into his TR4 as the police entered the house. The crime-scene tape was already in place. He took out the dry-cleaning receipt and his mobile, and punched in the number. After four rings, he heard the automatic voice mail message: *0207-938-1624 is not currently available.*

In twenty-five minutes he was back in Brecon. He parked in a short-stay lot, where he got directions to Lloyd's Cleaners. At Lloyd's, he introduced himself, presenting the receipt to the young woman at the desk, inquiring if anyone of their staff might know Mrs. Leslie or recall her having dropped off or picking up her clothes. He'd called the number on the receipt, with no success, he said. After the woman checked with another employee and the owner, the answer was negative. They all concurred that Mrs. Leslie was not a regular customer. They thought that she must have been an out of towner or a new resident. Kingston thanked them and left.

Twice on the journey home he committed driving errors, rare for him. On one occasion he ran a red light in a village. Luckily no cars were crossing at the time. Over and over, he replayed what had happened at Timothy Bell's house. Nothing made sense. Who had killed Julian Bell? Who had a motive? Why? Was it murder or the result of burglary gone wrong?

As far as the expedition was concerned, Bell had been the last man standing. Much as he wanted to think otherwise, there was one other inescapable fact. Of all the people surrounding the

274 • Anthony Eglin

case—those directly related or connected to any of the deceased—only one remained: Sally Mayhew. But she was in France—unless she'd lied. Could she have returned without telling him? It was possible. Why would she want to kill Bell, though? The only answer he could come up with was that, somehow or other, she'd found out or had concluded beyond doubt that Bell had had a hand in her brother's death. If, indeed, he had, surely he would never admit to it, though.

By the time Kingston reached the outskirts of London, having stopped twice to try the number again, he was even more confused than when he'd left the house in Wales. He'd been thinking too hard and was getting nowhere. It had been more than enough for one day, he decided. The mystery surrounding Bell's poetic demise would have to wait 'til morning, when he would speak to Inspector Sheffield. Pulling into Waverley Mews he couldn't help recalling Churchill's apt quote: "It's a riddle, wrapped in a mystery, inside an enigma; but perhaps there is a key."

Next morning, after another unsuccessful attempt to reach Mrs. Leslie, Kingston called the phone company to be told that they could not check if mobile numbers were in service; the phone was either off or disabled. It looked as though the serendipitous receipt, which he'd been pinning his hopes on, was not going to help.

Midmorning, Kingston caught up with Inspector Sheffield. It came as no surprise to hear that he already knew all the details of Bell's death and Kingston's involvement. The Welsh police had given him a full report. This saved Kingston a lot of explaining.

"I'm not going to ask you how you came to be at the house in Wales, Doctor," Sheffield said. "With our last and only suspect likely murdered, it hardly seems to matter anymore. For what it's worth, though, I might as well ask what you make of it all."

Kingston was mildly surprised at the question. "Of course," he

replied. "After having thought about it round the clock, I keep reaching the same conclusion. If we assume that Bell's death is connected to the Mayhew murders—which I believe is the case—then it leaves few suspects, five, if you want to include Kavanagh: the three Chinese and one woman—Sally Mayhew."

"Sally Mayhew?"

"Right." Kingston wondered if he should mention the drycleaning receipt, deciding it was irrelevant now.

"I thought you said that she'd gone to France."

"That's what she told me. I had no reason to disbelieve her. Doesn't mean that she couldn't have come back, though. Particularly if somehow she'd found out that Bell really did kill her brother. That would certainly be sufficient motive for her wanting revenge, wouldn't you think?"

"You're ruling out the Chinese, then?"

"For now, yes."

"What about the guide they never questioned, the chap who went back to Tibet?"

"Regardless, I still think Sally Mayhew is the person we should be looking for."

"Did she say where she was going?"

"To St. Émilion, to look after a friend's house, rent free."

"All right. We'll talk to the French police; see if they can track her down. Our immigration people will be able to tell us if she reentered the country."

"Or even left in the first place."

"Another possibility. I'll let you know what we find out, Doctor. Oh, and one thing more—please don't you go looking for her. If she did murder Bell, she won't be too happy if you show up. She may still have the weapon, too, a small-caliber handgun."

"Where on earth would I start to look for her?" Kingston replied. "I hardly know anything about the woman."

"Just a caution," Sheffield mumbled.

After putting down the phone, Kingston thought about his answer to Sheffield's question. Where *would* he start? he asked himself. The question was rhetorical. He shrugged it off. But he couldn't shake off the thought of Sally Mayhew on the run with a firearm.

THIRTY-TWO

The *Times* crossword puzzle not only kept Kingston mentally active but also took his mind off other problems. Today, one cryptic clue in particular had him stumped. He was certain that the answer was an anagram, hidden in the clue, which was: *One wouldn't expect to find pink, green rats at an animal enclosure here.* (2,7,4). On a pad, he jotted down the words "pink green rats," shuffling around the thirteen letters in his mind to make the three-word answer. At last, he figured it out: *in Regent's Park*, where London's zoo was located.

He put down his propelling pencil and looked out the window, thinking. Regent's Park... York Terrace... Sally Mayhew's friend's house, where the cab had dropped her off that day after their lunch. He remembered the black door with its classic fanlight and brass letter box. It was an awfully long shot, he knew, but if Sally were in Britain, and had killed Julian Bell, where *would* she hide? She could have rented a place, or might be holed up in a hotel, but the house at York Terrace would be as safe as anywhere and certainly provide the anonymity she would want. It was worth the try, he convinced himself as he tidied up the kitchen, preparing to leave.

An hour later, Kingston stood at the portico of the Georgian house and pressed the polished brass doorbell set in the shiny black door. After an adequate interval, he pressed again—still no response. He lifted the letter box flap, taking a quick peek. It was blocked from the other side. Disappointed, he turned and walked up the street. He'd have to come back and try again later. About to turn the corner, eyes open for a cab, he noticed an unoccupied bench. He turned and looked back. If he sat there, he would be able to see the house. He had all afternoon with nothing to do. At least he could camp on the bench for a half hour or so, to see if anyone showed up. He sat, crossed his legs, and tried to appear as if this was part of his daily routine. He soon wished he'd brought a newspaper or a book. He would have felt less conspicuous, and the time would have passed more quickly. He stuck it out for forty minutes, finally deciding to give up for the day. As it was, he might be left no choice. The skies had darkened and rain looked inevitable. The elegant limestone buildings opposite stood out in sharp contrast to the pitch-black thunderclouds.

He took one last look at the place. As he turned to leave, he saw a cab pull up outside the house. A woman emerged. She wore a cloche hat and was carrying a large carrier bag. She rummaged in her shoulder purse for money to pay the cabbie. He started to walk toward her. If he hurried, he figured he could get there before she had time to open the door and disappear, so he could get a close look at her.

Now only several yards away, Kingston could see that the woman's hair was dark and short. Sally's was auburn and shoulder length. It must be her friend, he thought. The cab was leaving, and she was halfway up the steps to the front door, key in hand.

"Excuse me, miss," he said.

Startled, she turned. "What?"

It was Sally.

"You look as surprised as I am," he said.

She shied away, flustered, fumbling to get the key in the lock.

"Sally, we need to talk," said Kingston, standing on the bottom step. It was more of a demand than a request.

"Please go away," she said angrily. "I can't see you." She'd opened the door, about to enter. "Go away, or I'll call the police."

She was now inside, Kingston on the top step. Just as she was about to slam the door in his face, he stretched out a leg and jammed his size-twelve shoe in the door. "I think you'd better let me in," he said. "I just came back from the house in Wales. We have a lot to talk about, Sally," he said calmly.

She made no attempt to stop him. It would have been futile anyway, and she knew it. She put down the carrier bag and walked into the living room, placing her purse on the coffee table. He followed her in. She stopped by the window and turned to face him. "You have to leave," she said, now more composed. "Don't force me to do anything I might regret, Doctor."

"What happened in Wales?" he asked soberly,

She shook her head. "I don't know what you're talking about. I've been here ever since I returned from France."

"Which was when?"

"About two weeks ago."

"So it didn't work out in St. Émilion?"

"No, it didn't."

"You don't know about Julian Bell, then?"

She frowned. "What about him?"

Kingston studied her face before answering. "He was murdered."

She put a hand to her mouth. "When?"

"We don't know yet, but let's say sometime during the last week."

"You said 'we.' Are you still working with the police?"

Kingston nodded. "I am, yes."

A pause followed. Kingston waited for her to say something, wondering how long the cat-and-mouse game would continue.

"How was he killed?" she said at last.

"He was shot—in the living room at his brother's house in Wales. At least that's where his body was found. Small-caliber handgun, so I'm told." Kingston decided on an impulse, for reasons he couldn't explain, not to say that it was he who had found the body.

She said nothing, simply stared at him.

"I'm curious," said Kingston, moving closer. At the sofa, he stopped and leaned on the back of it. "Did Julian tell you about his scheme to steal the bowl?"

Her impatience was starting to show. "I haven't the slightest idea what you're talking about. Would you please leave? Right now!" she snapped.

Kingston searched her face as he inched toward the coffee table. Was she telling the truth? Had he got it all wrong, been too clever for his boots? He started again. "I'm curious—"

"You have a bloody nerve coming here, all but accusing me of murder." She was close to screaming, her face reddening. "That's what you're saying, isn't it? Well, you couldn't be more wrong." She took a long breath. "Now just get out of here, damn you." She started toward the coffee table to get her purse.

A horrifying thought crossed Kingston's mind. Did she still have the gun? Was she about to pull it on him? Or was she really going to call the police? He was beginning to wish he'd taken a more conciliatory approach. "Wait. Wait," he barked.

She stopped in front of the table, staring at him, eyes smoldering.

Suddenly she lunged across the table, but it was too late. Kingston scooped up her purse and stepped back.

"What the hell are you doing?" she screamed. "Put that down! Put it *down*!"

"There's only one way to find out," he said calmly, rummaging in her bag, his eyes never leaving hers.

She started to come around the table. She grabbed the bag's leather strap and started pulling on it.

Keeping a tight grip on the purse, Kingston glanced into it. There it was. Not a gun, thank God, but her mobile. He took it out, letting go of the purse, which skidded across the coffee table onto the floor.

Sally Mayhew, still holding the strap, looked petrified. "What in hell's name do you think you're doing?"

Kingston said nothing. Looking at her, he opened her phone. It was off. He turned it on and placed it on the sofa immediately behind him.

Her face had now gone from flushed to ashen. It was clear that she was confused and at the same time frightened.

Kingston reached in his pocket, took out his mobile and the cleaner's receipt. Calmly, he dialed the number.

He let the phone on the sofa ring four times before picking it up and closing it.

"What was that about?" she said.

He held up the receipt. "I found your dry-cleaning receipt at the house in Wales, in your bedroom closet—'Mrs. Leslie.'"

An unnatural silence followed. Kingston watched the tears welling in her eyes, thinking that her legs might buckle at any moment, but she managed to make it to the sofa. She sat down and leaned forward. Elbows on her knees, she lowered her face into her outspread hands and let out a long sigh.

Kingston waited, mobile in hand.

"You wouldn't understand." She sobbed, without moving. "You've no idea what it's been like."

"I doubt I ever will," he said as compassionately as he could. He raised his mobile again and punched in 999.

THIRTY-THREE

A t three in the afternoon, two days after Sally Mayhew had been taken into custody, Kingston heard from Inspector Sheffield. He was calling from Metropolitan Police headquarters, where he'd just finished sitting in on a two-hour interview with Sally.

"She's confessed to murdering Bell and has been formally charged."

"Will she remain in London?" Kingston asked.

"No. Because the crime was committed in Wales, it comes under the jurisdiction of the Welsh force and initially she'll be sent there for questioning. We'll be interfacing with them, of course. Eventually though—because of her and Bell's connection to the Mayhew murders—the case will most certainly end up with us."

"How is she taking it?"

"Remarkably well, I'd say, all things considered. She has a solicitor, and everything she's told us thus far dovetails into what we know already—particularly concerning Bell's involvement in the case."

"So, as the saying goes, the pieces of the puzzle all fit?"

"It would appear so."

"Look, I know we'll all eventually learn the full story in the newspapers, but it would be good to know where you and I got it right—and wrong. When you've got the time, of course."

"You're reading my mind again, Doctor. The second reason I'm calling is that I've got a few hours to spare later this afternoon before I drive back up to Oxford, and I thought perhaps you might like to join me in a beer at your local watering hole. It'll be on me, of course. I owe you a lot more than that."

"I'd like that very much," Kingston replied, trying not to sound too enthused.

They agreed to meet at the Antelope at five thirty.

When Kingston arrived at the pub, Sheffield was already there, sitting at a table off the wood-paneled main bar, with a pint of beer, chatting with Zoe, the landlady.

"Here's your man, now," she said as Kingston approached. "It was nice meeting you, Inspector. Do come back when you're next in London." She left with a smile and Kingston's order for a pint of London Pride.

Kingston sat and shook Sheffield's hand, careful not to wobble the table as he pulled his chair closer. "Nice to see you again, Inspector," he said. "You must feel relieved to have the case more or less put to bed."

"Not half as much as my chief constable, I can tell you." He took a sip of beer and sighed. "But you're right, Lawrence, it is a weight off the old back."

Kingston didn't know whether Sheffield's use of his first name signaled a new turn in their relationship, or if it was just the informality of the occasion that had prompted it. He leaned back and shook his head. "When this whole business started—seems like ages ago now—who'd have guessed it would end up the way it did?" he said with a slight smile.

Sheffield nodded, taking his eyes off Kingston and gazing at his glass. "I know. Thank God cases like this come along only once in a blue moon."

"Do I see a promotion in the offing?"

"Not a chance. In a couple of years, I'll be packing it in, or taking a civilian job with the force." He took a long sip of beer. "In any case, you've done as much as or more than we have to solve this one. Now that we've got a clearer picture of the events—thanks in part from what we learned from Sally—there's no question that your ideas and theories were, for the best part, correct. She didn't hold back—she told us everything."

"For a while there, at the house in Regent's Park, I was starting to have second thoughts as to her guilt. She put on a damned good act."

"I heard about the dry cleaner receipt, mobile thing. Most ingenious, if I say so myself."

"Thanks. Did she say what brought her to kill Bell?"

Sheffield nodded. "She found out that Bell had a hand in her brother's death after all. She's claiming that she killed him after he threatened her with bodily harm. It happened during a violent argument."

"Where did she get the gun?"

"It was Bell's. She knew where he kept it."

Kingston frowned. "How did she find out that Bell had something to do with Mayhew's death?"

"From one of the guides. Actually, the one who took off, the chap who was never interviewed."

"I'm confused. How did she get to talk with him?"

"She said that, in the beginning, after the inquest, she began seeing Bell on a regular basis. Soon it blossomed into a close relationship. She was infatuated with Bell and she believed he felt the same. This was about the time she told you that she was moving to France. That, as we now know, was all hogwash. Bell had done a runner and she was living with him Wales. We'll never know what his true thoughts or motives were in hooking up with Sally, but she says that their affair gradually soured, and she became increasingly convinced that Bell was stitching her up. She's convinced that his ulterior motive was to enlist her help in stealing the bowl." The inspector took another draft of beer. Kingston did likewise.

"Makes sense. As far as he knew, the real bowl was still in the temple. But he couldn't go to China to get it."

"Right. He knew he'd never make it out of the country. Even if he did, he'd have to get back in. It was far too risky. He needed someone else to do it. Someone he could trust."

"Enter Sally?"

"Right. His plan, as she tells it, was for the guide to make the switch, then hand the bowl off to her, and she would bring it back. A small blue-and-white bowl, claimed as an inexpensive gift, wouldn't get a second look by customs."

"She didn't go, though."

"No. She didn't want any part of it. By this time, she feared that he might hurt her physically and wanted to get as far away from him as she could." Sheffield drained the remainder of his beer and continued. "Bell was in a bind. But he decided to go ahead anyway. Time was of the essence. In order to make the switch, he had to give the guide the fake bowl, tell him exactly where in the temple the bowl was located, and what to do with it afterward—in short, to set up the sting. So rather than send the bowl to China by post, he decided to have the guide come to England. Face-to-face, they could go over all the details, which included a hefty payment for the guide's services."

286 • Anthony Eglin

"It sounds as if he didn't fully trust the man."

"He didn't. According to Sally, he knew the Tibetan guide well. They'd been on other expeditions together. But there was no assurance that he wouldn't run off with the real bowl, since by this time the guide would have figured out that it was very valuable." He paused, eyeing Kingston with an amused look. "You're smiling."

"I'm sorry," said Kingston. "I just had a mental picture. By this time, of course, the real bowl had been taken out of the temple, replaced with the fake one that I'd found at Jenkins's house."

"That's right."

"If Bell *had* somehow managed to pull it off, that would have been some surprise when he found out that he'd swapped a fake for another fake."

Sheffield smiled back. "I'd like to have witnessed that."

"Me, too."

Sheffield continued. "So when the Tibetan arrived in England, the three met at the Marriott, Heathrow to give the bowl to the guide and go over the plan."

"Bell took Sally, although she'd already refused to cooperate?"

Sheffield nodded. "He was afraid she might do a bunk. She claims that by this time, Bell was concerned about leaving her alone at the house in Wales. She said that he'd become paranoid and abusive, and didn't trust her. He was holding her there against her will and she was starting to fear for her life."

"Having met him the one time, I can see that he's someone you wouldn't want to mess with if he were crossed."

Sheffield glanced at his watch. "Time for one more, Lawrence?"

"Fine. Let me do the honors." Kingston picked up their empty glasses. "What were you drinking?"

"ESB draft, thanks."

Kingston left for the bar and was back in a couple of minutes, gently lowering the beer glasses to the table.

Kingston took a sip of Pride. "You were saying that the three met at the Marriott."

"Right. During the day they were there, Sally managed to spend time alone with the Tibetan, in the hotel bar—he spoke passable English, by the way. Without telling him that she was Peter Mayhew's sister, she quizzed him about what had happened on the day the man was killed in the fall. He'd had a couple of drinks and was talkative. He said that early on the morning of the accident, he'd seen the other guide put something into the man's tea. When he'd confronted the guide later, asking what it was, the man said he didn't know, that Bell had paid him to do it. The Tibetan said he was scared of Bell so didn't say anything. He didn't want to be part of it. That's why he vanished soon after it happened."

"And all along we'd concluded it was an accident."

Sheffield nodded, hoisting his glass again.

"Has there been any news from China? I mean, the fake bowl is still in the temple, I take it?"

"As far as I know, yes. We've heard nothing to the contrary."

A brief silence followed, then Kingston spoke again.

"Tell me about Hobbs. Given everything we know, I'm guessing that Bell's fingerprints were on his murder, too. Bell no doubt put him up to murder Jenkins."

"Up until yesterday, that had been a question mark. There'd been little or no evidence to implicate Bell in Hobbs's death. But something that Sally said tends to suggest that he could have had a good motive."

"Really?"

"She said that one evening she'd eavesdropped on a phone conversation that Bell had had with a man named Hobbs. He'd dropped Hobbs's name twice, she said. They were having a heated argument and the man was threatening Bell. Obviously, she didn't know with what."

"One would think that with his brother arrested, and your

chaps breathing down his neck, Hobbs might be starting to panic. Could be that Bell had stiffed him, and Hobbs was demanding payment for his services—eliminating Jenkins."

"I doubt we'll ever know." Sheffield shook his head. "Your theory's as good as any."

Kingston sighed. "All in the name of roses."

"What?"

"Well, one could argue that was the original purpose of the expedition. None of this would have happened were it not for them."

"That's one way of looking at it, I suppose." Sheffield lifted his glass, holding it up in front of him. "Lawrence," he said, pausing, "in addition to bringing you up to speed with Sally Mayhew's confession, there was another reason I wanted to see you."

Kingston watched the inspector take another gulp of beer, wondering just what that reason might be. With his beer glass still held aloft, Sheffield continued. "I'd like to offer not only my sincere thanks for everything you've done to help solve the case, but also that of the department. Your contribution has been invaluable—I really mean that. Lord knows how or where you acquired this knack for crime solving, but I must confess you've become damned good at it. Just one thing, though," he said, smiling. "Like Robbie Carmichael in Hampshire cautioned you—with any future investigations, please try to steer clear of Thames Valley."

"That's a promise." Kingston raised his glass, clinking it in a toast with Sheffield's. "Your words are deeply appreciated."

Five minutes later, in a steady rain, Sheffield's cab splashed up to the curb in front of the Antelope. He and Kingston were waiting in the shelter of the door.

"Perhaps you would do something for me," said Kingston before Sheffield could make a dash to the cab.

"Sure."

"When you next talk to Sally, would you please tell her that

I'm thinking of her? Now that I know what really happened, I understand better why she did what she did. If it's permissible and providing she wants to, of course, I would be happy to visit her."

"I'll tell her," Sheffield replied with a wink.

They shook hands. "Take care, Lawrence," he said. "We never predict how these things might turn out—that's not our job. But just between you, me, and the gatepost, with a good barrister, I don't think Sally will spend a long time in jail."

Kingston watched the cab disappear into the Kings Road, then went back into the warmth of the pub. He felt especially good. A double Macallan was called for.

EPILOGUE

Ten days later, Chelsea

Turning his key in the front door, Kingston heard the phone ringing. He reached the living room just in time to hear the answering machine kick in: "Inspector Sheffield. Sorry I missed you, Doctor. Thought you might like to know we got a call yesterday from the Chinese police in Lijiang. A couple of days ago they apprehended Tenzin Choden, a Tibetan national, attempting to switch the temple bowl. Well, I guess that just about wraps things up in a neat bow, you might say. Give me a call sometime— perhaps before you start on your next case." A chuckle followed.